DEDICATED TO THE MEMORY OF
PRESIDENT AND CO-PUBLISHER
RICHARD H. GOLDWATER
1936-2007

CHAIRMAN /CEO/ PUBLISHER
MICHAEL I. SILBERKLEIT

VP/ EDITOR-IN-CHIEF
VICTOR GORELICK

VP/ DIRECTOR OF CIRCULATION
FRED MAUSSER

MANAGING EDITOR
MIKE PELLERITO

COMPILATION EDITOR
PAUL CASTIGLIA

ART DIRECTOR
JOE PEP

COVER ART
REX LINDSEY

COVER COLORIST
ROSARIO "TITO" PEÑA

PRODUCTION
STEPHEN OSWALD
CARLOS ANTUNES
JOE MORCIGLIO

STAND CLEAR

ARCHIE AMERICANA SERIES, Volume 8
BEST OF THE SIXTIES, BOOK 2, 2008.
Printed in CANADA.
Published by Archie Comic Publications, Inc.,
325 Fayette Avenue, Mamaroneck, New York
10543-2318. The individual characters' names
and likenesses are the exclusive trademarks of
Archie Comic Publications, Inc.
All stories previously published and copyrighted
by Archie Comic Publications, Inc.
(or its predecessors) in magazine form in
1961-1969.
This compilation copyright © 2008
Archie Comic Publications, Inc. All rights
reserved. Nothing may be reprinted in whole
or part without written permission from
Archie Comic Publications, Inc.
WWW.ARCHIECOMICS.COM
ISBN-13: 978-1-879794-31-3
ISBN-10:1-879794-31-4

T5-AFR-751

ROCKET WALKWAY KEEP CLEAR

LAUNCH PAD
61
AUTHORIZED
PERSONNEL
ONLY!

TABLE OF CONTENTS

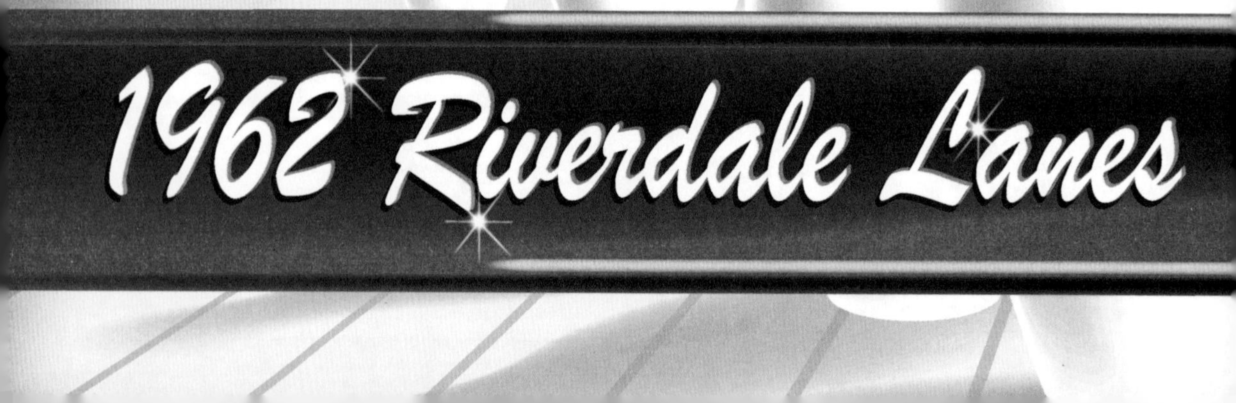
1962 Riverdale Lanes

Bowling Championship

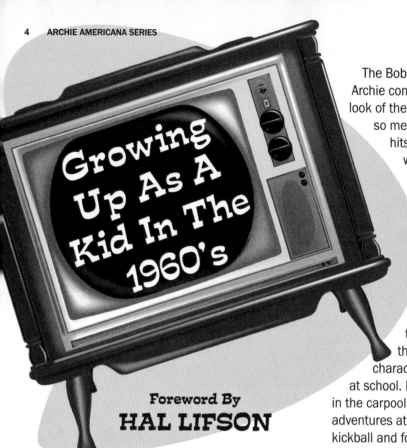

Growing Up As A Kid In The 1960's

Foreword By

HAL LIFSON

Growing up as a kid in the 1960's I was exposed to the best pop culture expanse of the last 100 years. Music, television, movies, toys, and certainly comic books were at their creative peak it seemed, due to the imagination, the writing, the style, and the colors that were being utilized during this very artistic and progressive time. ARCHIE comics were a major part of the '60s experience for me, as I am sure they were for you as well. ARCHIE and his buddies Reggie and Jughead, and "hot chicks" Betty and Veronica, resonated as being so "real" to me, that I felt I was actually a teenager years before I actually was. I learned about teen culture, romance, and overall teen behavior in large part from reading ARCHIE comic books.

The Bob Montana inspired artwork of the Archie comics prevailed in the '60s, and the look of the characters, especially the girls, was so memorable. When you are 5 years old it hits you on a primal level I suppose, the way Mary Poppins did around that same time in 1965. While cartoons were flourishing on TV in the mid '60s, Archie comics gave you a more personal feeling about following the exploits of Riverdale's wacky bunch of teenagers. Betty was the nice girl next door, Veronica was the rich heartbreaker for Archie, Reggie the narcissistic bully, and Jughead the comic eccentric. We all knew characters like this in our neighborhood or at school. I used to take my Archie comics along in the carpool to grade school, so I could follow the adventures at recess and lunchtime. Forget about kickball and football... I didn't want to get my flared pants and Hang Ten shirts all messed up! If I wanted to procure my own Betty and Veronica, I needed to look smooth! Besides, I found by playing the tamer Hopscotch during recess, it was a much better way to meet girls. I used my rubber coin purse quite handily to treat a few of the ladies to a carton of milk. I was the man!

In this new compendium of Archie Americana, you get a wonderful and very comprehensive overview of many of the biggest trends of the '60s decade. Betty beats the bongo drums in a Beatnik furor, Veronica experiments with the Annette Funicello bubble hairstyle that would have made Gidget proud, Betty and Veronica sport their tight "Bye Bye Birdie" era capri pants, Betty and Veronica also wear their hip huggers with wide belts and miniskirts in some of the later pages here.

TIME LINE
1960
Archie's
MAD HOUSE
1961
Only...
10¢
LET'S GO BOWLING!
1962
Archie's
Joke Book
IT'S MY COWBOY GRANDFATHER! THEY USED TO CALL HIM "THE TWO-GUN KID"!
1963
LOOK AT ME. I'M A BEETLE!
1964

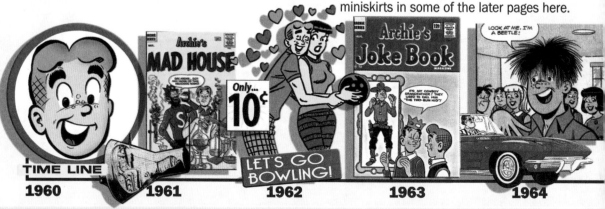

It's a tour guide of everything that made the '60s so eternally cool and of course, Archie comics were right there to capture it in full color! The writing and the art of the Archie comics of the '60s was unlike anything on the stands. I was too young to read the heavyweight Super Hero comics at the time, and even when I began to do that, I still loved my Archie books as they had my 'friends' inside. I can remember really having a 'crush' on Betty when I was first reading these stories. I don't know that it ever stopped really, as I am still reading Archie today and now, even more importantly, am sharing them with my two daughters. My eldest, Sofia, who's only a little over two, already knows all the names of the characters and loves watching the Archie cartoons (recently released on DVD) from the '60s and carrying her Archie Digests wherever she goes! Like Father, Like Daughter, right?

It was a major thrill for me in 1968, when the Archie gang debuted on TV with "The Archie Show" on Saturday mornings. The addition of music to the world of Archie was amazing and I remember vividly cutting out the cardboard 45 single (that's like a CD for those of you too young to remember!) from the back of a box of Sugar Crisp cereal with the song, "Jingle Jangle" on it. That singer Ron Dante really captured the essence of the sound of the Archies group and of course, "Sugar Sugar" became one of the biggest hits of the '60s the next year, in 1969. The Archie Show, The Archie Comedy Hour, and Archie's Funhouse all became '60s Hall of Fame classics and paved the way for more Archie cartoon shows in the '70s. Now, the Archie characters had come to life on TV and yet, I still loved reading the actual comic books. I could really escape with these to Riverdale and join the gang at Pop's Chocklit Shoppe or in Archie's jalopy on the way to school or on a big date with Ronnie. (Watch out, Arch, there's Betty!) With Archie comics, I was part of something truly special...teen life 7 years early! Other than watching Gidget on TV with Sally Field in 1965 and seeing the myriad Beach Party movies, nothing provided with me with this vicarious thrill quite like the Archie comic books of the '60s.

Today, life has changed so much since the '60s. Reading this compilation of Archie stories from that era will show us that. But at the same time, there is a precious consistency about Archie comics and we can thank Editor-in-Chief Victor Gorelick and his fine staff of writers and of course, the great artists for keeping Archie innocent and timeless. We want Archie to stay the same in a way, as we can't accomplish that feat in our own lives. The magic of Archie is that no matter what current trends of the day the Archie gang experiences, you can always trace their behavior and insouciance back to the "glory days" of the '60s. Even Jughead's drum kit he still uses when playing with the Archies band today is so '60s looking!

So, as Sonny and Cher so eloquently sung in 1968, the year of Archie's big TV breakthrough, "The Beat Goes On" for Archie and The Gang and hopefully, it will for many more years to come. Before long, my kids will be reading the "Best of 2000's" Americana Series and joking to each other about those crazy cell phones that people used to use before the Dick Tracy style TV and wrist telephones were invented!

HAL
LIFSON

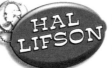

Hal is the author of the book, "1966; The Coolest Year in Pop Culture History" which chronicles many of the brightest and most memorable aspects of that landmark year. Hal is an entertainment writer and publicist who also pens a story now and then for Archie comics. Oh, and he still carries his rubber coin purse with him!

NEW YORK WORLD'S FAIR
UNISPHERE
1964
1965
YOU KIDS HAVE BEEN WATCHING TOO MANY U.N.C.L.E. T.V. SHOWS!
THE MAN FROM R.I.V.E.R.D.A.L.E.
Archie
SUGAR, SUGAR 45
1965
1966
1967
1968
1969

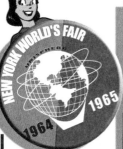

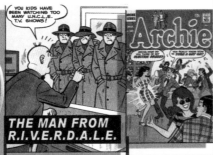

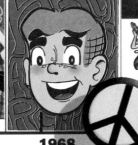

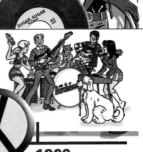

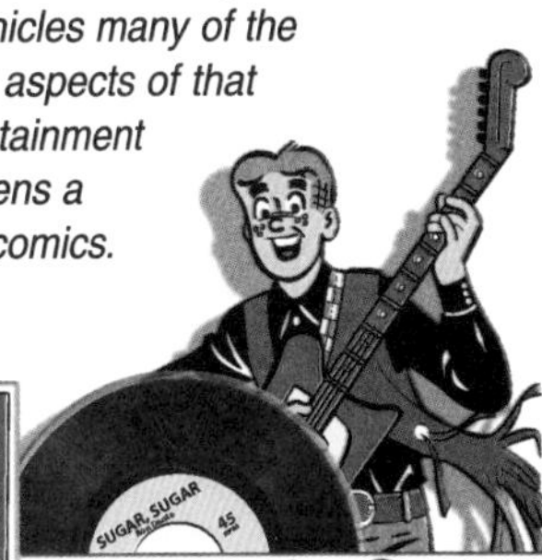

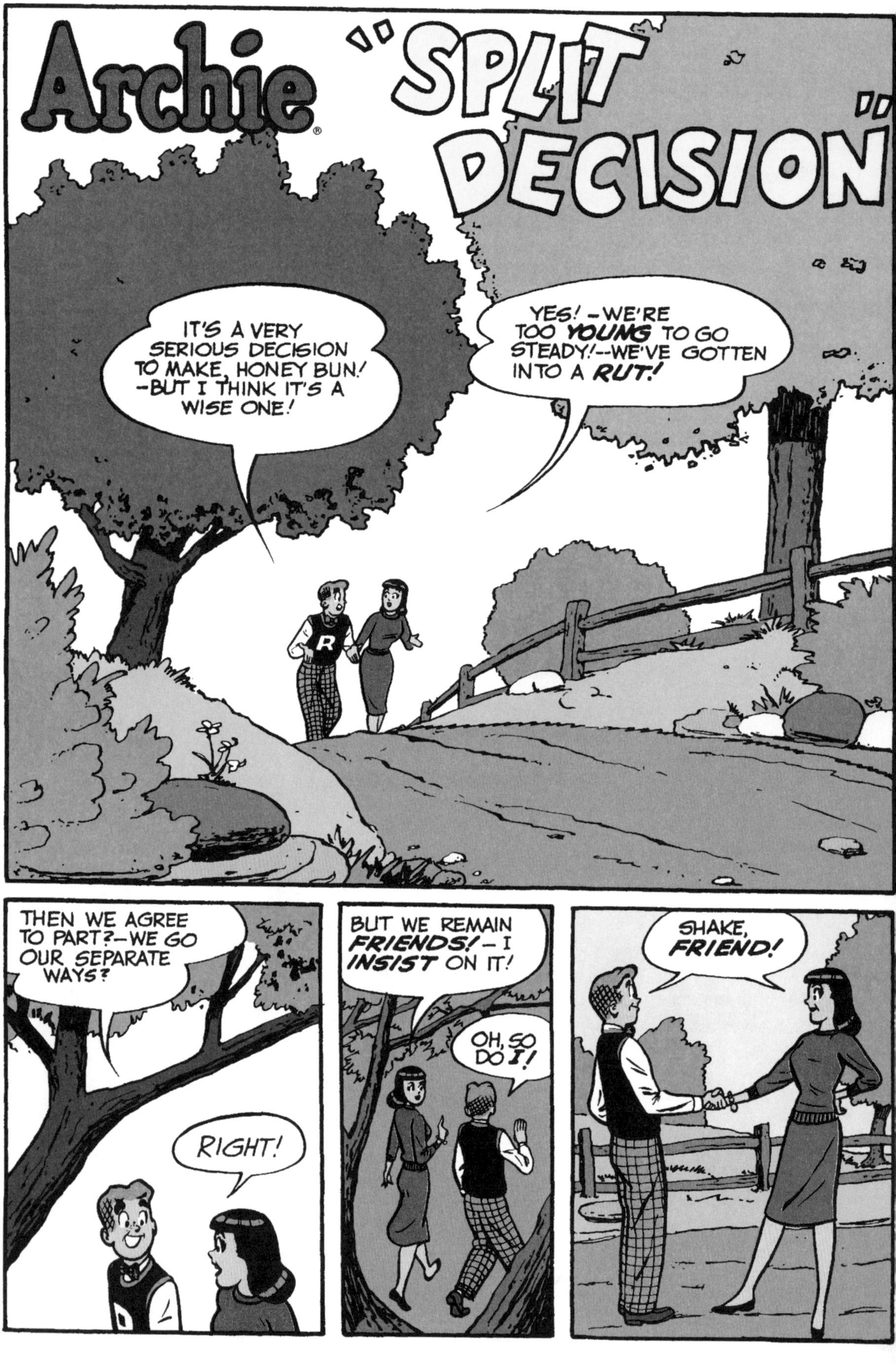
Archie®
"SPLIT DECISION"
IT'S A VERY SERIOUS DECISION TO MAKE, HONEY BUN! -BUT I THINK IT'S A WISE ONE!
YES! -WE'RE TOO YOUNG TO GO STEADY!--WE'VE GOTTEN INTO A RUT!
THEN WE AGREE TO PART?-WE GO OUR SEPARATE WAYS?
RIGHT!
BUT WE REMAIN FRIENDS! -I INSIST ON IT!
OH, SO DO I!
SHAKE, FRIEND!

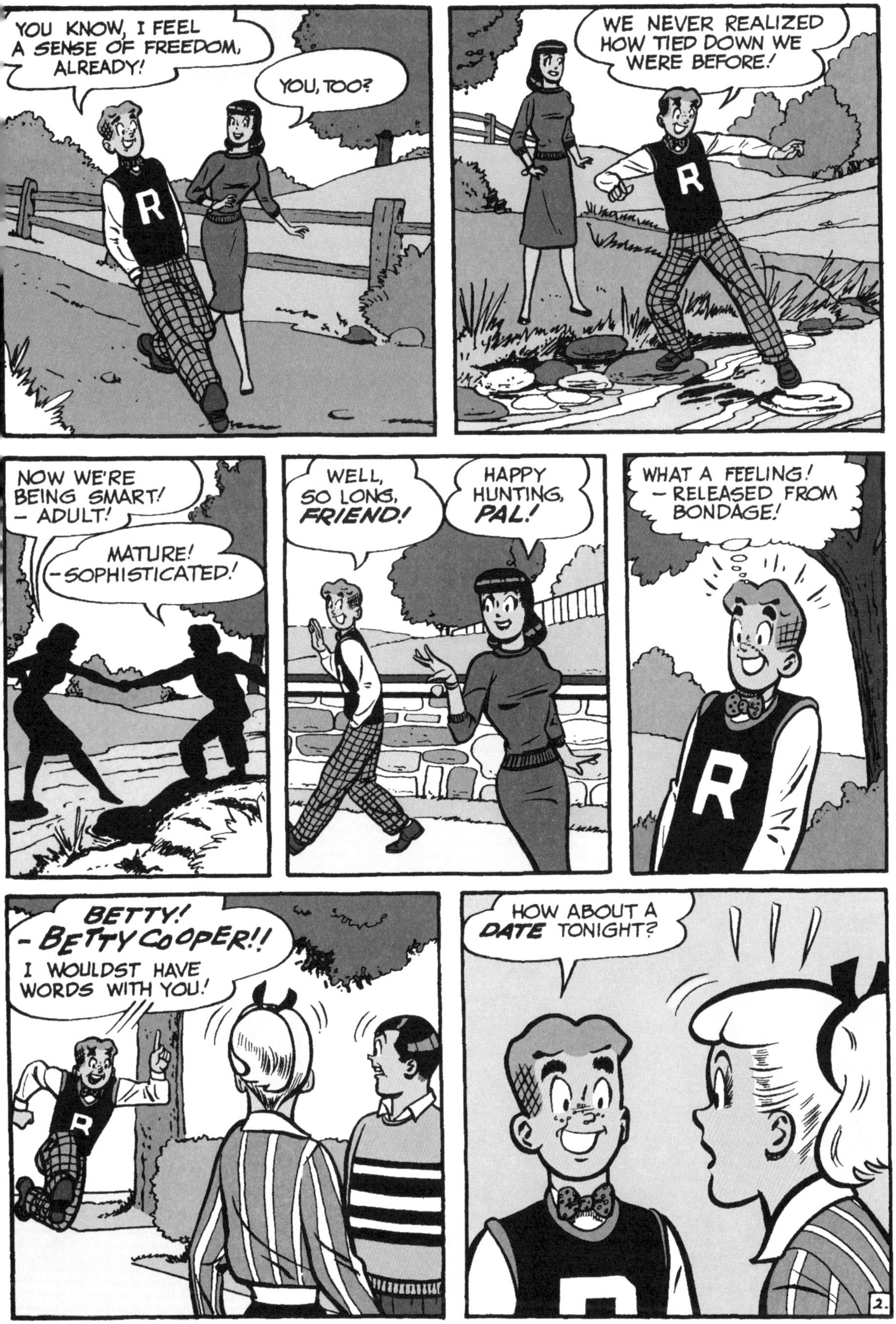
YOU KNOW, I FEEL A SENSE OF FREEDOM, ALREADY!
YOU, TOO?
WE NEVER REALIZED HOW TIED DOWN WE WERE BEFORE!
NOW WE'RE BEING SMART! - ADULT!
MATURE! -SOPHISTICATED!
WELL, SO LONG, FRIEND!
HAPPY HUNTING, PAL!
WHAT A FEELING! - RELEASED FROM BONDAGE!
BETTY! - BETTY COOPER!! I WOULDST HAVE WORDS WITH YOU!
HOW ABOUT A DATE TONIGHT?
2.

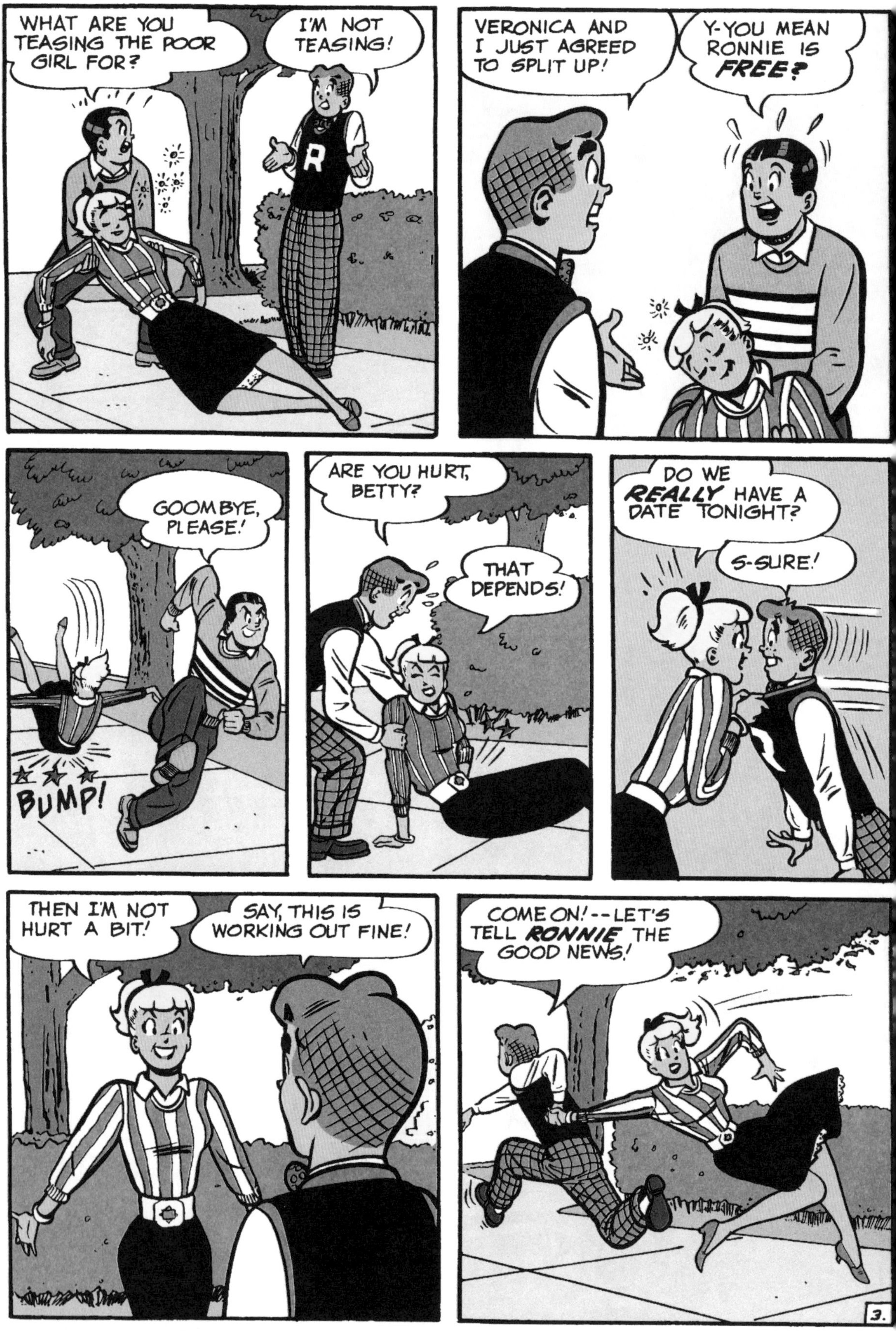
WHAT ARE YOU TEASING THE POOR GIRL FOR?
I'M NOT TEASING!
VERONICA AND I JUST AGREED TO SPLIT UP!
Y-YOU MEAN RONNIE IS FREE?
GOOMBYE, PLEASE!
BUMP!
ARE YOU HURT, BETTY?
THAT DEPENDS!
DO WE REALLY HAVE A DATE TONIGHT?
S-SURE!
THEN I'M NOT HURT A BIT!
SAY, THIS IS WORKING OUT FINE!
COME ON!--LET'S TELL RONNIE THE GOOD NEWS!
3.

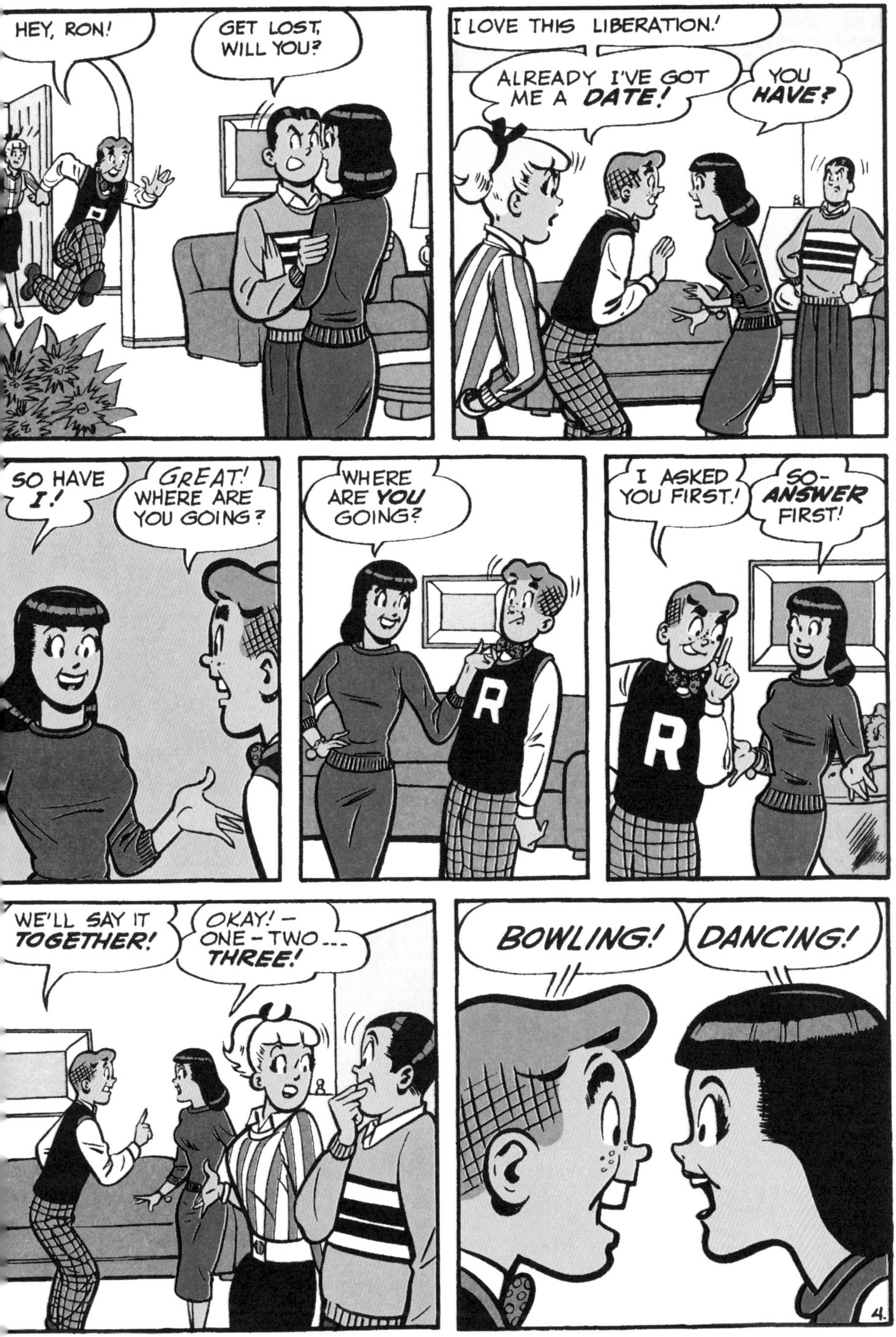
HEY, RON!
GET LOST, WILL YOU?
I LOVE THIS LIBERATION!
ALREADY I'VE GOT ME A DATE!
YOU HAVE?
SO HAVE I!
GREAT! WHERE ARE YOU GOING?
WHERE ARE YOU GOING?
I ASKED YOU FIRST!
SO- ANSWER FIRST!
WE'LL SAY IT TOGETHER!
OKAY! - ONE - TWO... THREE!
BOWLING!
DANCING!
4.

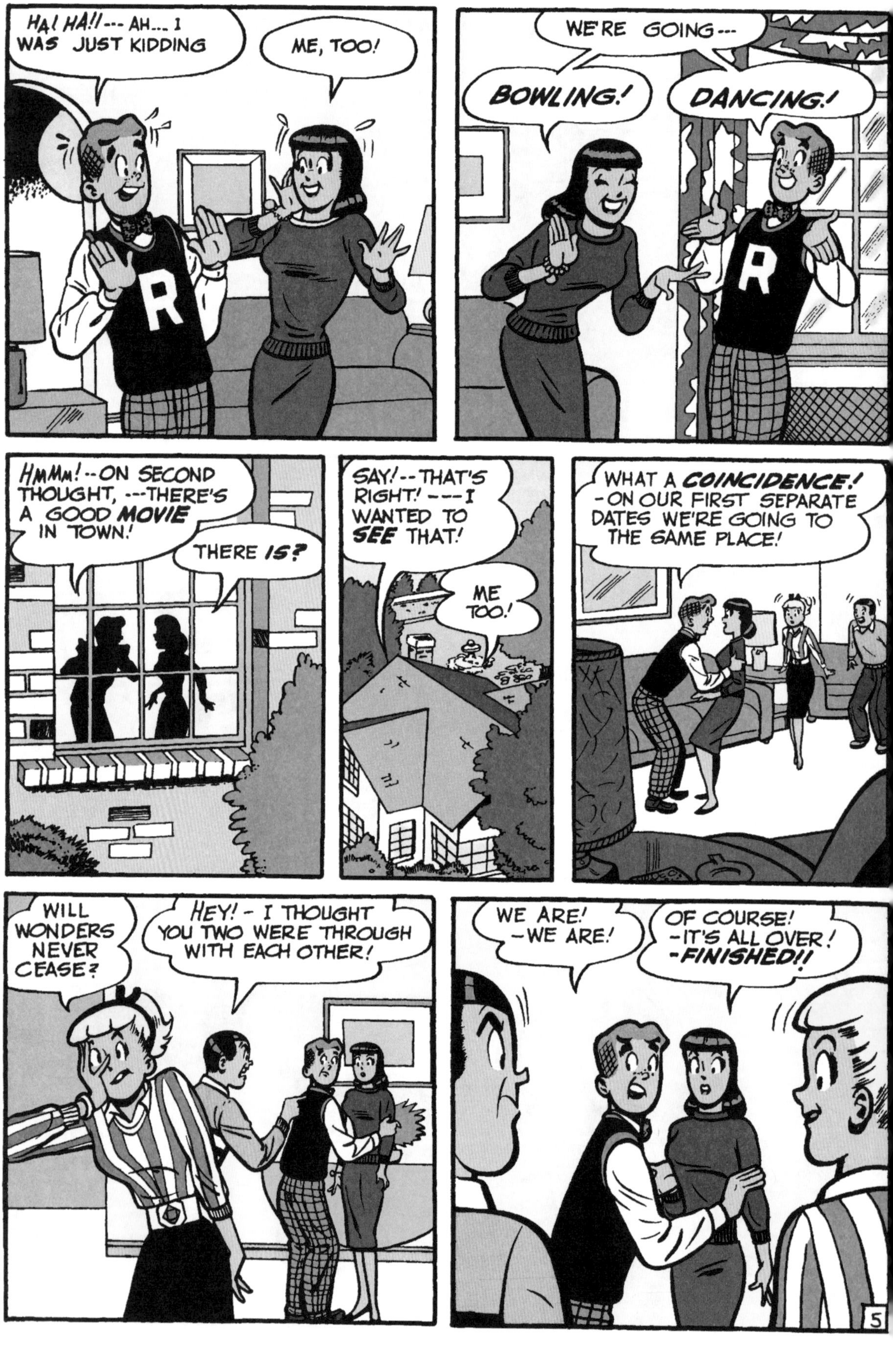
HA! HA!! --- AH... I WAS JUST KIDDING
ME, TOO!
WE'RE GOING---
BOWLING!
DANCING!
HMMM! --ON SECOND THOUGHT, ---THERE'S A GOOD MOVIE IN TOWN!
THERE IS?
SAY! --THAT'S RIGHT! ---I WANTED TO SEE THAT!
ME TOO!
WHAT A COINCIDENCE! -ON OUR FIRST SEPARATE DATES WE'RE GOING TO THE SAME PLACE!
WILL WONDERS NEVER CEASE?
HEY! - I THOUGHT YOU TWO WERE THROUGH WITH EACH OTHER!
WE ARE! -WE ARE!
OF COURSE! -IT'S ALL OVER! -FINISHED!!
5

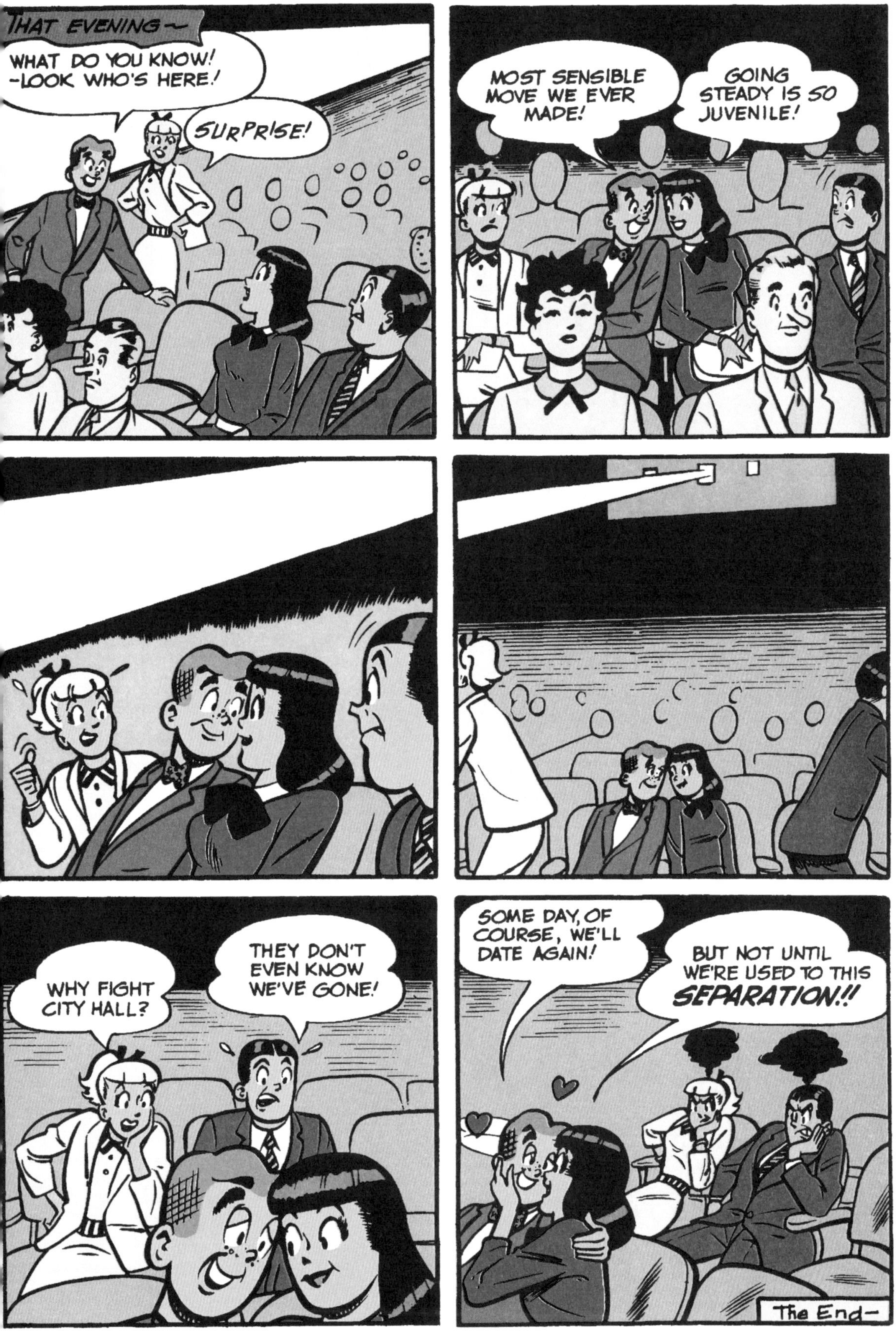
THAT EVENING~
WHAT DO YOU KNOW! -LOOK WHO'S HERE!
SURPRISE!
MOST SENSIBLE MOVE WE EVER MADE!
GOING STEADY IS SO JUVENILE!
WHY FIGHT CITY HALL?
THEY DON'T EVEN KNOW WE'VE GONE!
SOME DAY, OF COURSE, WE'LL DATE AGAIN!
BUT NOT UNTIL WE'RE USED TO THIS SEPARATION!!
The End-

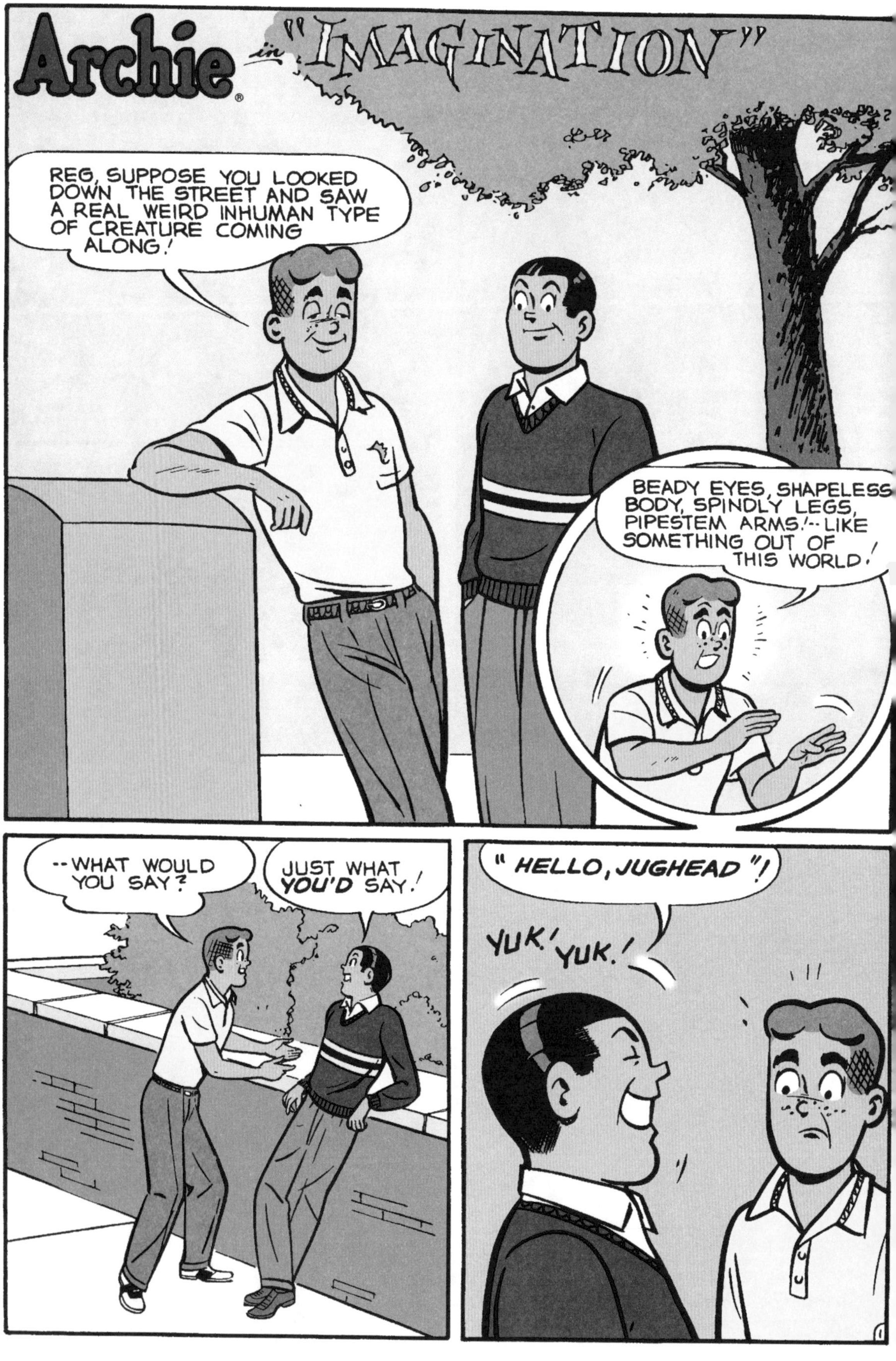
Archie in "IMAGINATION"
REG, SUPPOSE YOU LOOKED DOWN THE STREET AND SAW A REAL WEIRD INHUMAN TYPE OF CREATURE COMING ALONG!
BEADY EYES, SHAPELESS BODY, SPINDLY LEGS, PIPESTEM ARMS! -- LIKE SOMETHING OUT OF THIS WORLD!
-- WHAT WOULD YOU SAY?
JUST WHAT YOU'D SAY!
" HELLO, JUGHEAD "!
YUK! YUK!

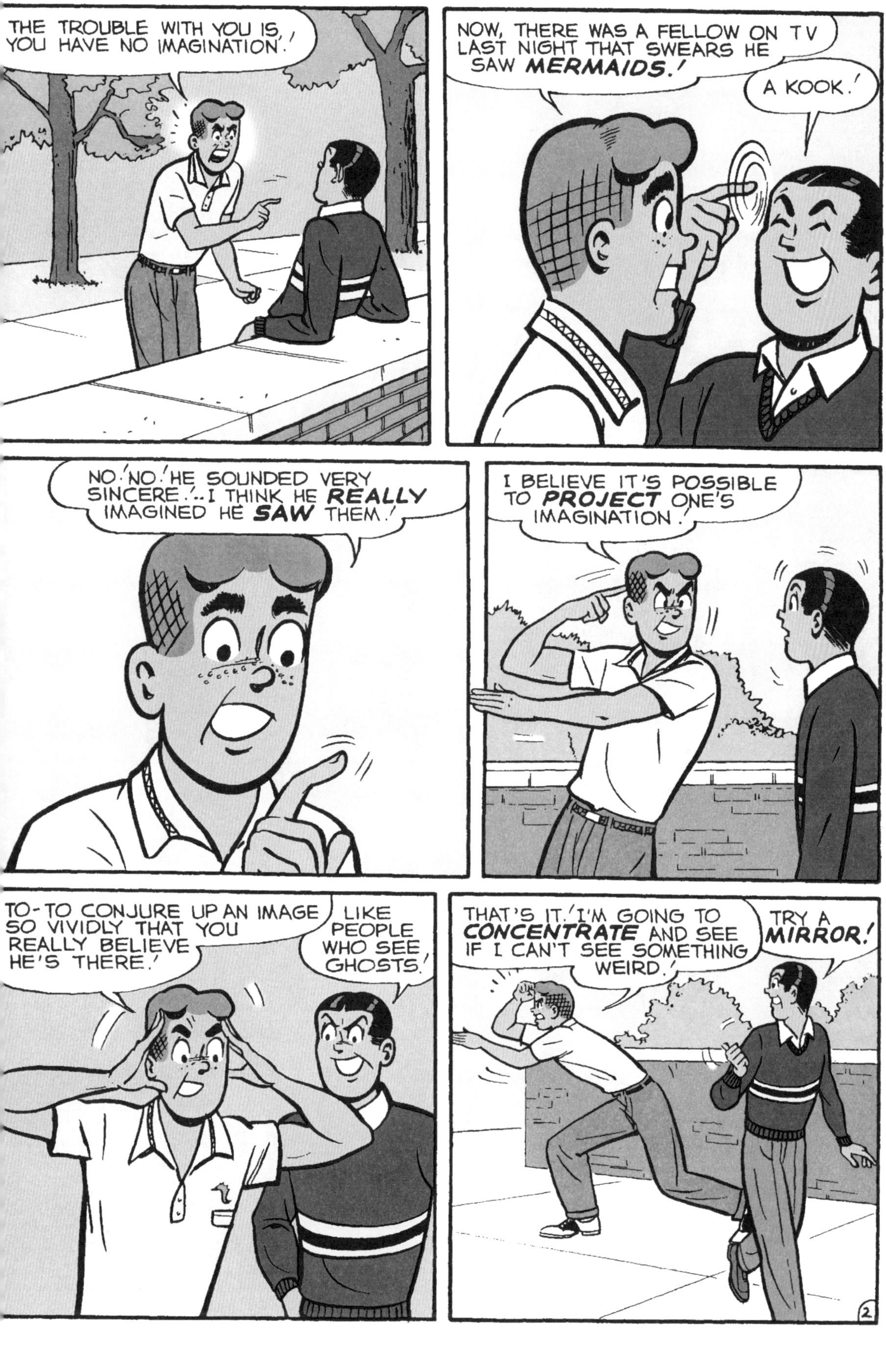
THE TROUBLE WITH YOU IS, YOU HAVE NO IMAGINATION!
NOW, THERE WAS A FELLOW ON TV LAST NIGHT THAT SWEARS HE SAW MERMAIDS!
A KOOK!
NO! NO! HE SOUNDED VERY SINCERE!.. I THINK HE REALLY IMAGINED HE SAW THEM!
I BELIEVE IT'S POSSIBLE TO PROJECT ONE'S IMAGINATION!
TO-TO CONJURE UP AN IMAGE SO VIVIDLY THAT YOU REALLY BELIEVE HE'S THERE!
LIKE PEOPLE WHO SEE GHOSTS!
THAT'S IT! I'M GOING TO CONCENTRATE AND SEE IF I CAN'T SEE SOMETHING WEIRD!
TRY A MIRROR!
2

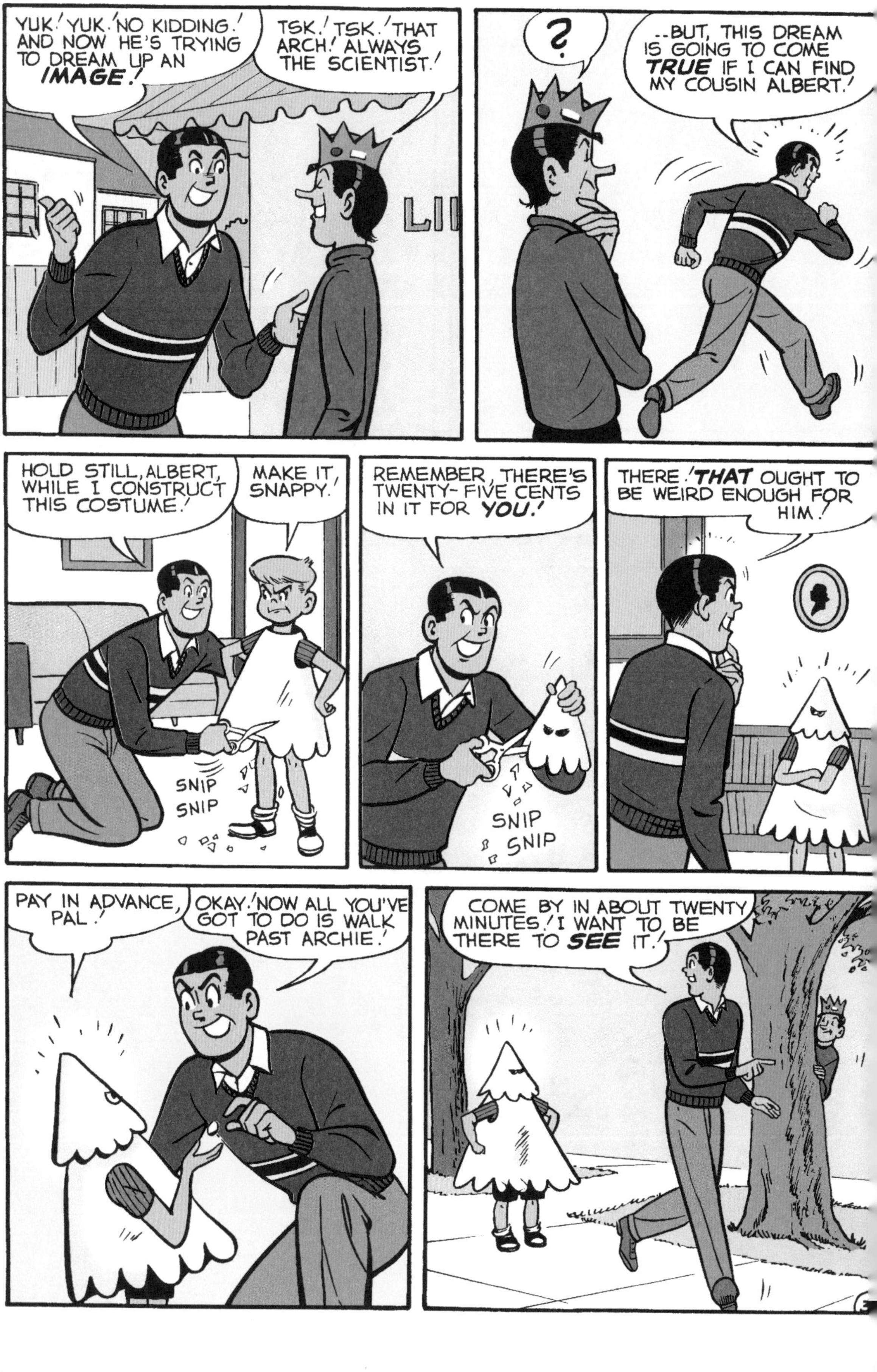
YUK! YUK! NO KIDDING! AND NOW HE'S TRYING TO DREAM UP AN IMAGE!
TSK! TSK! THAT ARCH! ALWAYS THE SCIENTIST!
LII
?
..BUT, THIS DREAM IS GOING TO COME TRUE IF I CAN FIND MY COUSIN ALBERT!
HOLD STILL, ALBERT, WHILE I CONSTRUCT THIS COSTUME!
MAKE IT SNAPPY!
SNIP SNIP
REMEMBER, THERE'S TWENTY-FIVE CENTS IN IT FOR YOU!
SNIP SNIP
THERE! THAT OUGHT TO BE WEIRD ENOUGH FOR HIM!
PAY IN ADVANCE, PAL!
OKAY! NOW ALL YOU'VE GOT TO DO IS WALK PAST ARCHIE!
COME BY IN ABOUT TWENTY MINUTES! I WANT TO BE THERE TO SEE IT!

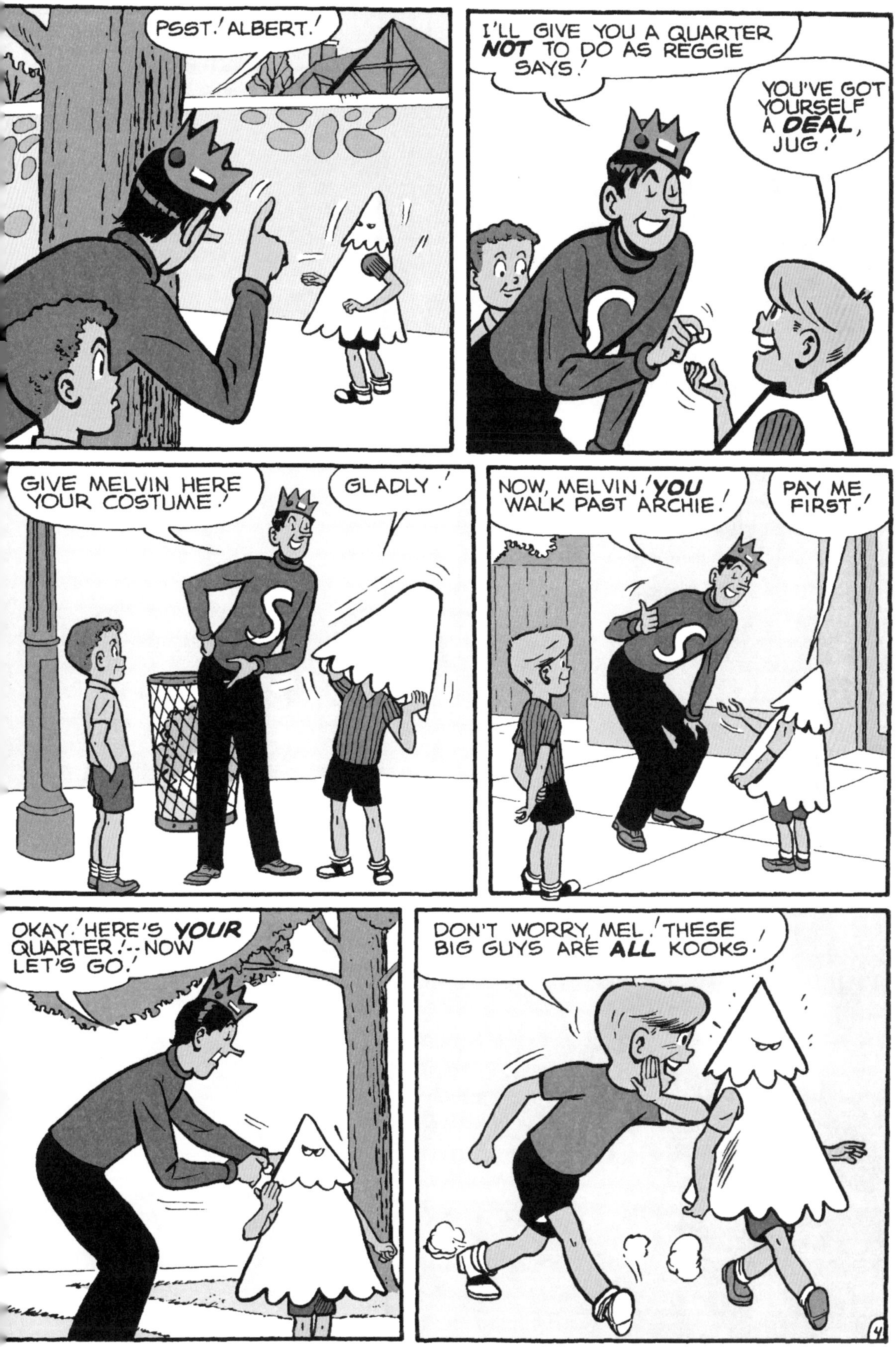
PSST.! ALBERT.!
I'LL GIVE YOU A QUARTER NOT TO DO AS REGGIE SAYS.!
YOU'VE GOT YOURSELF A DEAL, JUG.!
GIVE MELVIN HERE YOUR COSTUME.!
GLADLY.!
NOW, MELVIN.! YOU WALK PAST ARCHIE.!
PAY ME FIRST.!
OKAY.! HERE'S YOUR QUARTER.!--NOW LET'S GO.!
DON'T WORRY, MEL.! THESE BIG GUYS ARE ALL KOOKS.!
4

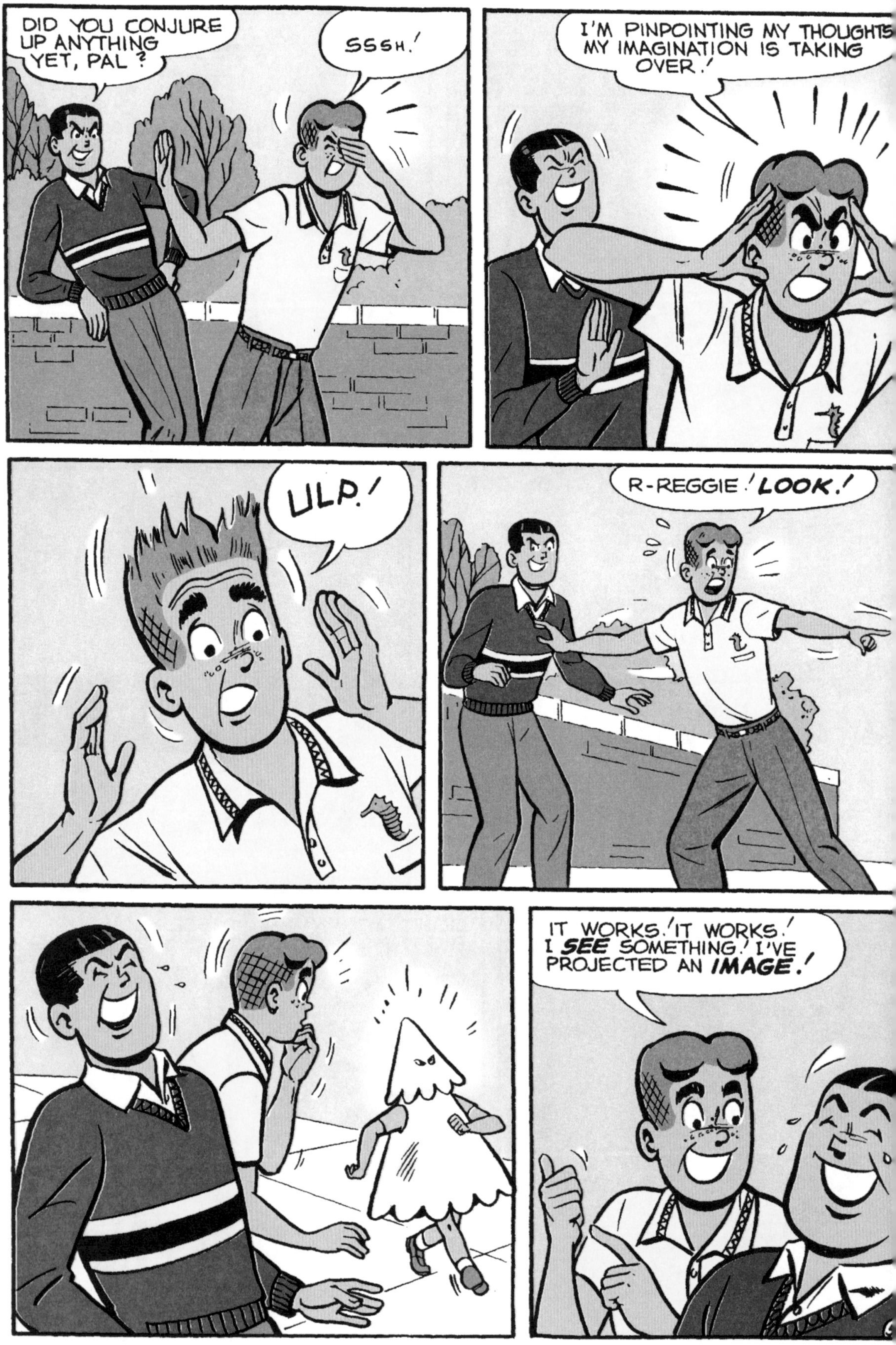
DID YOU CONJURE UP ANYTHING YET, PAL ?
SSSH.!
I'M PINPOINTING MY THOUGHTS MY IMAGINATION IS TAKING OVER.!
ULP.!
R-REGGIE.! LOOK.!
IT WORKS.! IT WORKS.! I SEE SOMETHING.! I'VE PROJECTED AN IMAGE.!

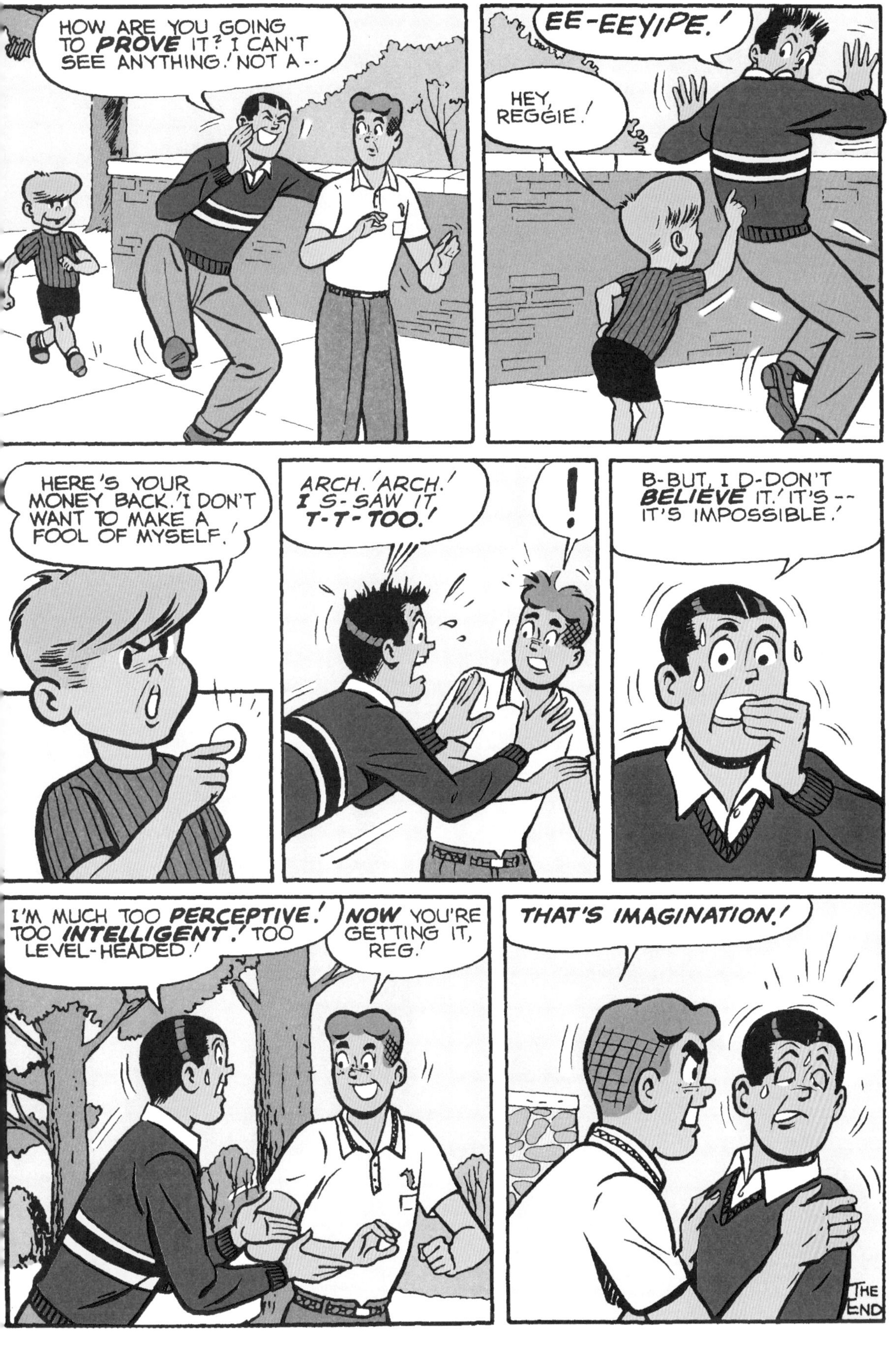
HOW ARE YOU GOING TO **PROVE** IT? I CAN'T SEE ANYTHING! NOT A--
EE-EEYIPE!
HEY, REGGIE!
HERE'S YOUR MONEY BACK! I DON'T WANT TO MAKE A FOOL OF MYSELF!
ARCH! ARCH! I S-SAW IT, T-T-TOO!
!
B-BUT, I D-DON'T **BELIEVE** IT! IT'S -- IT'S IMPOSSIBLE!
I'M MUCH TOO **PERCEPTIVE**! TOO **INTELLIGENT**! TOO LEVEL-HEADED!
NOW YOU'RE GETTING IT, REG!
THAT'S IMAGINATION!
THE END

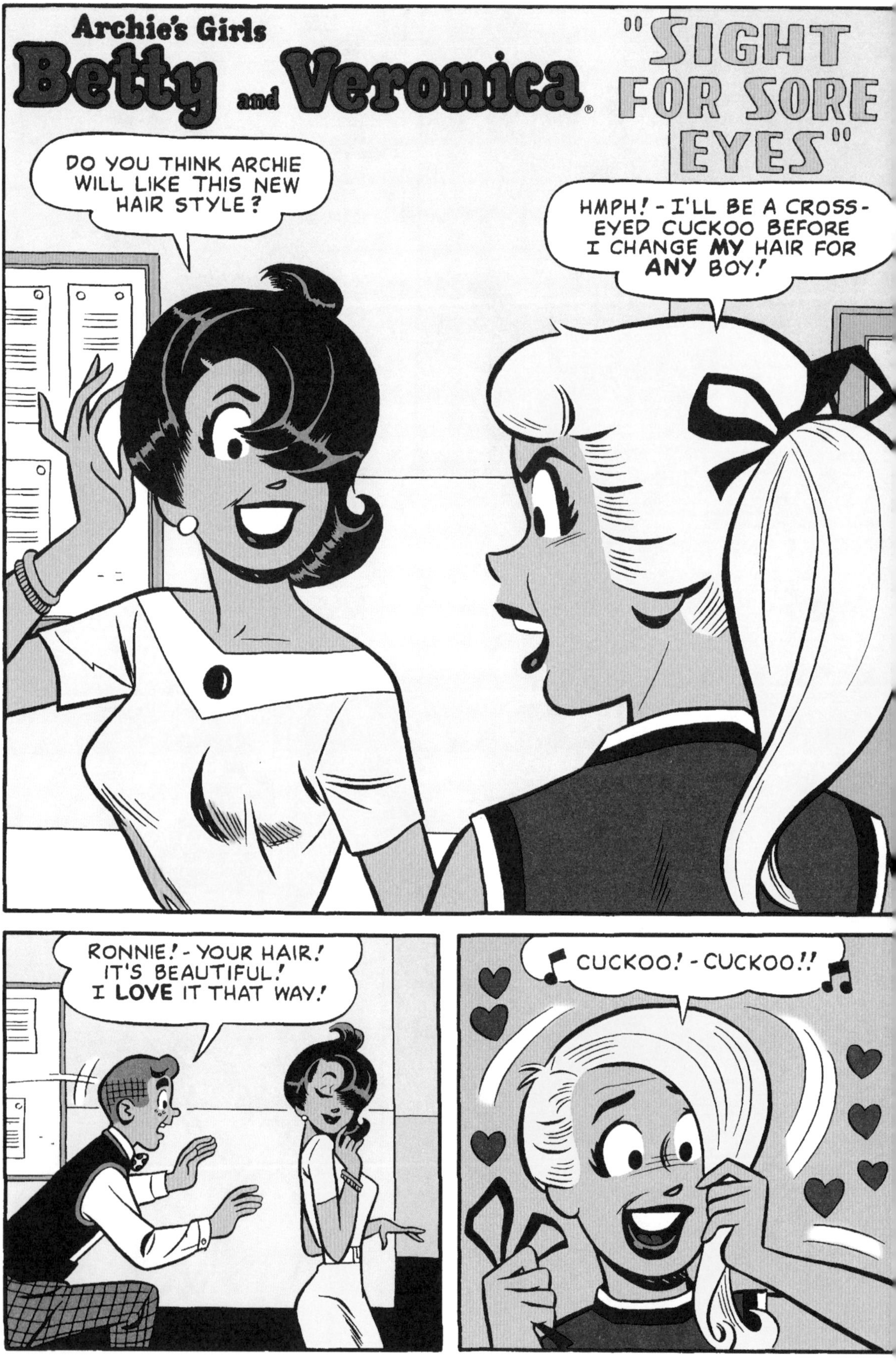
Archie's Girls Betty and Veronica
"SIGHT FOR SORE EYES"
DO YOU THINK ARCHIE WILL LIKE THIS NEW HAIR STYLE?
HMPH! - I'LL BE A CROSS-EYED CUCKOO BEFORE I CHANGE MY HAIR FOR ANY BOY!
RONNIE! - YOUR HAIR! IT'S BEAUTIFUL! I LOVE IT THAT WAY!
CUCKOO! - CUCKOO!!

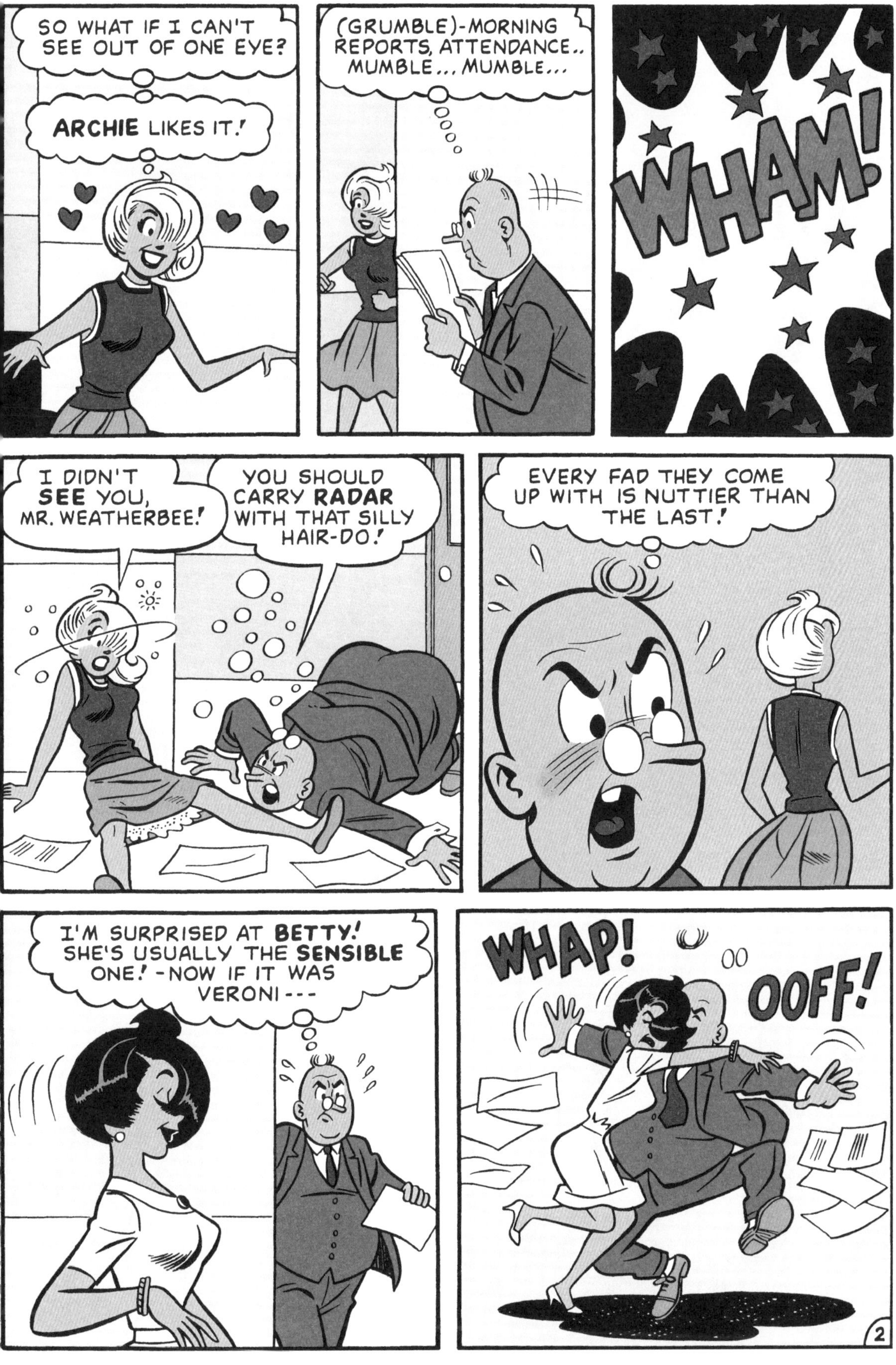
SO WHAT IF I CAN'T SEE OUT OF ONE EYE?
ARCHIE LIKES IT!
(GRUMBLE)-MORNING REPORTS, ATTENDANCE.. MUMBLE..., MUMBLE...
WHAM!
I DIDN'T SEE YOU, MR. WEATHERBEE!
YOU SHOULD CARRY RADAR WITH THAT SILLY HAIR-DO!
EVERY FAD THEY COME UP WITH IS NUTTIER THAN THE LAST!
I'M SURPRISED AT BETTY! SHE'S USUALLY THE SENSIBLE ONE! -NOW IF IT WAS VERONI---
WHAP!
OOFF!
2

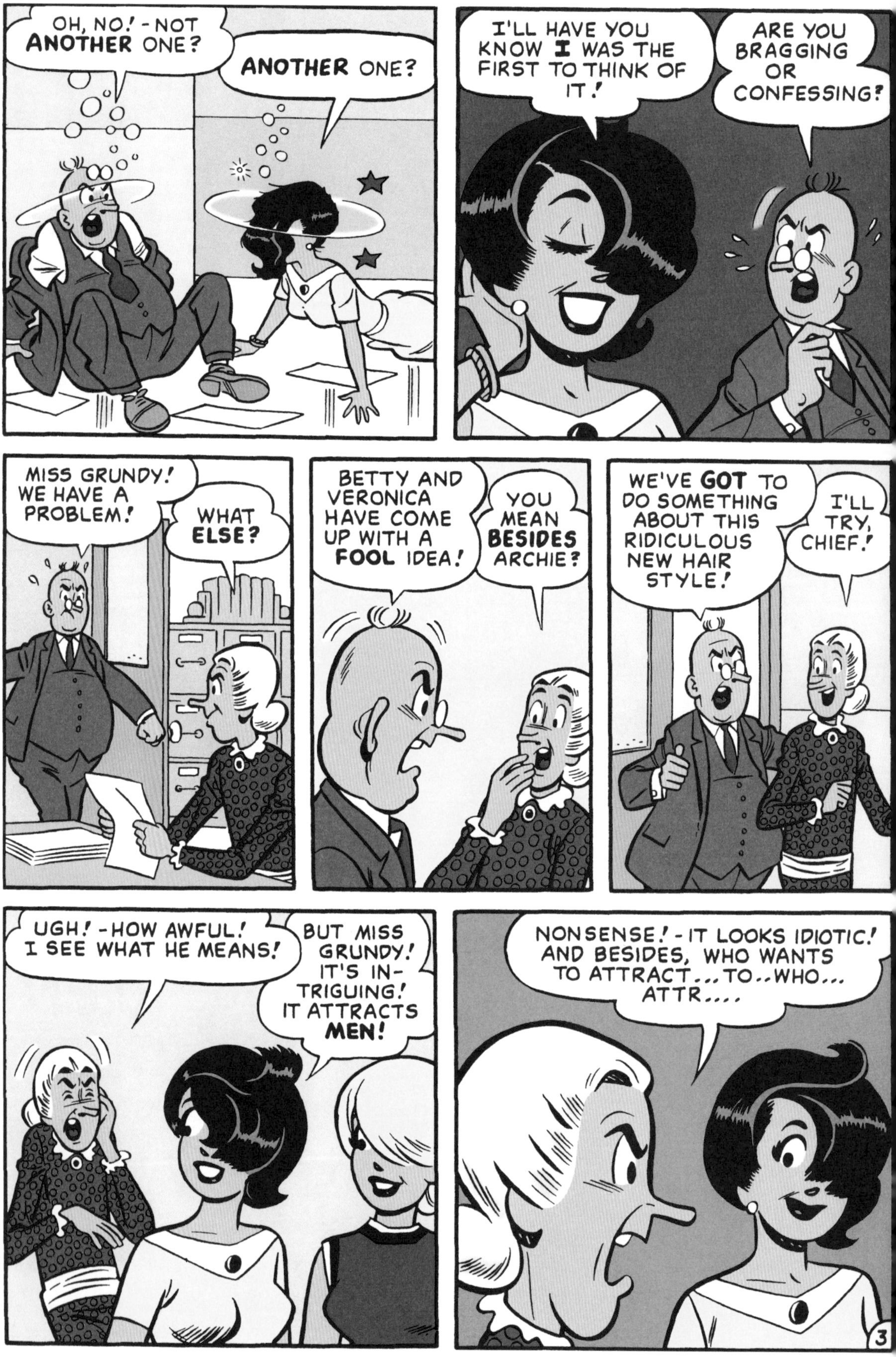
OH, NO! - NOT ANOTHER ONE?
ANOTHER ONE?
I'LL HAVE YOU KNOW I WAS THE FIRST TO THINK OF IT!
ARE YOU BRAGGING OR CONFESSING?
MISS GRUNDY! WE HAVE A PROBLEM!
WHAT ELSE?
BETTY AND VERONICA HAVE COME UP WITH A FOOL IDEA!
YOU MEAN BESIDES ARCHIE?
WE'VE GOT TO DO SOMETHING ABOUT THIS RIDICULOUS NEW HAIR STYLE!
I'LL TRY, CHIEF!
UGH! - HOW AWFUL! I SEE WHAT HE MEANS!
BUT MISS GRUNDY! IT'S IN-TRIGUING! IT ATTRACTS MEN!
NONSENSE! - IT LOOKS IDIOTIC! AND BESIDES, WHO WANTS TO ATTRACT... TO.. WHO... ATTR....
3

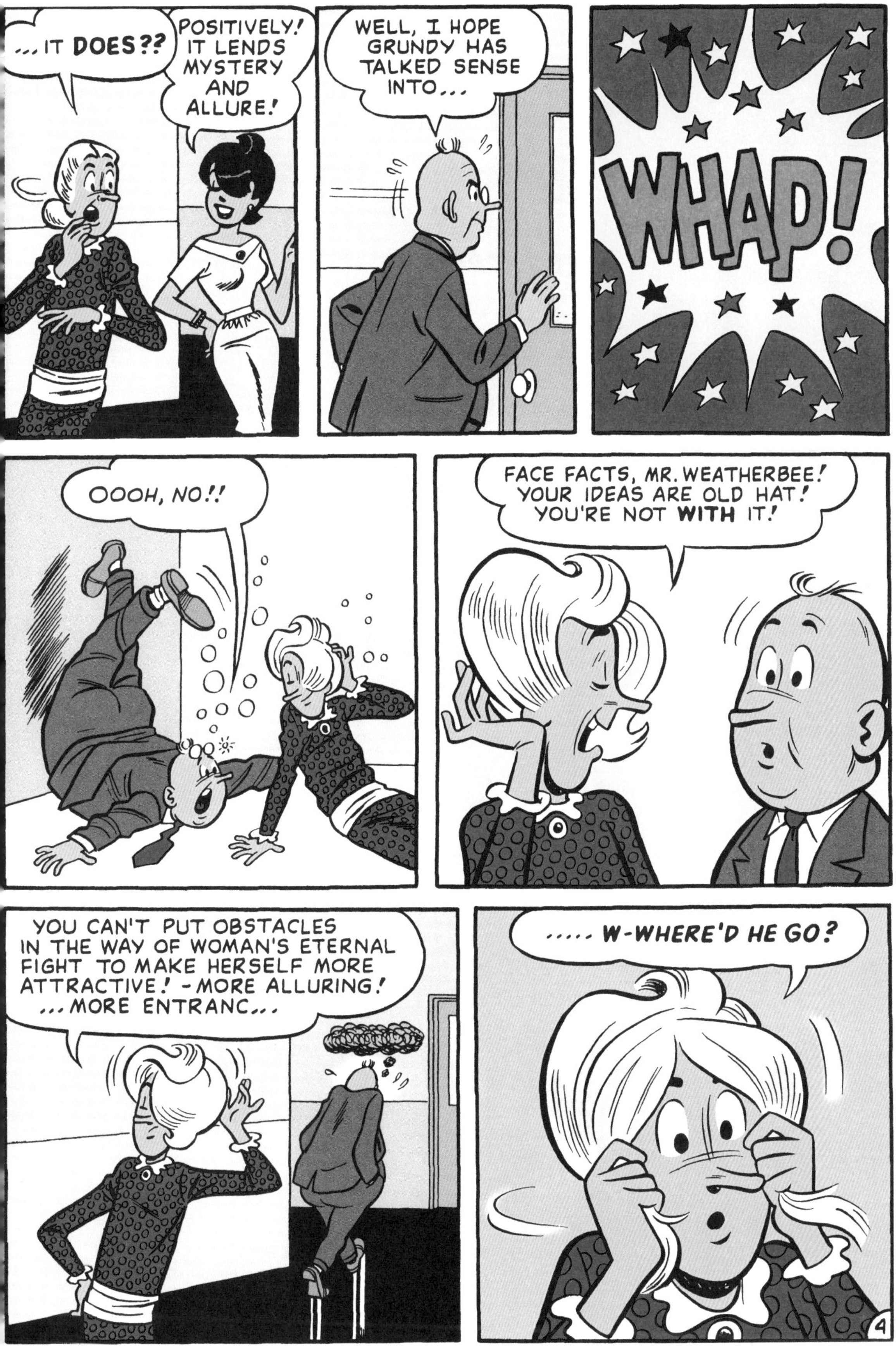
...IT **DOES??**
POSITIVELY! IT LENDS MYSTERY AND ALLURE!
WELL, I HOPE GRUNDY HAS TALKED SENSE INTO...
WHAP!
OOOH, NO!!
FACE FACTS, MR. WEATHERBEE! YOUR IDEAS ARE OLD HAT! YOU'RE NOT **WITH** IT!
YOU CAN'T PUT OBSTACLES IN THE WAY OF WOMAN'S ETERNAL FIGHT TO MAKE HERSELF MORE ATTRACTIVE! -MORE ALLURING! ...MORE ENTRANC...
..... W-WHERE'D HE GO?
4

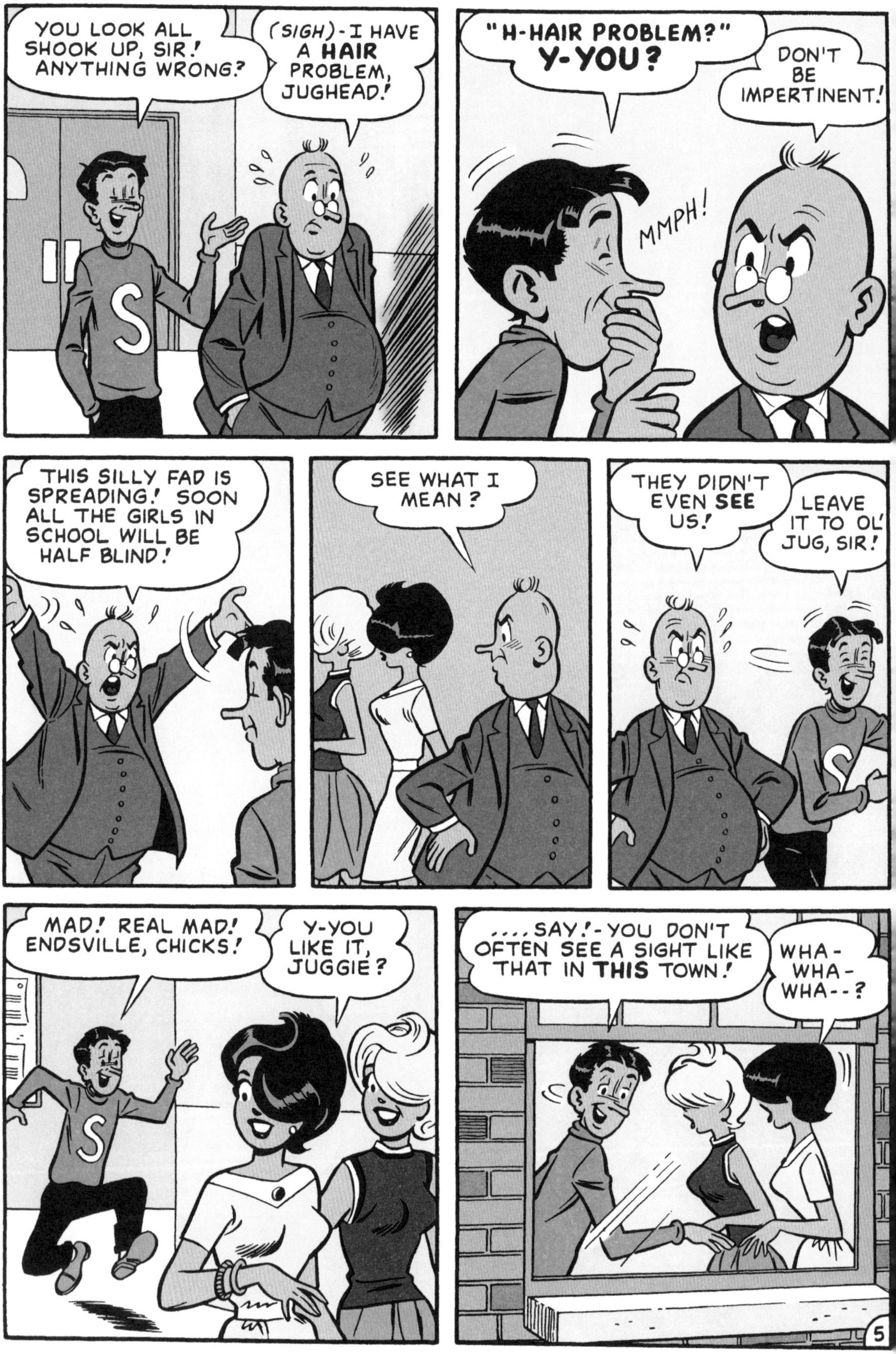
YOU LOOK ALL SHOOK UP, SIR! ANYTHING WRONG?
(SIGH)-I HAVE A HAIR PROBLEM, JUGHEAD!
"H-HAIR PROBLEM?" Y-YOU?
DON'T BE IMPERTINENT!
MMPH!
THIS SILLY FAD IS SPREADING! SOON ALL THE GIRLS IN SCHOOL WILL BE HALF BLIND!
SEE WHAT I MEAN?
THEY DIDN'T EVEN SEE US!
LEAVE IT TO OL' JUG, SIR!
MAD! REAL MAD! ENDSVILLE, CHICKS!
Y-YOU LIKE IT, JUGGIE?
....SAY!-YOU DON'T OFTEN SEE A SIGHT LIKE THAT IN THIS TOWN!
WHA-WHA-WHA--?
5

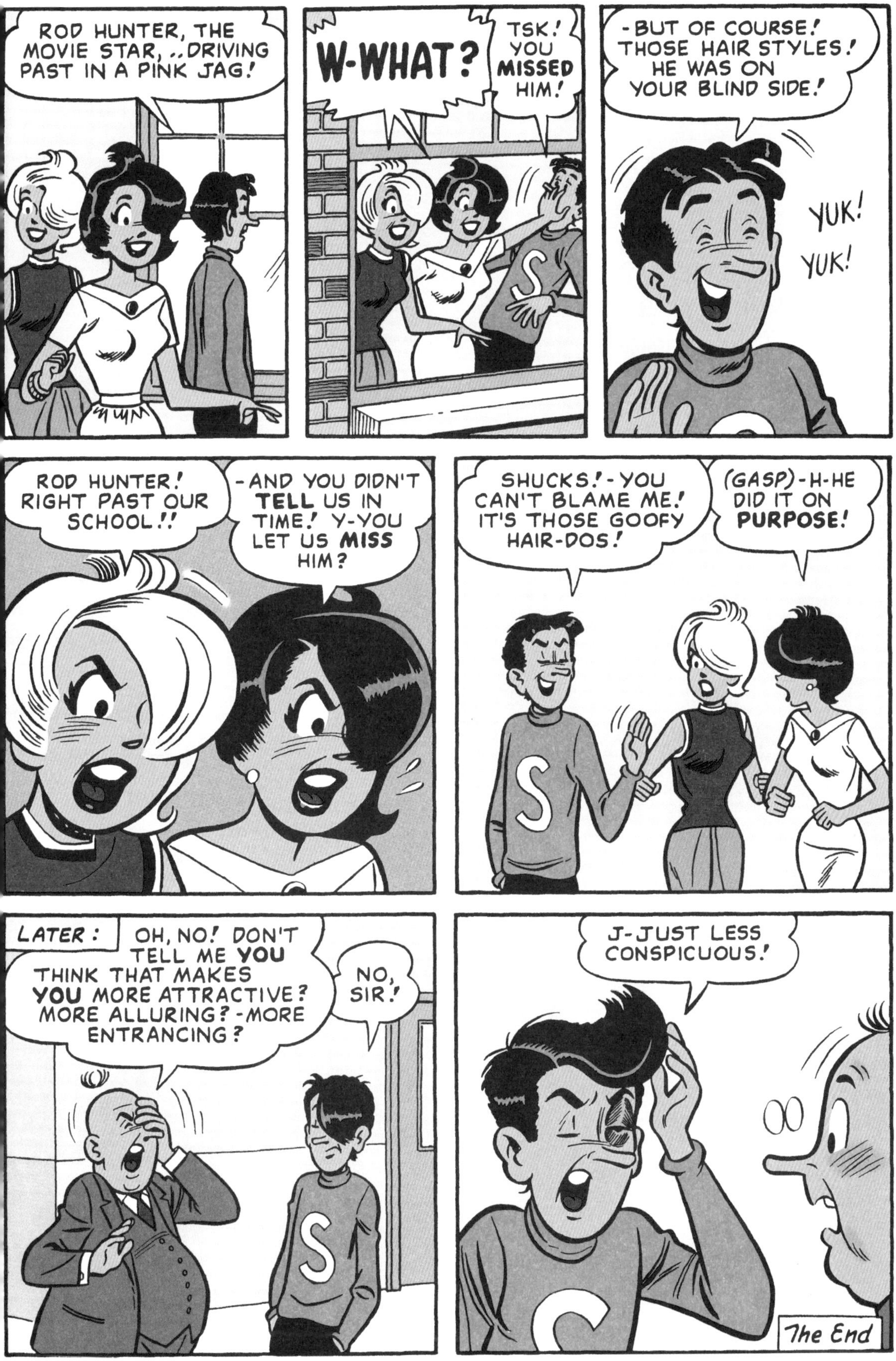
ROD HUNTER, THE MOVIE STAR, ..DRIVING PAST IN A PINK JAG!
W-WHAT?
TSK! YOU MISSED HIM!
-BUT OF COURSE! THOSE HAIR STYLES! HE WAS ON YOUR BLIND SIDE!
YUK!
YUK!
ROD HUNTER! RIGHT PAST OUR SCHOOL!!
-AND YOU DIDN'T TELL US IN TIME! Y-YOU LET US MISS HIM?
SHUCKS!-YOU CAN'T BLAME ME! IT'S THOSE GOOFY HAIR-DOS!
(GASP)-H-HE DID IT ON PURPOSE!
LATER:
OH, NO! DON'T TELL ME YOU THINK THAT MAKES YOU MORE ATTRACTIVE? MORE ALLURING? -MORE ENTRANCING?
NO, SIR!
J-JUST LESS CONSPICUOUS!
The End

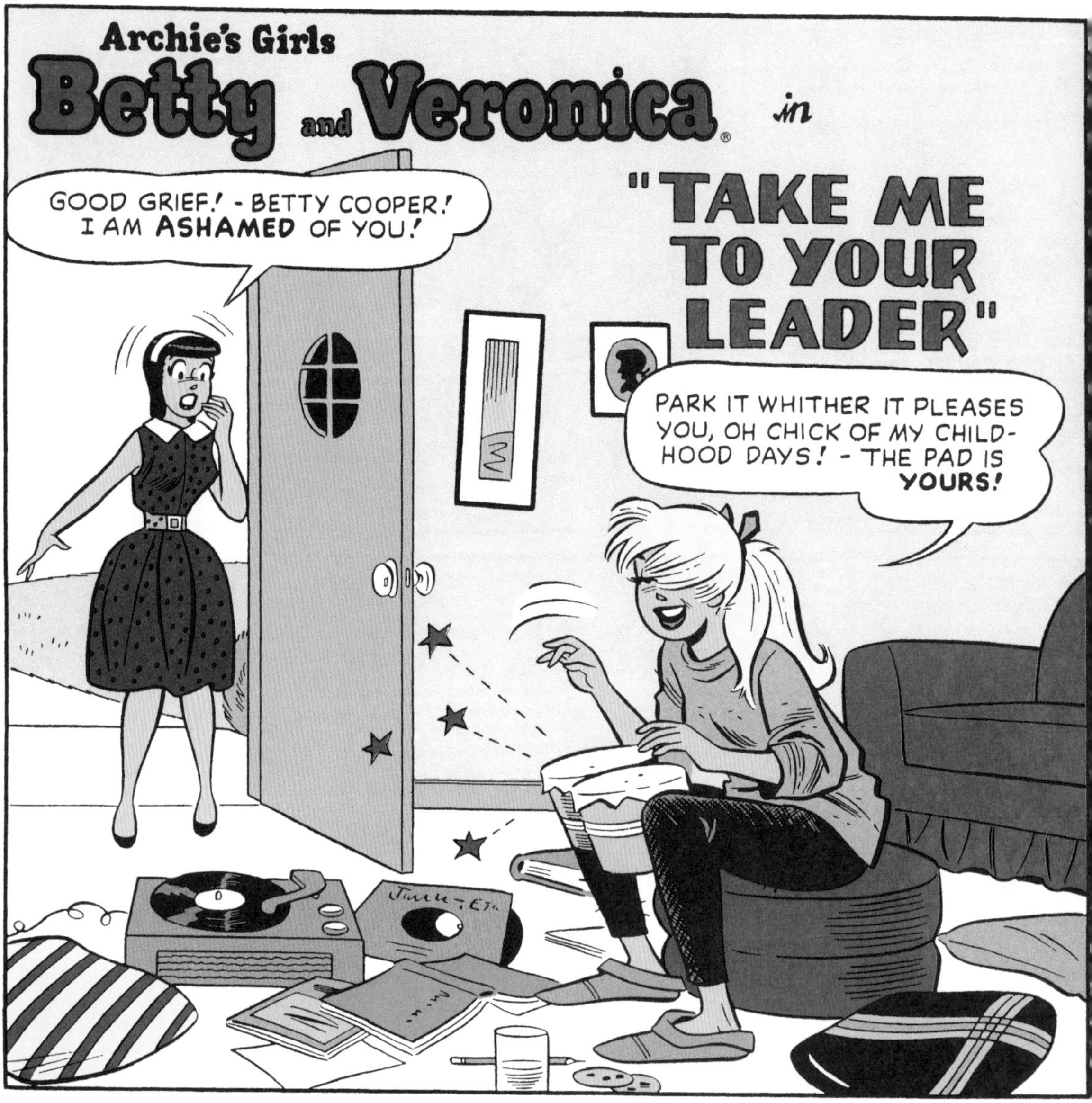
Archie's Girls
Betty and Veronica in
"TAKE ME TO YOUR LEADER"
GOOD GRIEF! - BETTY COOPER! I AM ASHAMED OF YOU!
PARK IT WHITHER IT PLEASES YOU, OH CHICK OF MY CHILD-HOOD DAYS! - THE PAD IS YOURS!

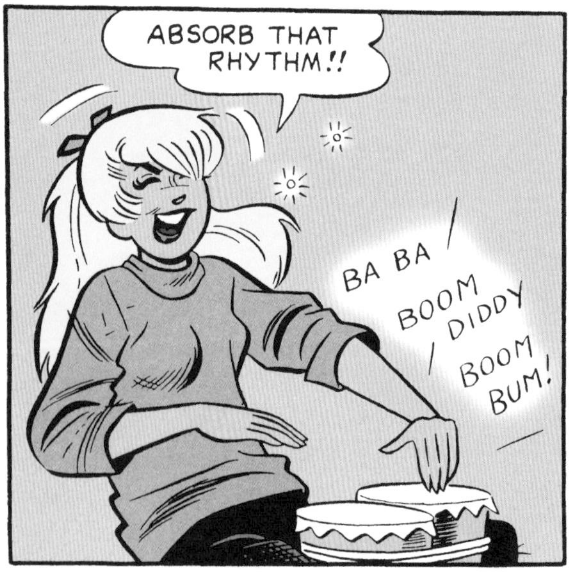
ABSORB THAT RHYTHM!!
BA BA / BOOM DIDDY / BOOM BUM!

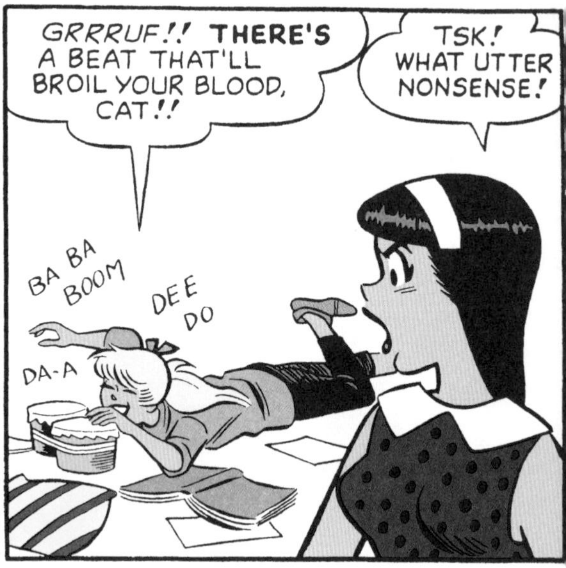
GRRRUF!! THERE'S A BEAT THAT'LL BROIL YOUR BLOOD, CAT!!
TSK! WHAT UTTER NONSENSE!
BA BA BOOM
DEE DO
DA-A

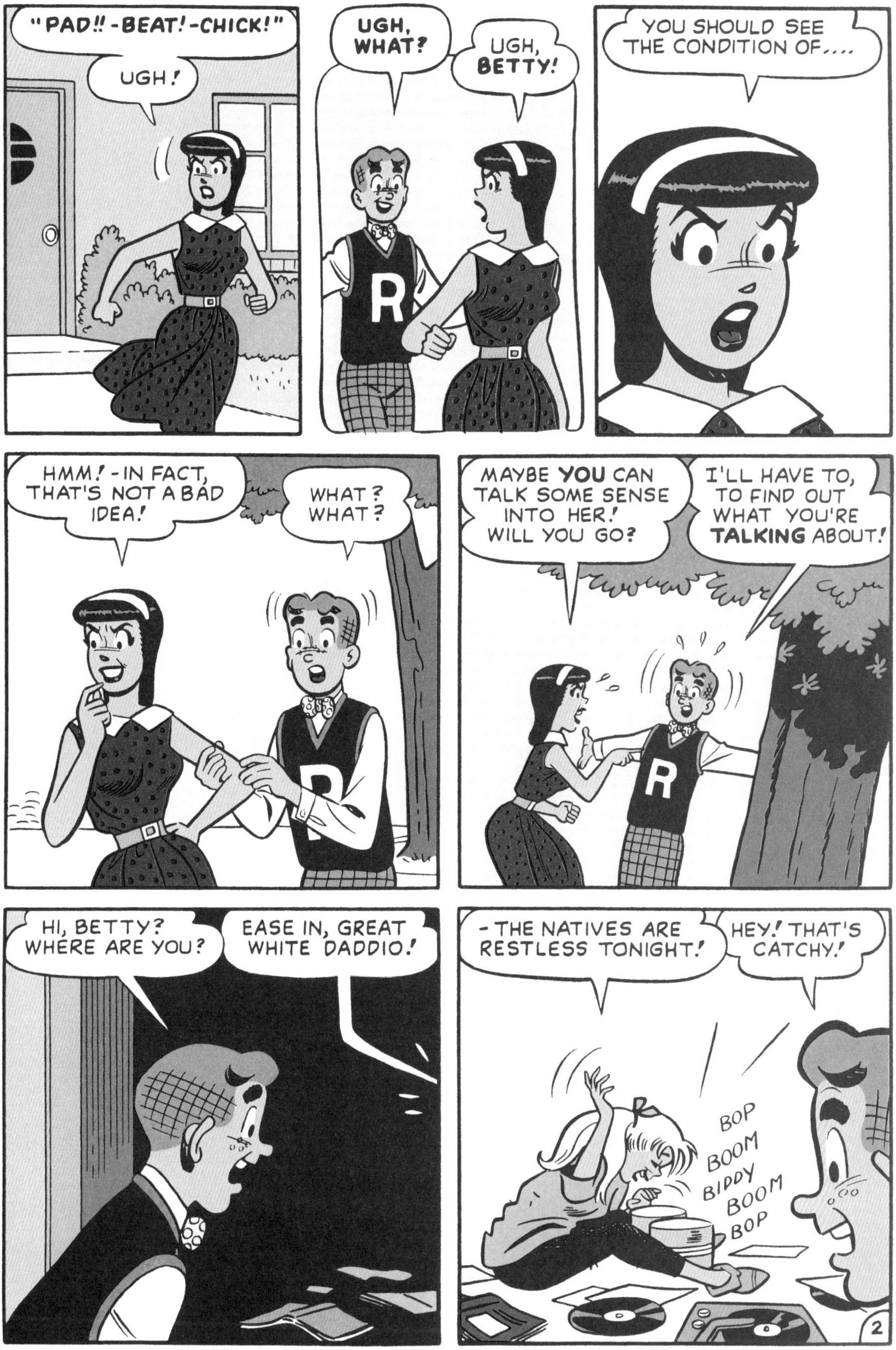
"PAD!! -BEAT! -CHICK!"
UGH!
UGH, WHAT?
UGH, BETTY!
YOU SHOULD SEE THE CONDITION OF....
HMM! -IN FACT, THAT'S NOT A BAD IDEA!
WHAT? WHAT?
MAYBE YOU CAN TALK SOME SENSE INTO HER! WILL YOU GO?
I'LL HAVE TO, TO FIND OUT WHAT YOU'RE TALKING ABOUT!
HI, BETTY? WHERE ARE YOU?
EASE IN, GREAT WHITE DADDIO!
-THE NATIVES ARE RESTLESS TONIGHT!
HEY! THAT'S CATCHY!
BOP
BOOM
BIDDY
BOOM
BOP
2

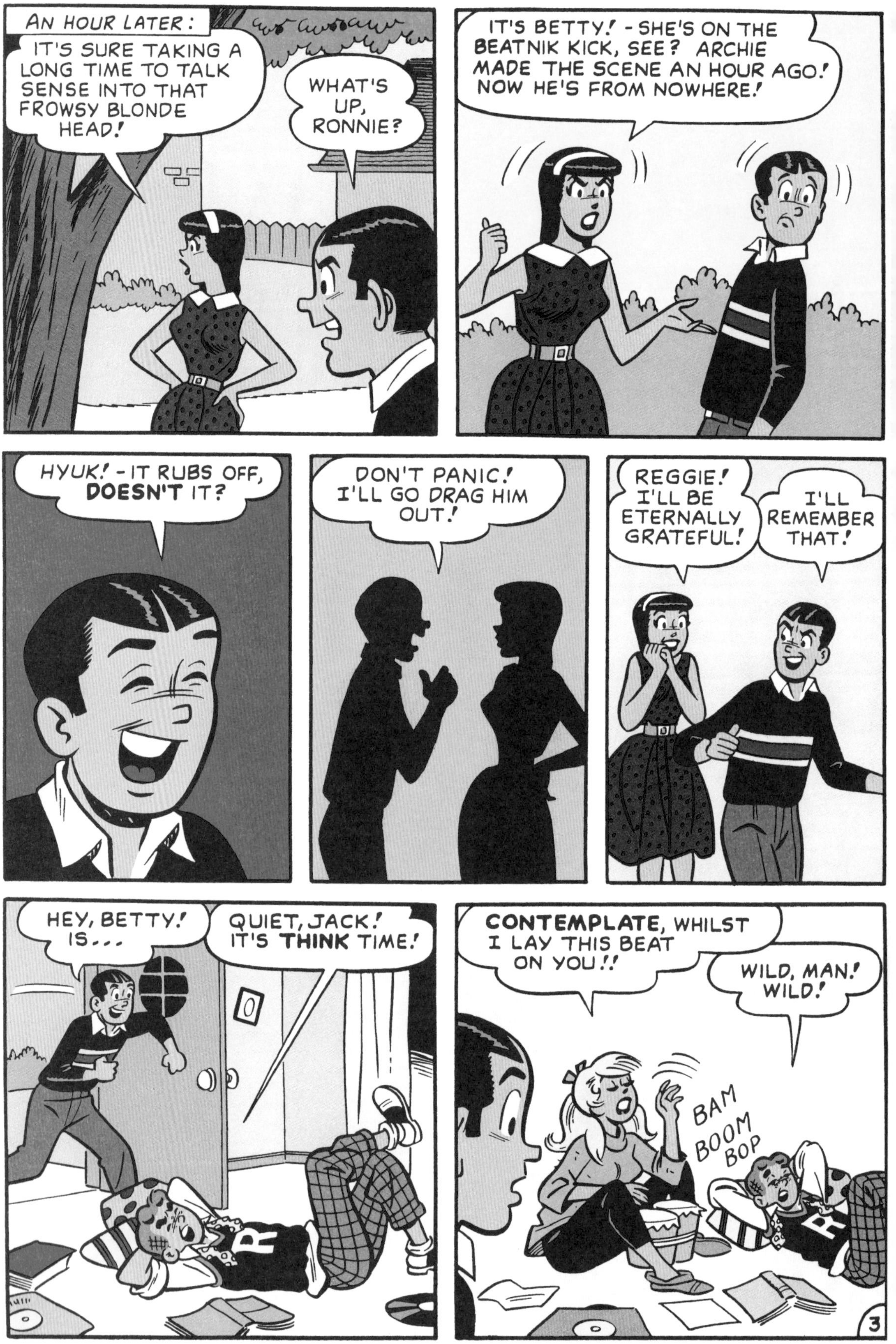
AN HOUR LATER:
IT'S SURE TAKING A LONG TIME TO TALK SENSE INTO THAT FROWSY BLONDE HEAD!
WHAT'S UP, RONNIE?
IT'S BETTY! - SHE'S ON THE BEATNIK KICK, SEE? ARCHIE MADE THE SCENE AN HOUR AGO! NOW HE'S FROM NOWHERE!
HYUK! - IT RUBS OFF, DOESN'T IT?
DON'T PANIC! I'LL GO DRAG HIM OUT!
REGGIE! I'LL BE ETERNALLY GRATEFUL!
I'LL REMEMBER THAT!
HEY, BETTY! IS...
QUIET, JACK! IT'S THINK TIME!
CONTEMPLATE, WHILST I LAY THIS BEAT ON YOU!!
WILD, MAN! WILD!
BAM BOOM BOP
3

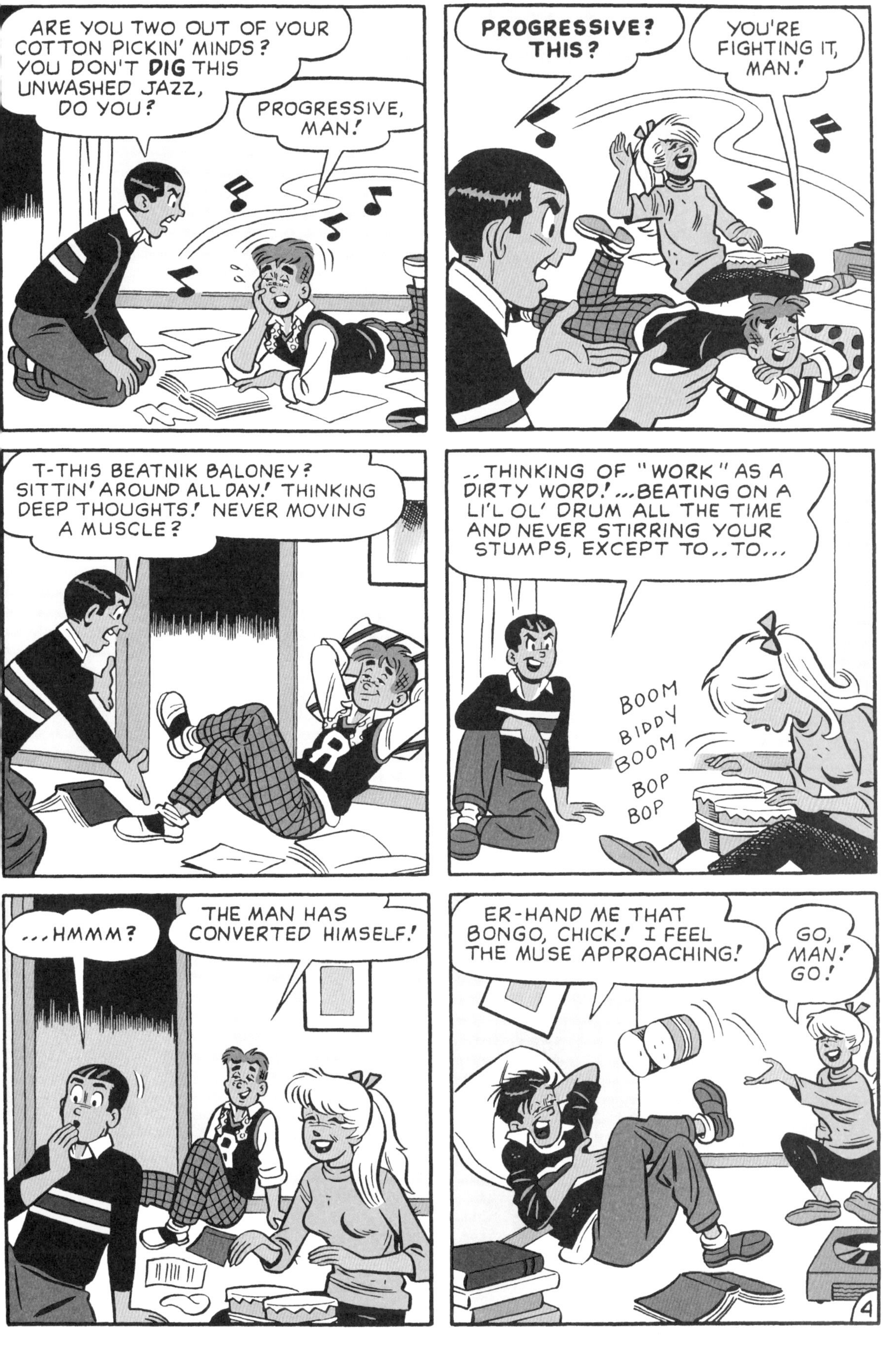
ARE YOU TWO OUT OF YOUR COTTON PICKIN' MINDS? YOU DON'T **DIG** THIS UNWASHED JAZZ, DO YOU?
PROGRESSIVE, MAN!
PROGRESSIVE? THIS?
YOU'RE FIGHTING IT, MAN!
T-THIS BEATNIK BALONEY? SITTIN' AROUND ALL DAY! THINKING DEEP THOUGHTS! NEVER MOVING A MUSCLE?
..THINKING OF "WORK" AS A DIRTY WORD! ...BEATING ON A LI'L OL' DRUM ALL THE TIME AND NEVER STIRRING YOUR STUMPS, EXCEPT TO..TO...
BOOM BIDDY BOOM BOP BOP
...HMMM?
THE MAN HAS CONVERTED HIMSELF!
ER-HAND ME THAT BONGO, CHICK! I FEEL THE MUSE APPROACHING!
GO, MAN! GO!
4

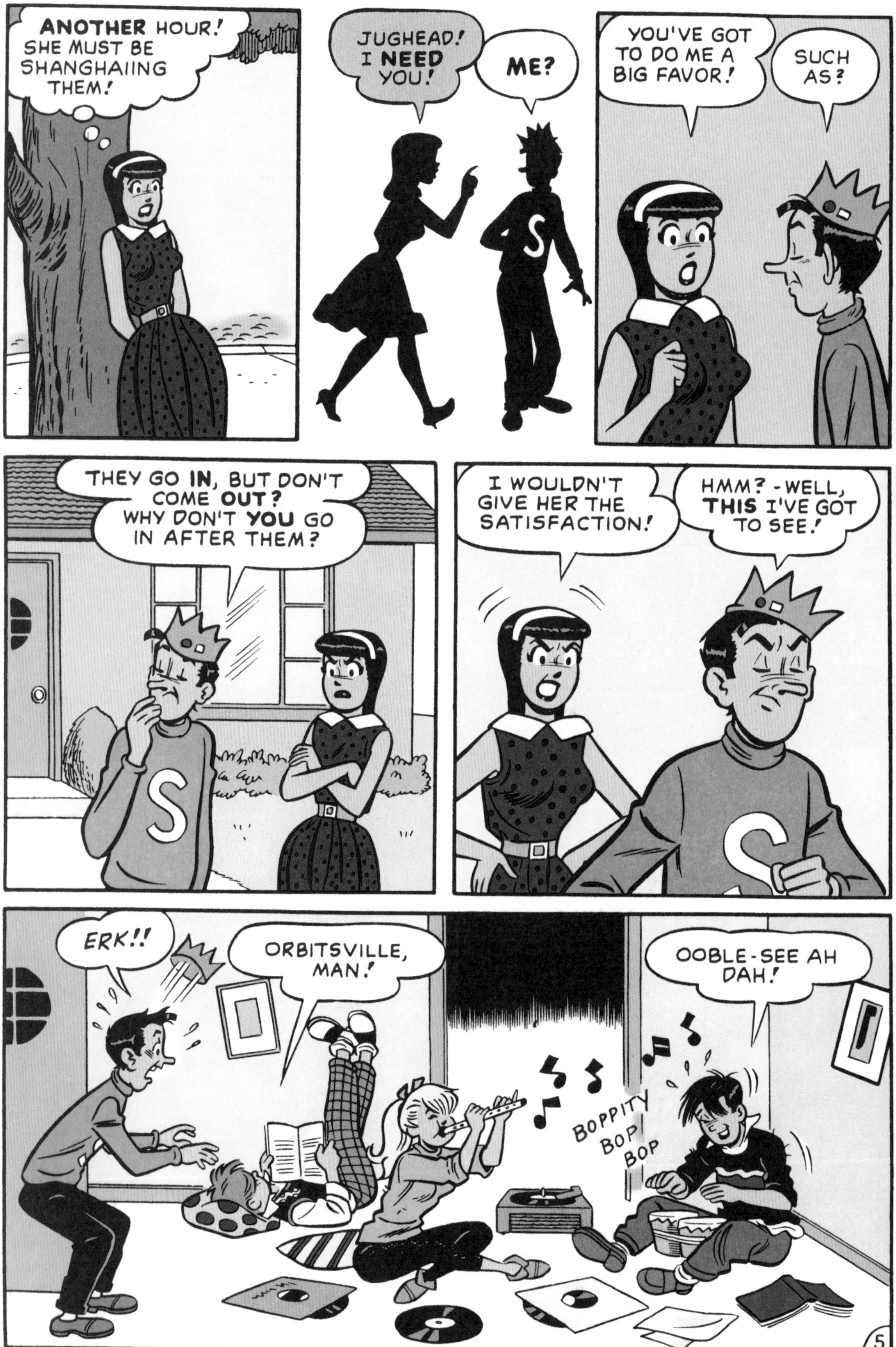
ANOTHER HOUR! SHE MUST BE SHANGHAIING THEM!
JUGHEAD! I NEED YOU!
ME?
YOU'VE GOT TO DO ME A BIG FAVOR!
SUCH AS?
THEY GO IN, BUT DON'T COME OUT? WHY DON'T YOU GO IN AFTER THEM?
I WOULDN'T GIVE HER THE SATISFACTION!
HMM? -WELL, THIS I'VE GOT TO SEE!
ERK!!
ORBITSVILLE, MAN!
OOBLE-SEE AH DAH!
BOPPITY BOP BOP
5

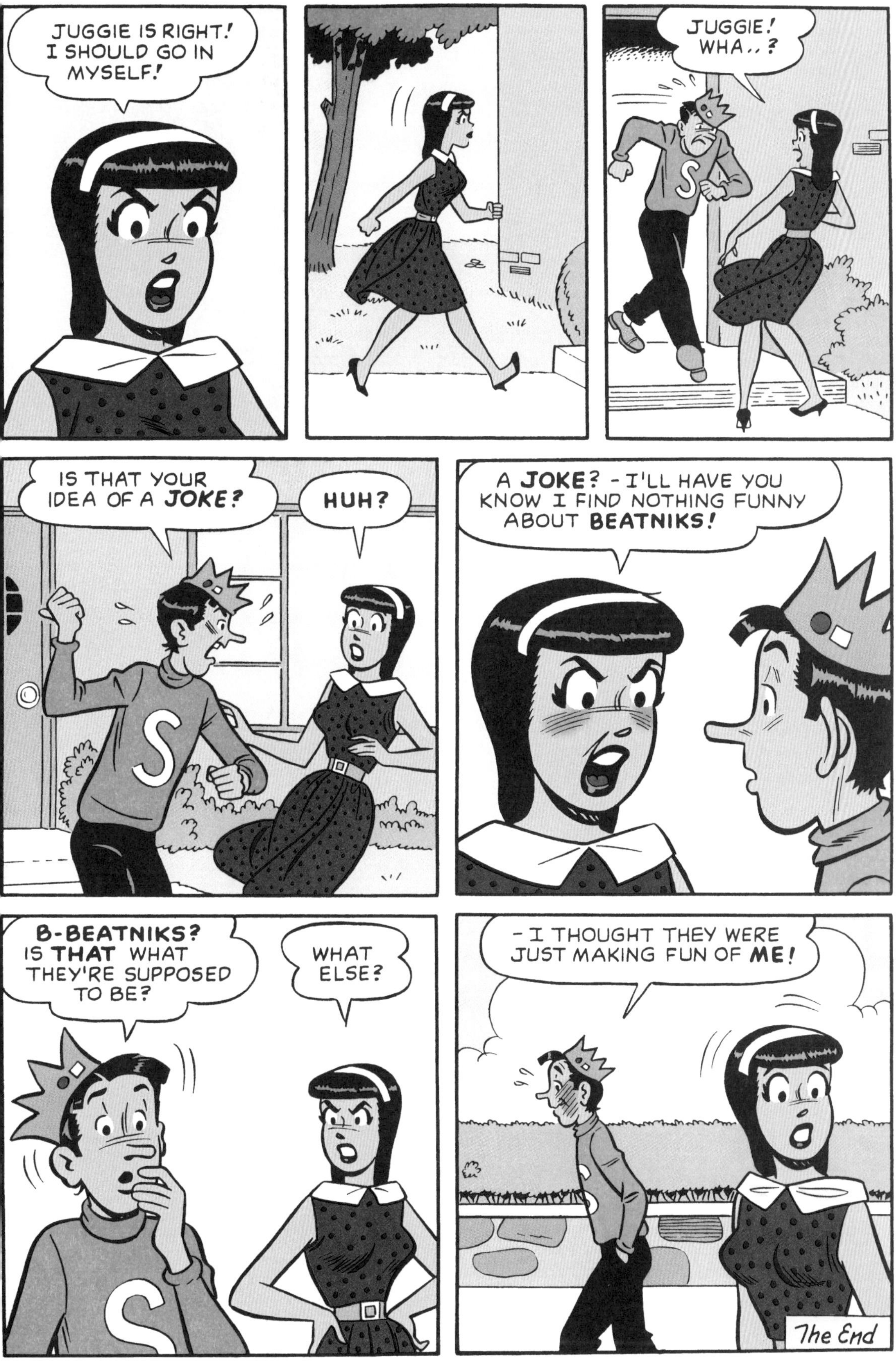
JUGGIE IS RIGHT! I SHOULD GO IN MYSELF!
JUGGIE! WHA.. ?
IS THAT YOUR IDEA OF A **JOKE?**
HUH?
A **JOKE?** - I'LL HAVE YOU KNOW I FIND NOTHING FUNNY ABOUT **BEATNIKS!**
B-BEATNIKS? IS **THAT** WHAT THEY'RE SUPPOSED TO BE?
WHAT ELSE?
- I THOUGHT THEY WERE JUST MAKING FUN OF **ME!**
The End

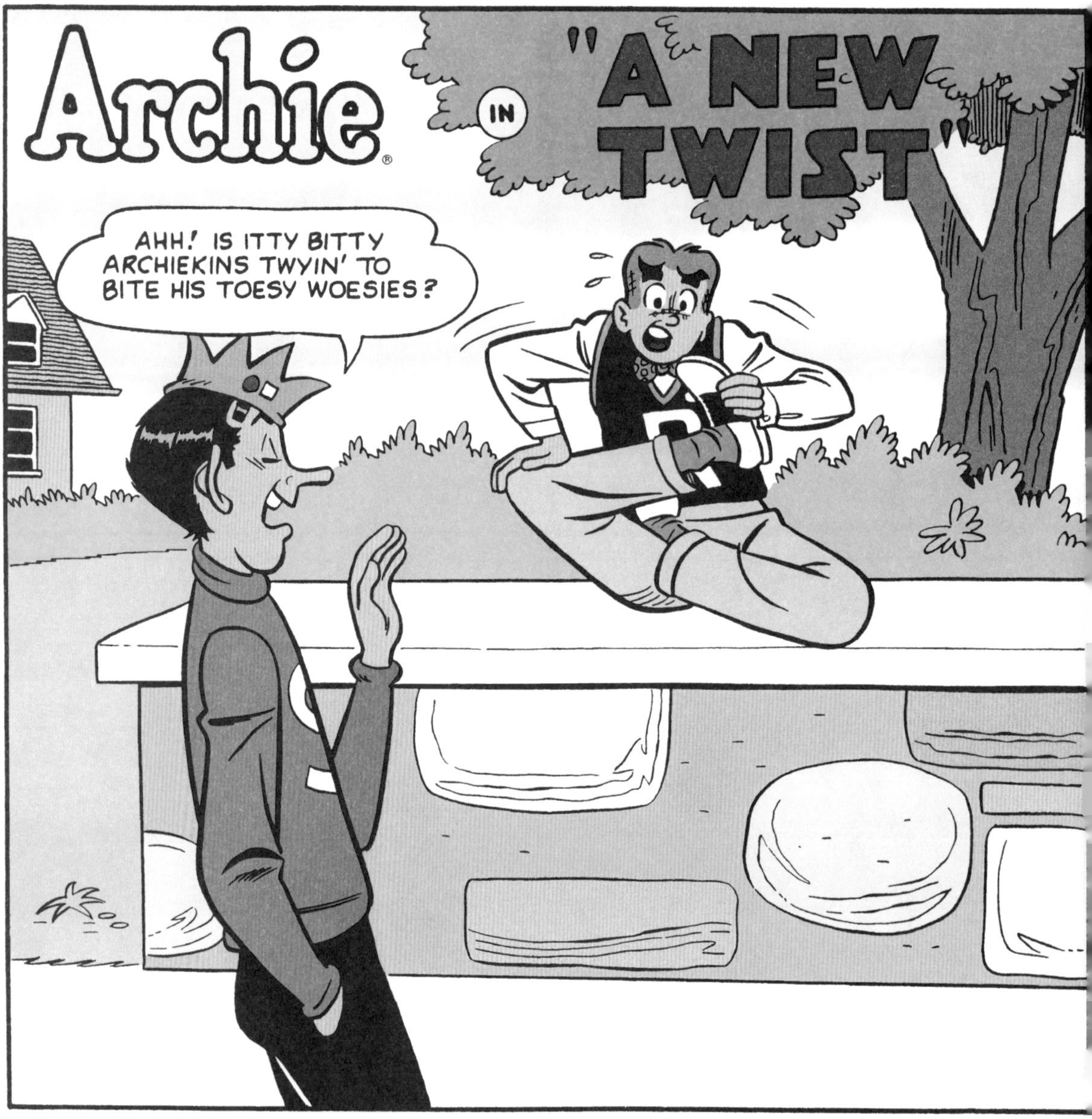
Archie®
IN
"A NEW TWIST"
AHH! IS ITTY BITTY ARCHIEKINS TWYIN' TO BITE HIS TOESY WOESIES?

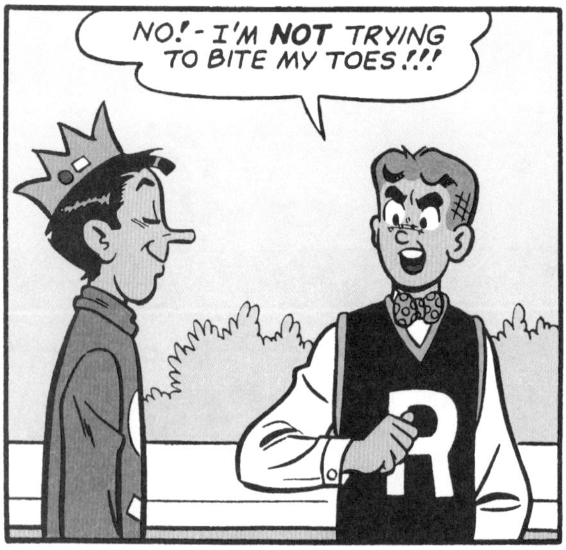
NO! - I'M NOT TRYING TO BITE MY TOES!!!

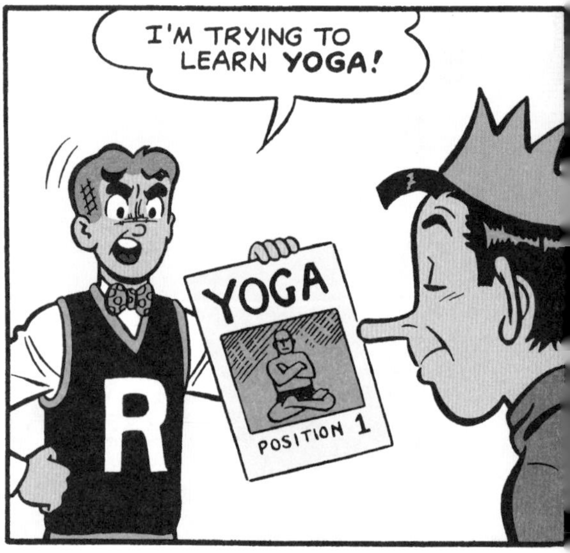
I'M TRYING TO LEARN YOGA!
YOGA
POSITION 1

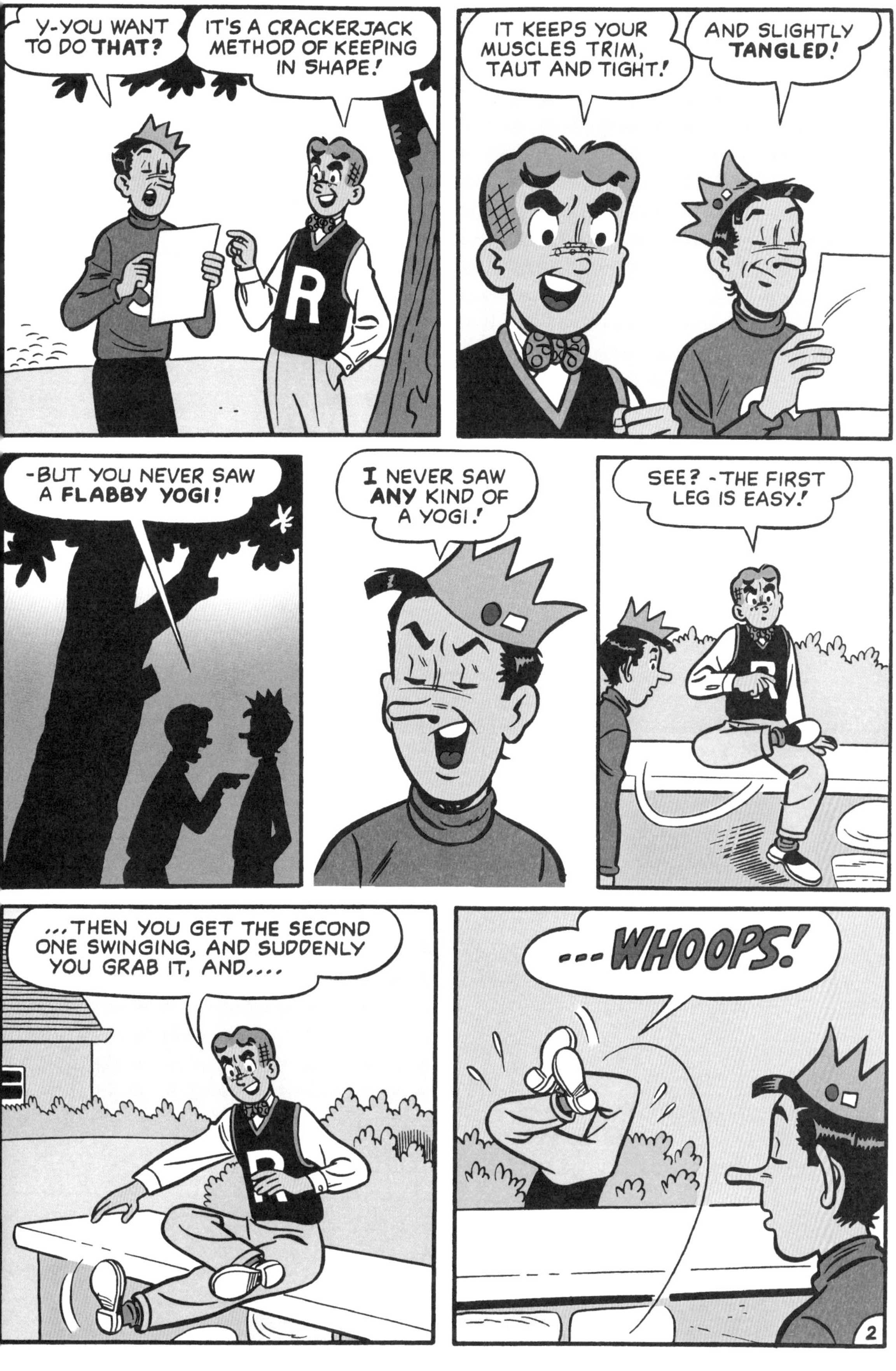
Y-YOU WANT TO DO **THAT?**
IT'S A CRACKERJACK METHOD OF KEEPING IN SHAPE!
IT KEEPS YOUR MUSCLES TRIM, TAUT AND TIGHT!
AND SLIGHTLY **TANGLED!**
-BUT YOU NEVER SAW A **FLABBY YOGI!**
I NEVER SAW **ANY** KIND OF A YOGI!
SEE? -THE FIRST LEG IS EASY!
...THEN YOU GET THE SECOND ONE SWINGING, AND SUDDENLY YOU GRAB IT, AND....
---WHOOPS!
2

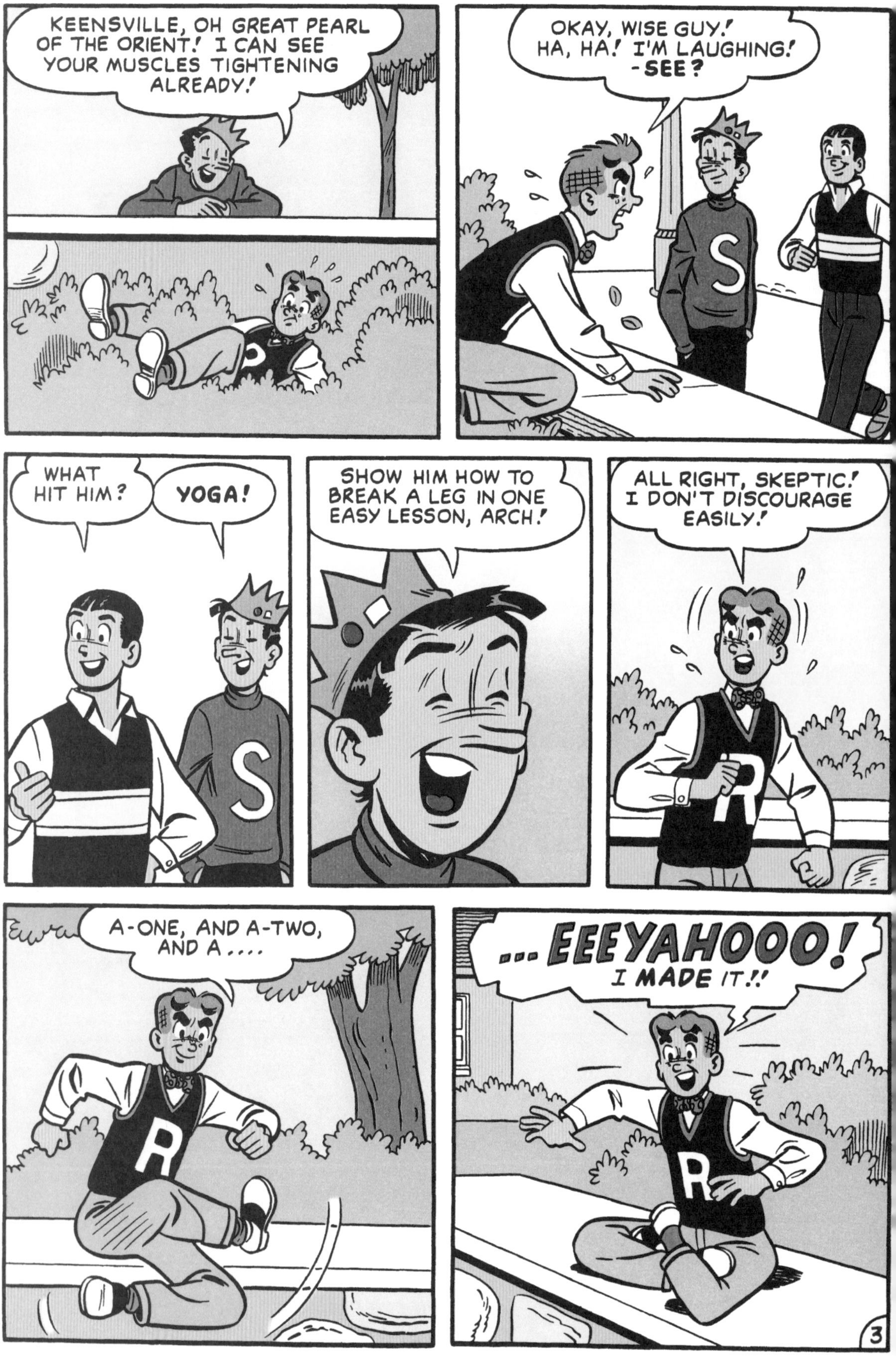
KEENSVILLE, OH GREAT PEARL OF THE ORIENT! I CAN SEE YOUR MUSCLES TIGHTENING ALREADY!
OKAY, WISE GUY! HA, HA! I'M LAUGHING! -SEE?
WHAT HIT HIM?
YOGA!
SHOW HIM HOW TO BREAK A LEG IN ONE EASY LESSON, ARCH!
ALL RIGHT, SKEPTIC! I DON'T DISCOURAGE EASILY!
A-ONE, AND A-TWO, AND A....
...EEEYAHOOO! I MADE IT!!
3

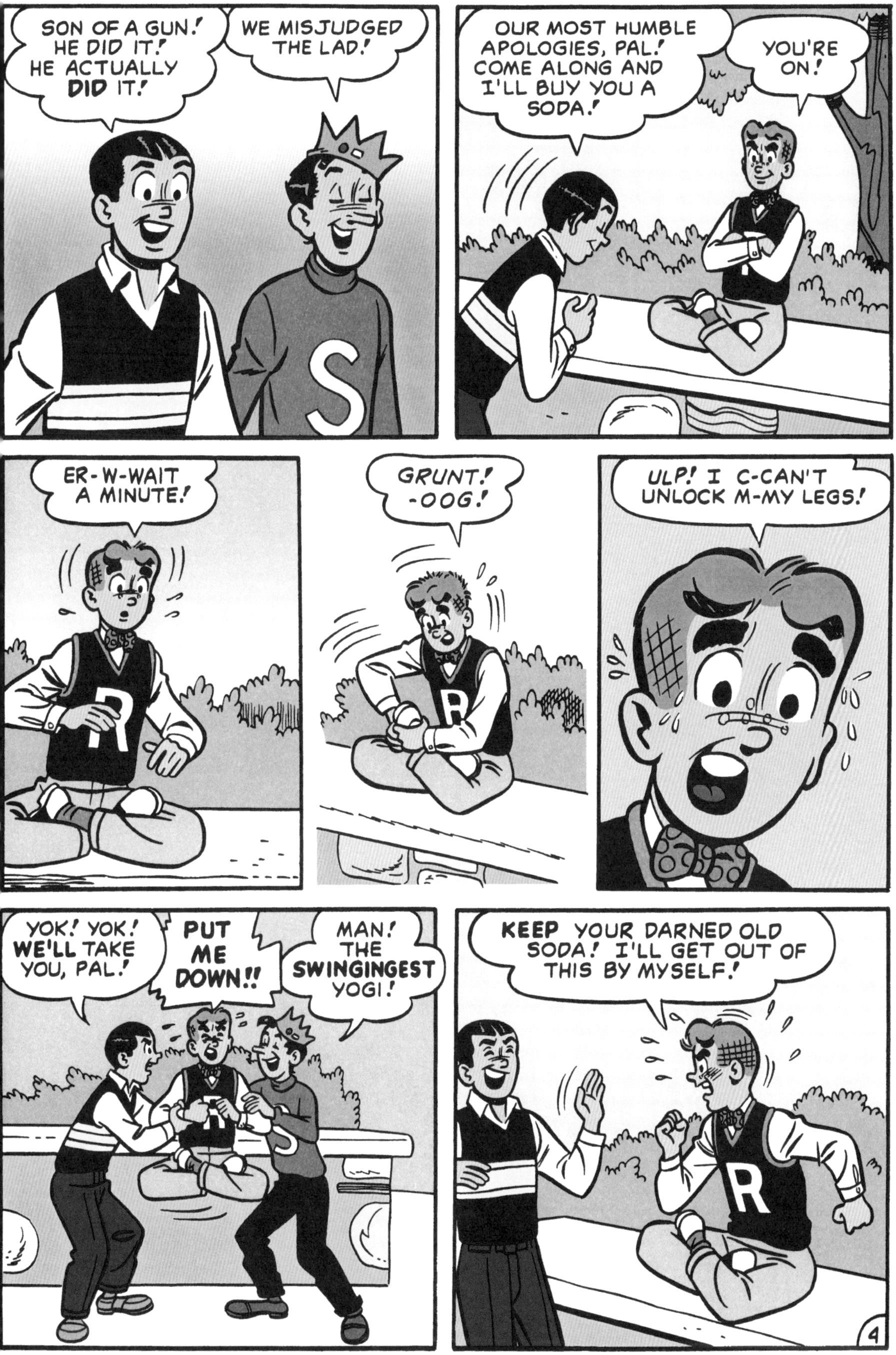
SON OF A GUN! HE DID IT! HE ACTUALLY **DID** IT!
WE MISJUDGED THE LAD!
OUR MOST HUMBLE APOLOGIES, PAL! COME ALONG AND I'LL BUY YOU A SODA!
YOU'RE ON!
ER-W-WAIT A MINUTE!
GRUNT! -OOG!
ULP! I C-CAN'T UNLOCK M-MY LEGS!
YOK! YOK! **WE'LL** TAKE YOU, PAL!
PUT ME DOWN!!
MAN! THE **SWINGINGEST** YOGI!
KEEP YOUR DARNED OLD SODA! I'LL GET OUT OF THIS BY MYSELF!
4

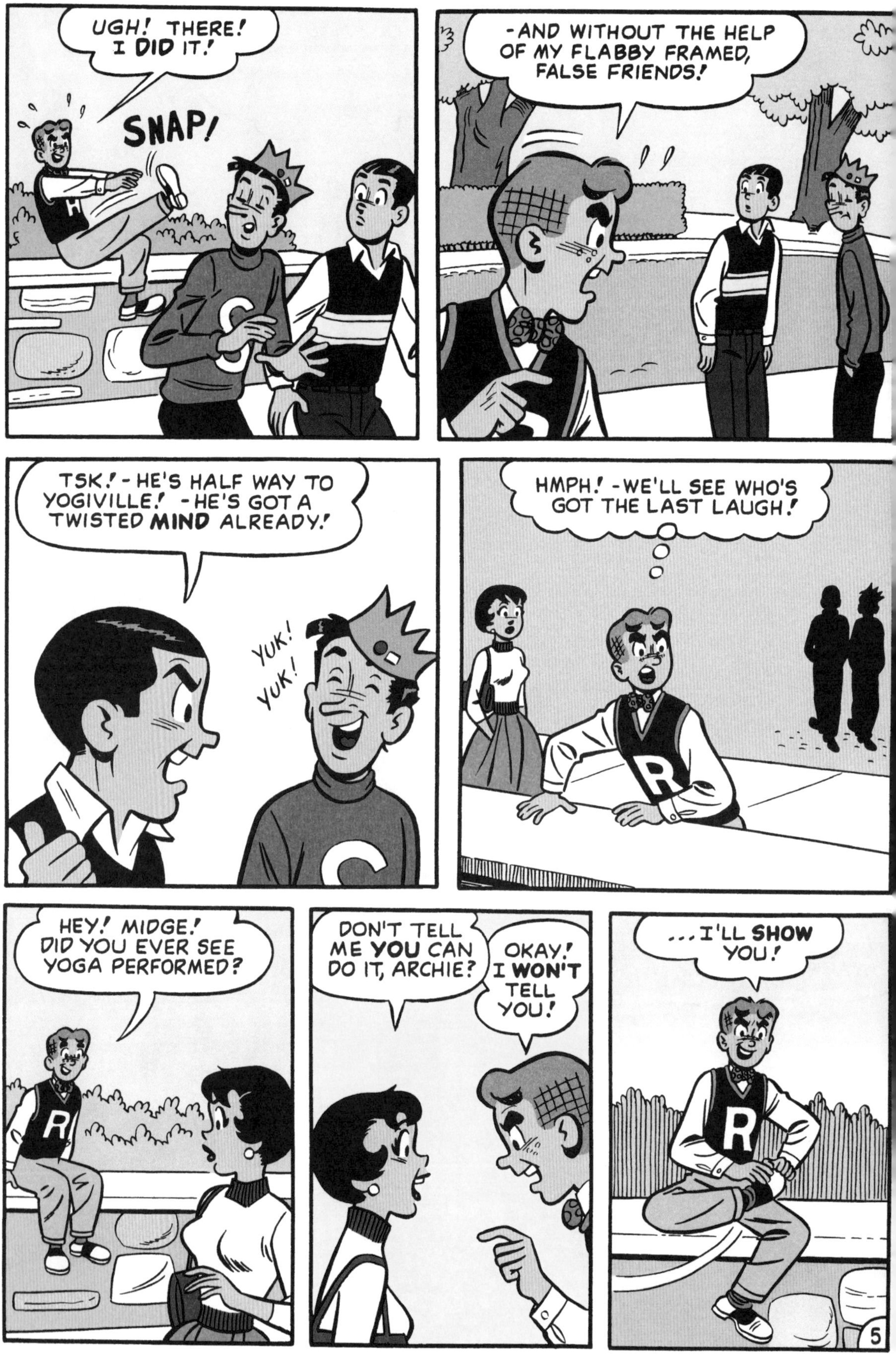
UGH! THERE! I DID IT!
SNAP!
-AND WITHOUT THE HELP OF MY FLABBY FRAMED, FALSE FRIENDS!
TSK! -HE'S HALF WAY TO YOGIVILLE! -HE'S GOT A TWISTED MIND ALREADY!
YUK! YUK!
HMPH! -WE'LL SEE WHO'S GOT THE LAST LAUGH!
HEY! MIDGE! DID YOU EVER SEE YOGA PERFORMED?
DON'T TELL ME YOU CAN DO IT, ARCHIE?
OKAY! I WON'T TELL YOU!
...I'LL SHOW YOU!
5

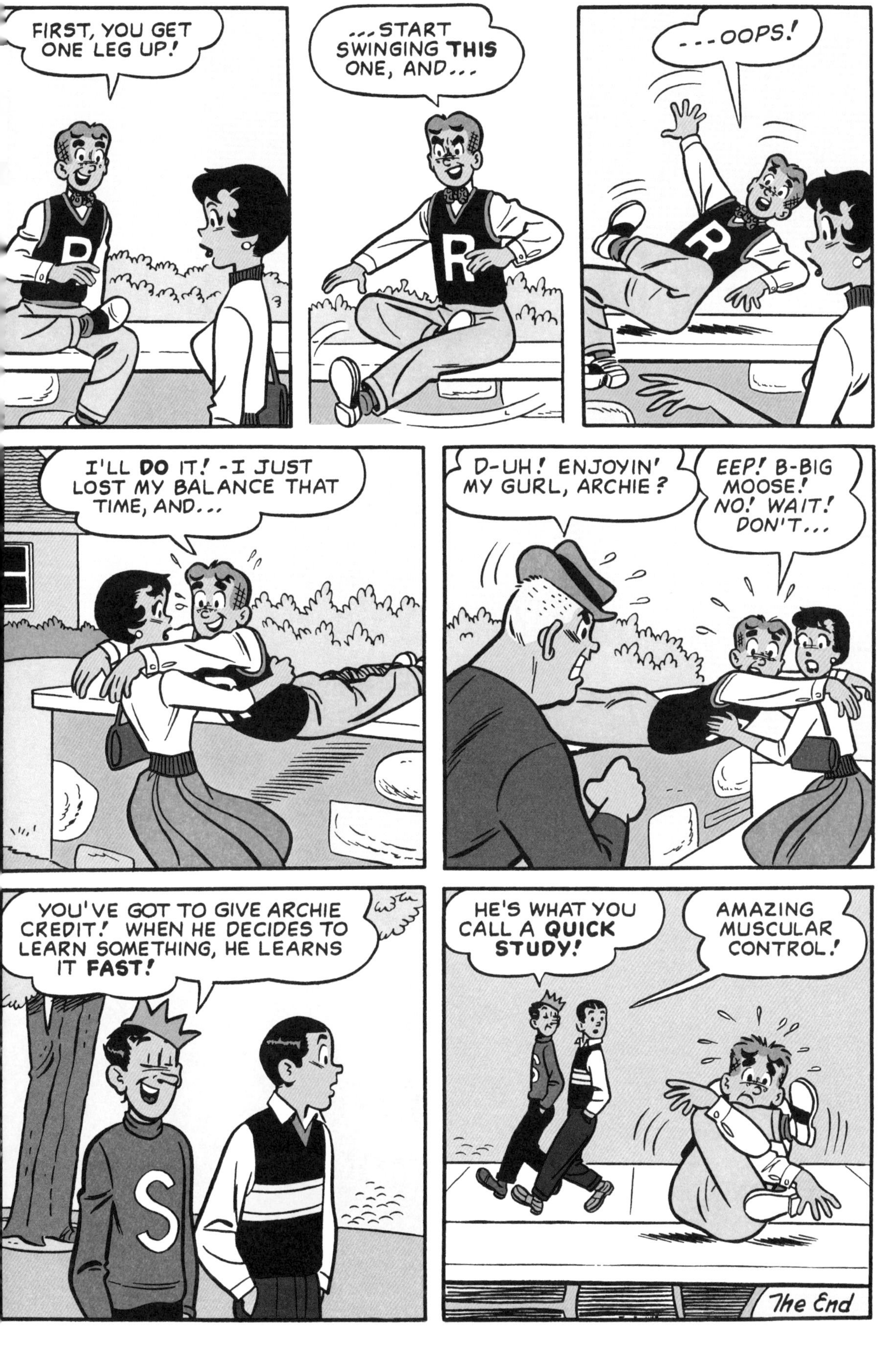
FIRST, YOU GET ONE LEG UP!
...START SWINGING THIS ONE, AND...
---OOPS!
I'LL DO IT! -I JUST LOST MY BALANCE THAT TIME, AND...
D-UH! ENJOYIN' MY GURL, ARCHIE?
EEP! B-BIG MOOSE! NO! WAIT! DON'T...
YOU'VE GOT TO GIVE ARCHIE CREDIT! WHEN HE DECIDES TO LEARN SOMETHING, HE LEARNS IT FAST!
HE'S WHAT YOU CALL A QUICK STUDY!
AMAZING MUSCULAR CONTROL!
The End

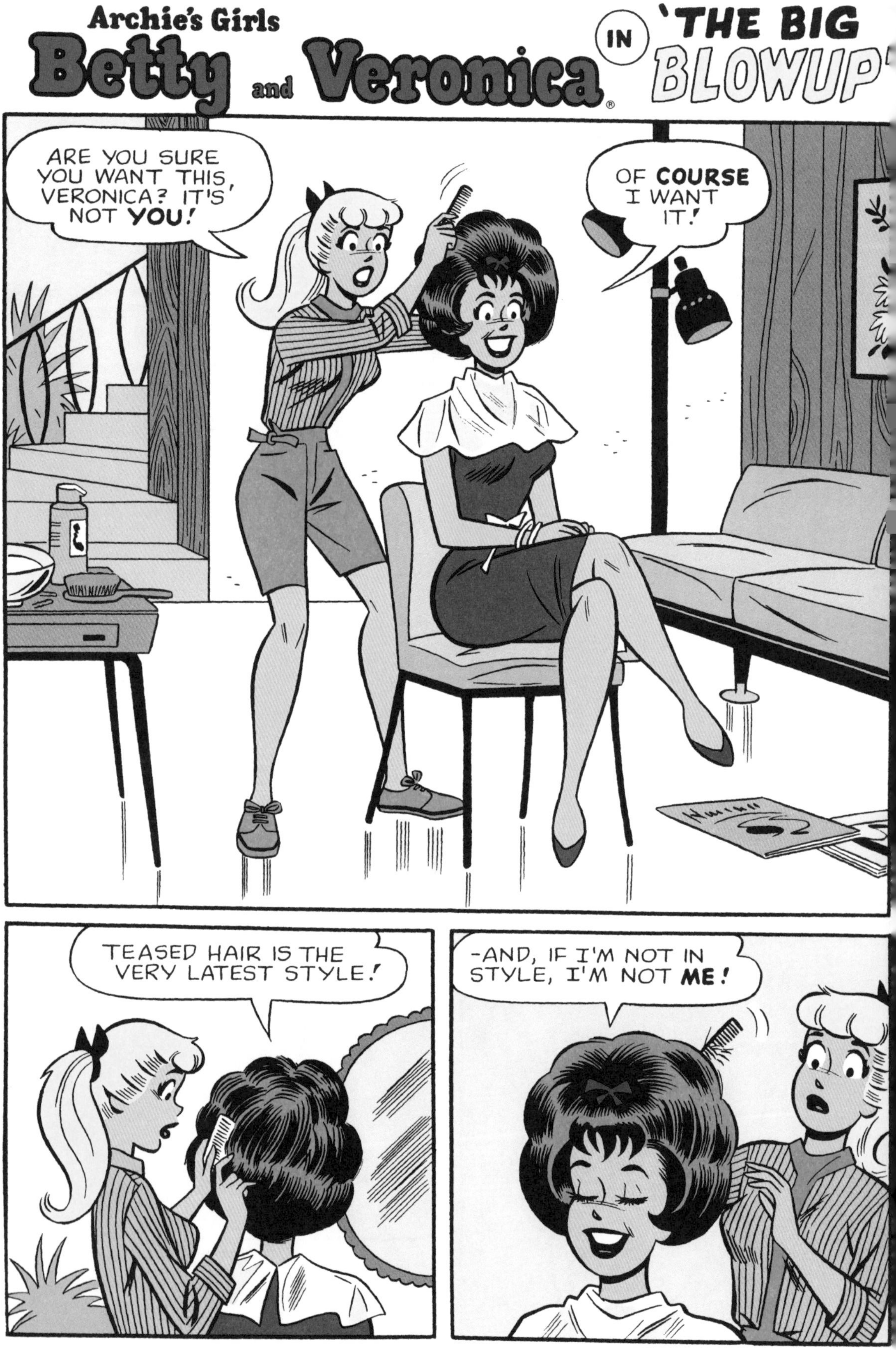
Archie's Girls Betty and Veronica® IN 'THE BIG BLOWUP'
ARE YOU SURE YOU WANT THIS, VERONICA? IT'S NOT **YOU**!
OF **COURSE** I WANT IT!
TEASED HAIR IS THE VERY LATEST STYLE!
-AND, IF I'M NOT IN STYLE, I'M NOT **ME**!

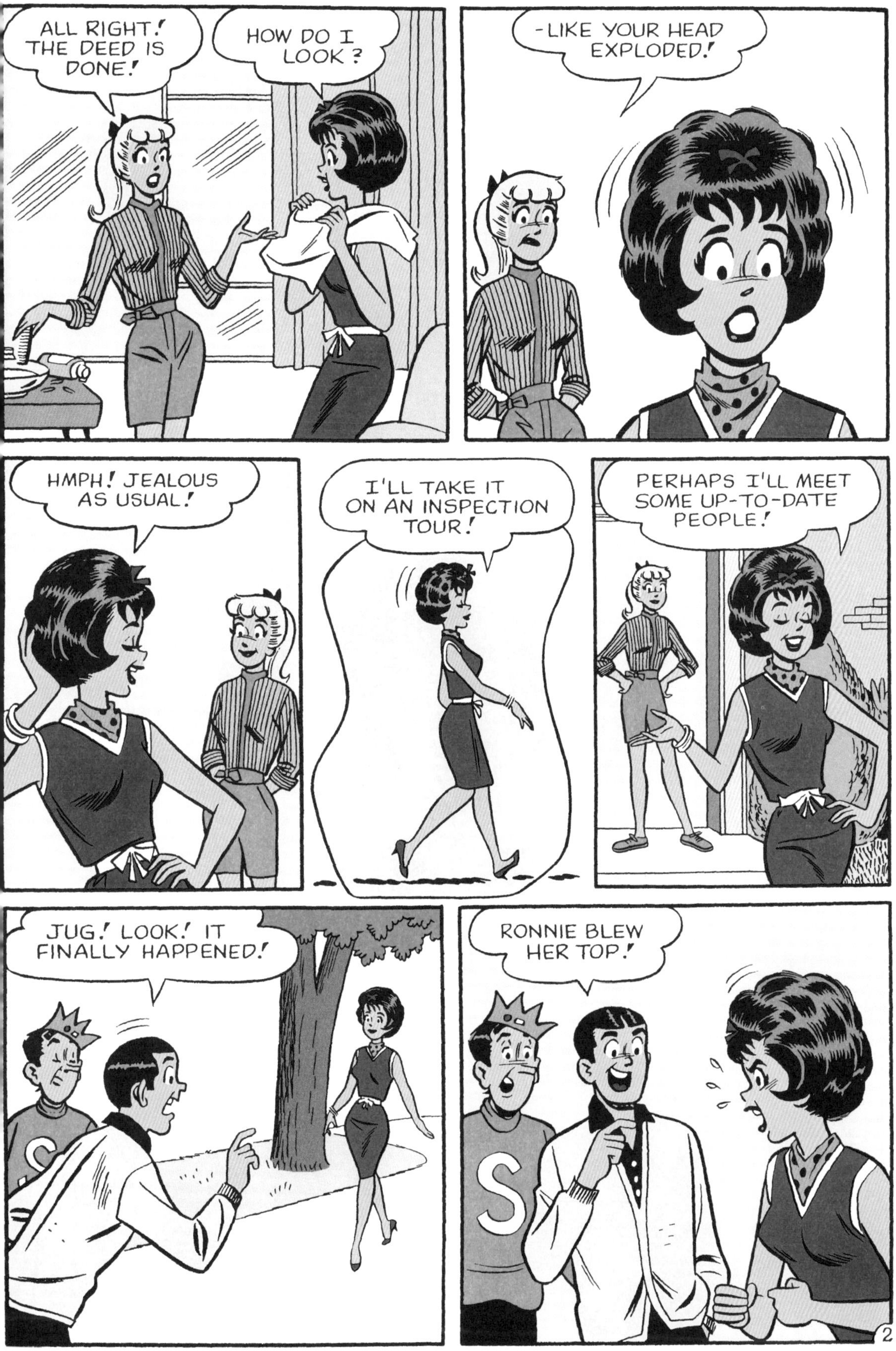
ALL RIGHT! THE DEED IS DONE!
HOW DO I LOOK?
-LIKE YOUR HEAD EXPLODED!
HMPH! JEALOUS AS USUAL!
I'LL TAKE IT ON AN INSPECTION TOUR!
PERHAPS I'LL MEET SOME UP-TO-DATE PEOPLE!
JUG! LOOK! IT FINALLY HAPPENED!
RONNIE BLEW HER TOP!
2

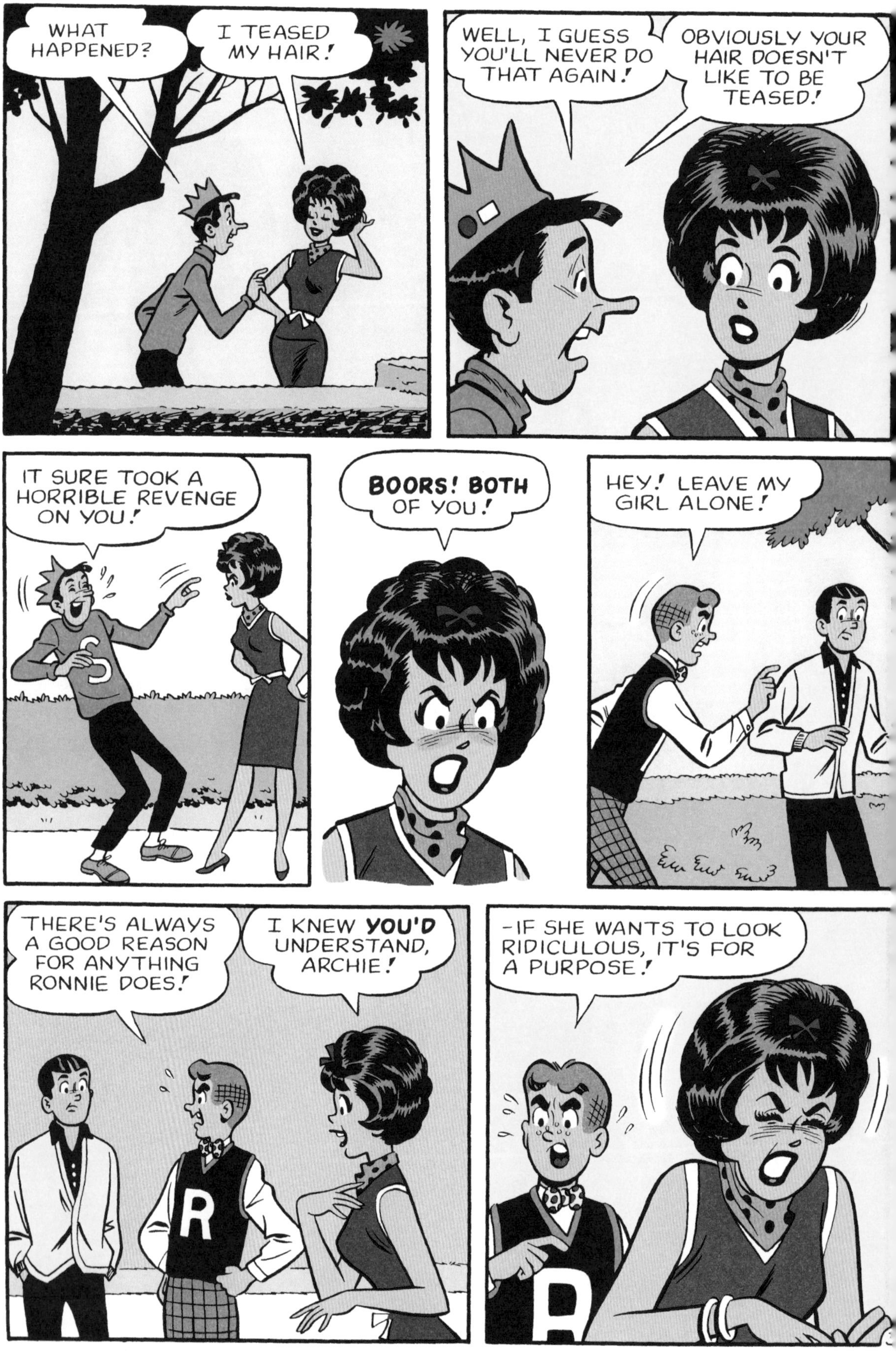
WHAT HAPPENED?
I TEASED MY HAIR!
WELL, I GUESS YOU'LL NEVER DO THAT AGAIN!
OBVIOUSLY YOUR HAIR DOESN'T LIKE TO BE TEASED!
IT SURE TOOK A HORRIBLE REVENGE ON YOU!
BOORS! BOTH OF YOU!
HEY! LEAVE MY GIRL ALONE!
THERE'S ALWAYS A GOOD REASON FOR ANYTHING RONNIE DOES!
I KNEW YOU'D UNDERSTAND, ARCHIE!
-IF SHE WANTS TO LOOK RIDICULOUS, IT'S FOR A PURPOSE!

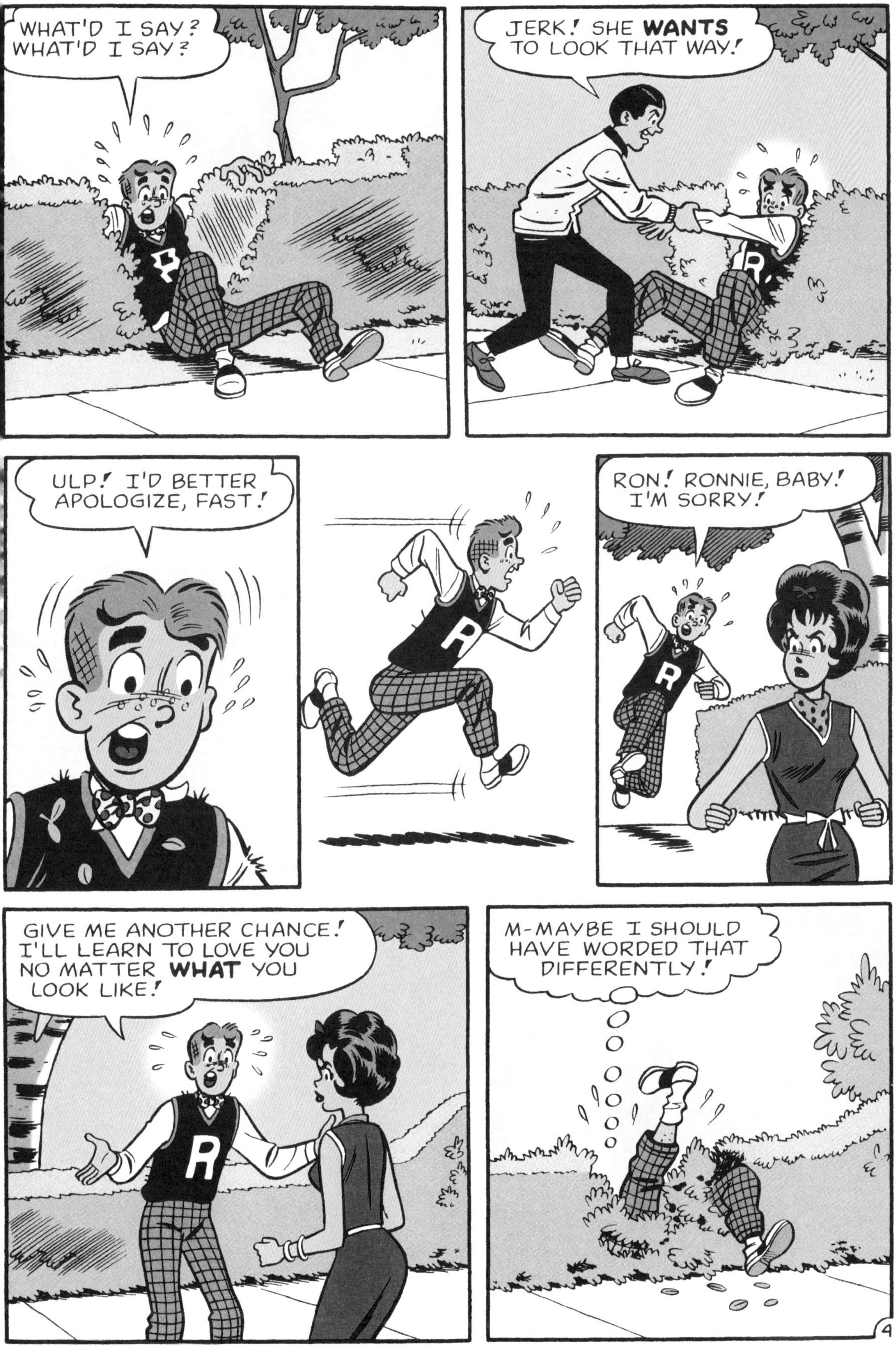
WHAT'D I SAY? WHAT'D I SAY?
JERK! SHE **WANTS** TO LOOK THAT WAY!
ULP! I'D BETTER APOLOGIZE, FAST!
RON! RONNIE, BABY! I'M SORRY!
GIVE ME ANOTHER CHANCE! I'LL LEARN TO LOVE YOU NO MATTER **WHAT** YOU LOOK LIKE!
M-MAYBE I SHOULD HAVE WORDED THAT DIFFERENTLY!
4

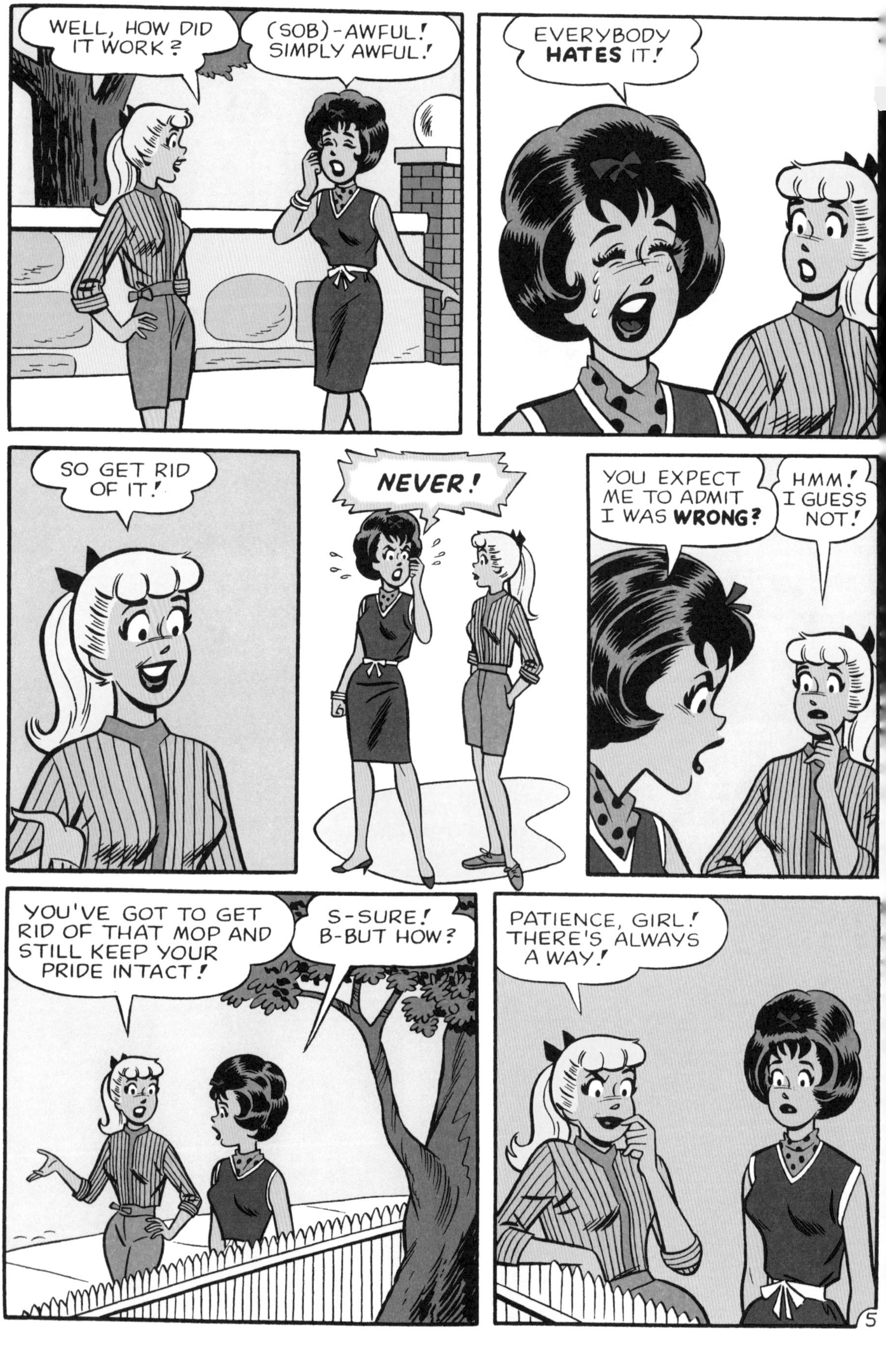
WELL, HOW DID IT WORK?
(SOB)-AWFUL! SIMPLY AWFUL!
EVERYBODY **HATES** IT!
SO GET RID OF IT!
NEVER!
YOU EXPECT ME TO ADMIT I WAS **WRONG**?
HMM! I GUESS NOT!
YOU'VE GOT TO GET RID OF THAT MOP AND STILL KEEP YOUR PRIDE INTACT!
S-SURE! B-BUT HOW?
PATIENCE, GIRL! THERE'S ALWAYS A WAY!
5

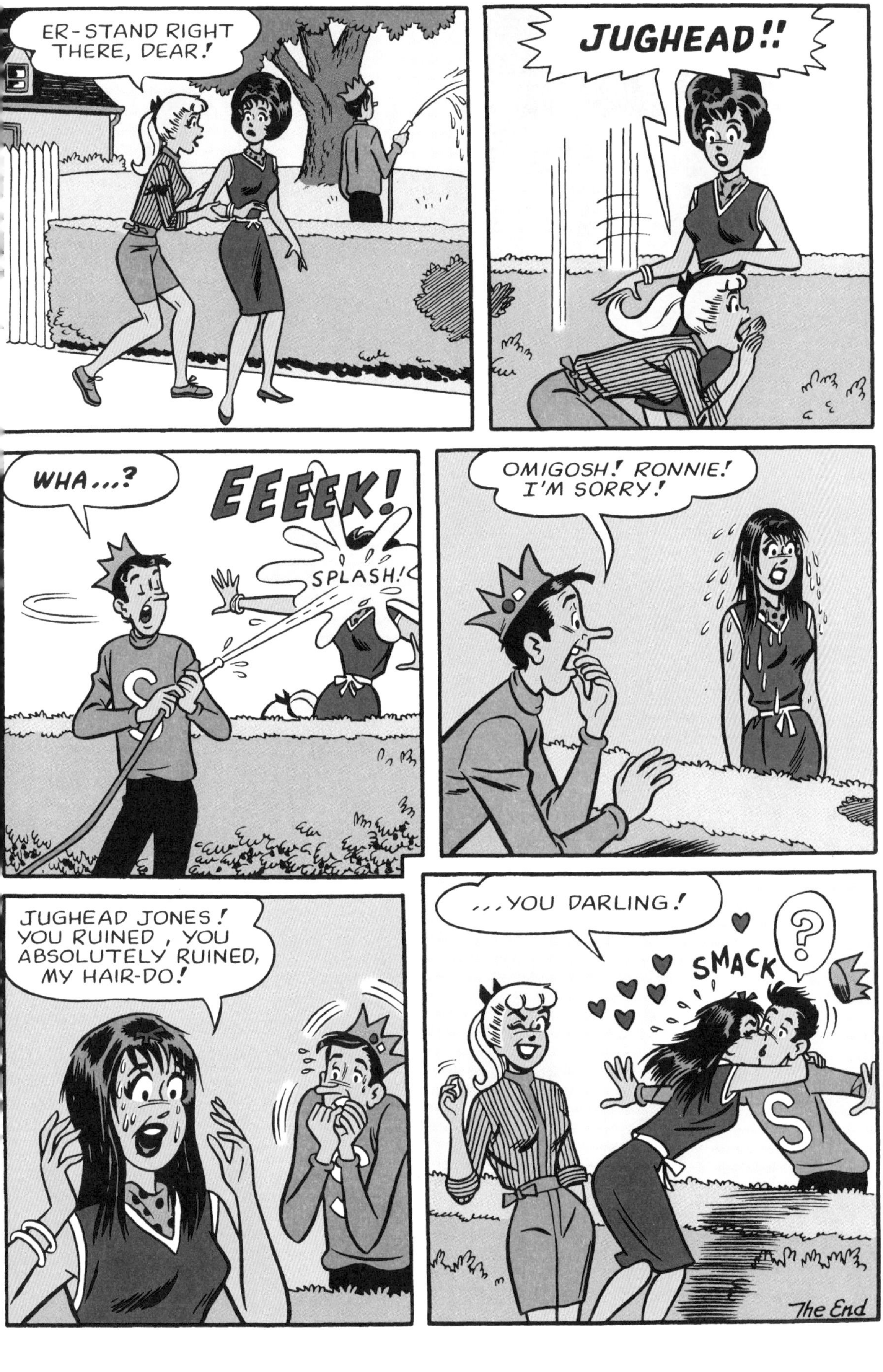
ER-STAND RIGHT THERE, DEAR!
JUGHEAD!!
WHA...?
EEEEK!
SPLASH!
OMIGOSH! RONNIE! I'M SORRY!
JUGHEAD JONES! YOU RUINED, YOU ABSOLUTELY RUINED, MY HAIR-DO!
...YOU DARLING!
SMACK
?
The End

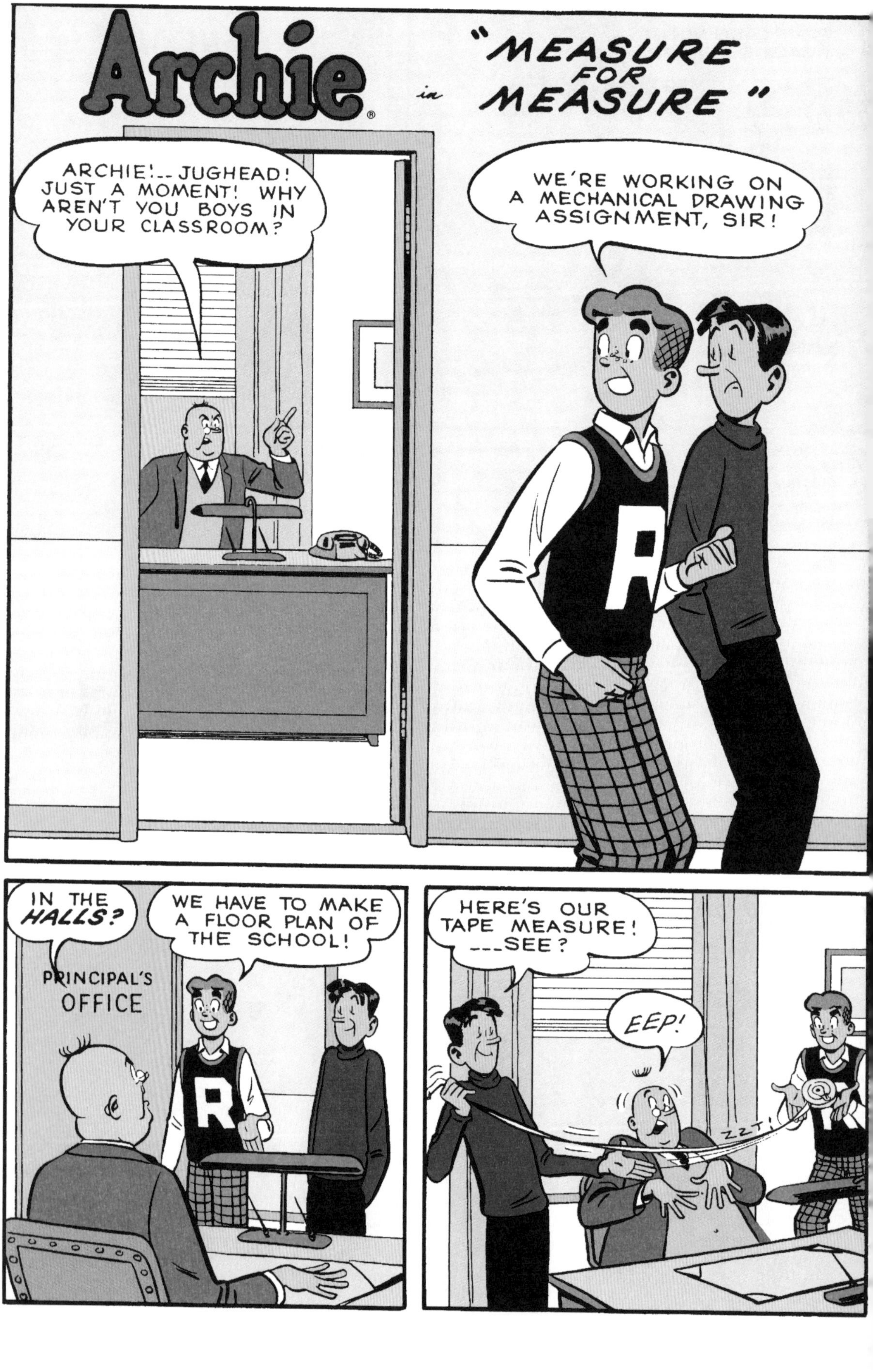
Archie in "MEASURE FOR MEASURE"
ARCHIE!-- JUGHEAD! JUST A MOMENT! WHY AREN'T YOU BOYS IN YOUR CLASSROOM?
WE'RE WORKING ON A MECHANICAL DRAWING ASSIGNMENT, SIR!
IN THE HALLS?
WE HAVE TO MAKE A FLOOR PLAN OF THE SCHOOL!
PRINCIPAL'S OFFICE
HERE'S OUR TAPE MEASURE! ---SEE?
EEP!
ZZT!

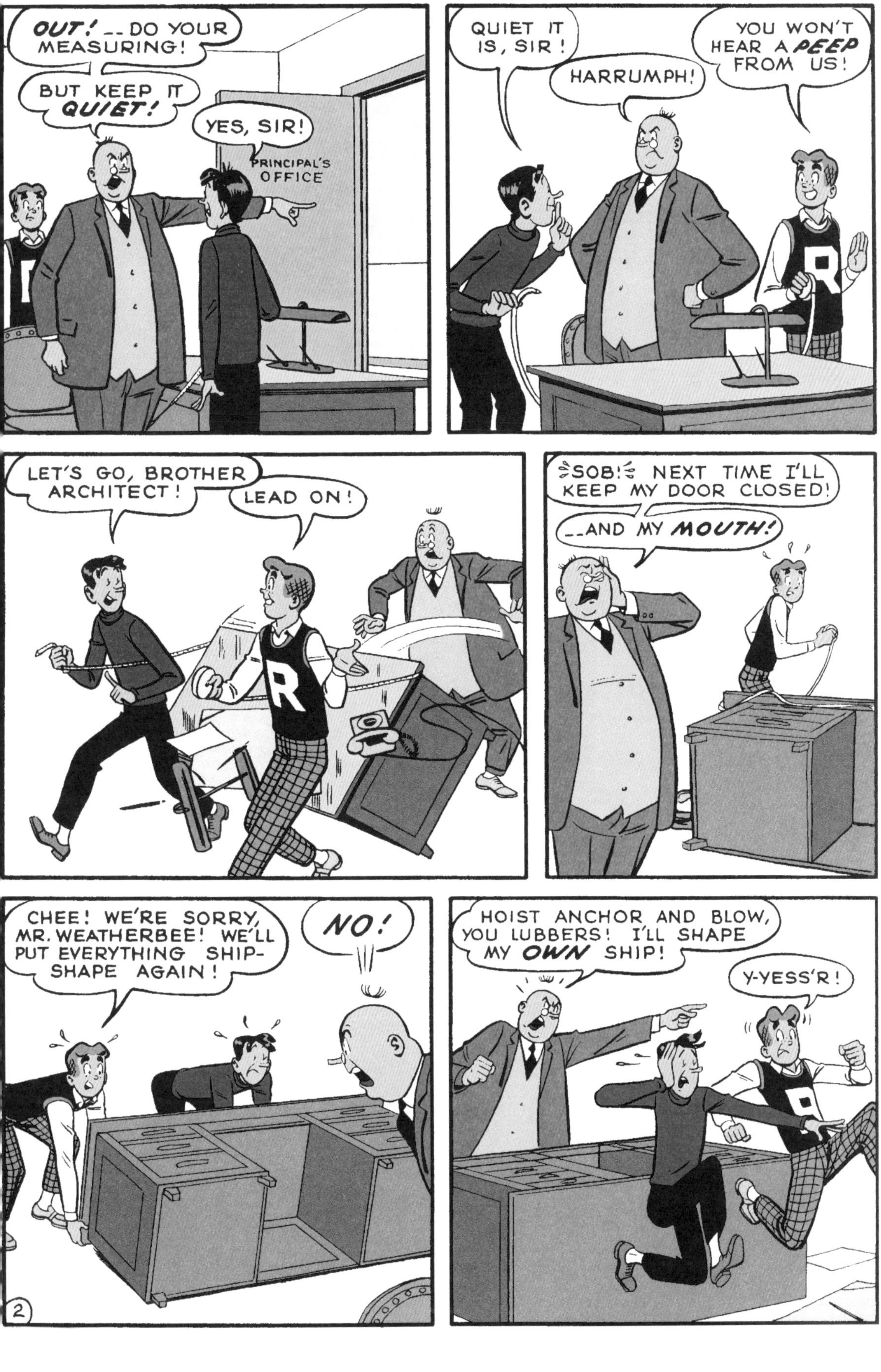
OUT! --DO YOUR MEASURING!
BUT KEEP IT QUIET!
YES, SIR!
PRINCIPAL'S OFFICE
QUIET IT IS, SIR!
HARRUMPH!
YOU WON'T HEAR A PEEP FROM US!
LET'S GO, BROTHER ARCHITECT!
LEAD ON!
SOB! NEXT TIME I'LL KEEP MY DOOR CLOSED!
--AND MY MOUTH!
CHEE! WE'RE SORRY, MR. WEATHERBEE! WE'LL PUT EVERYTHING SHIP-SHAPE AGAIN!
NO!
HOIST ANCHOR AND BLOW, YOU LUBBERS! I'LL SHAPE MY OWN SHIP!
Y-YESS'R!
2

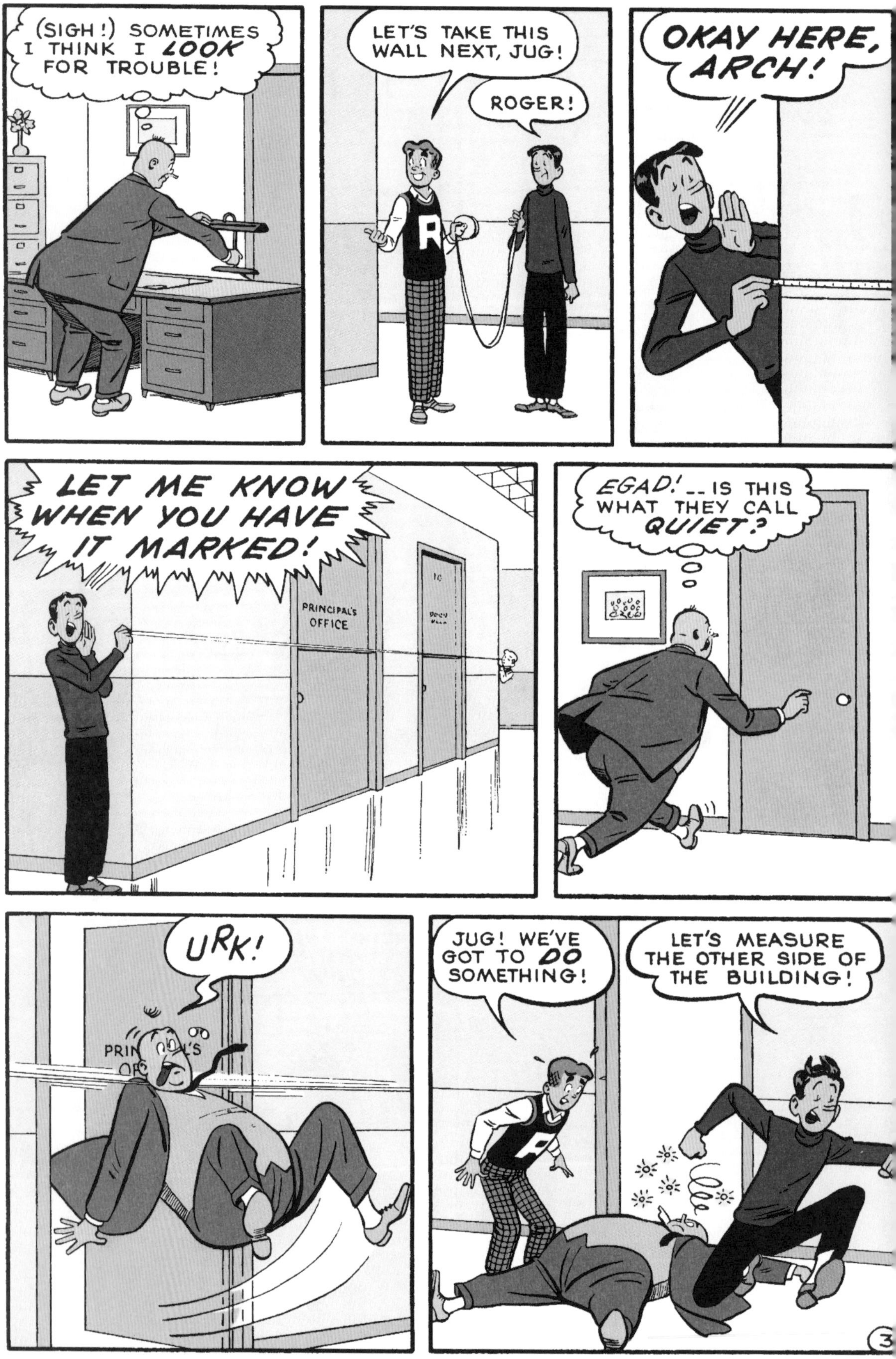

(SIGH!) SOMETIMES I THINK I LOOK FOR TROUBLE!
LET'S TAKE THIS WALL NEXT, JUG!
ROGER!
OKAY HERE, ARCH!
LET ME KNOW WHEN YOU HAVE IT MARKED!
PRINCIPAL'S OFFICE
IC
EGAD! -- IS THIS WHAT THEY CALL QUIET?
URK!
PRIN L'S OF
JUG! WE'VE GOT TO DO SOMETHING!
LET'S MEASURE THE OTHER SIDE OF THE BUILDING!
3

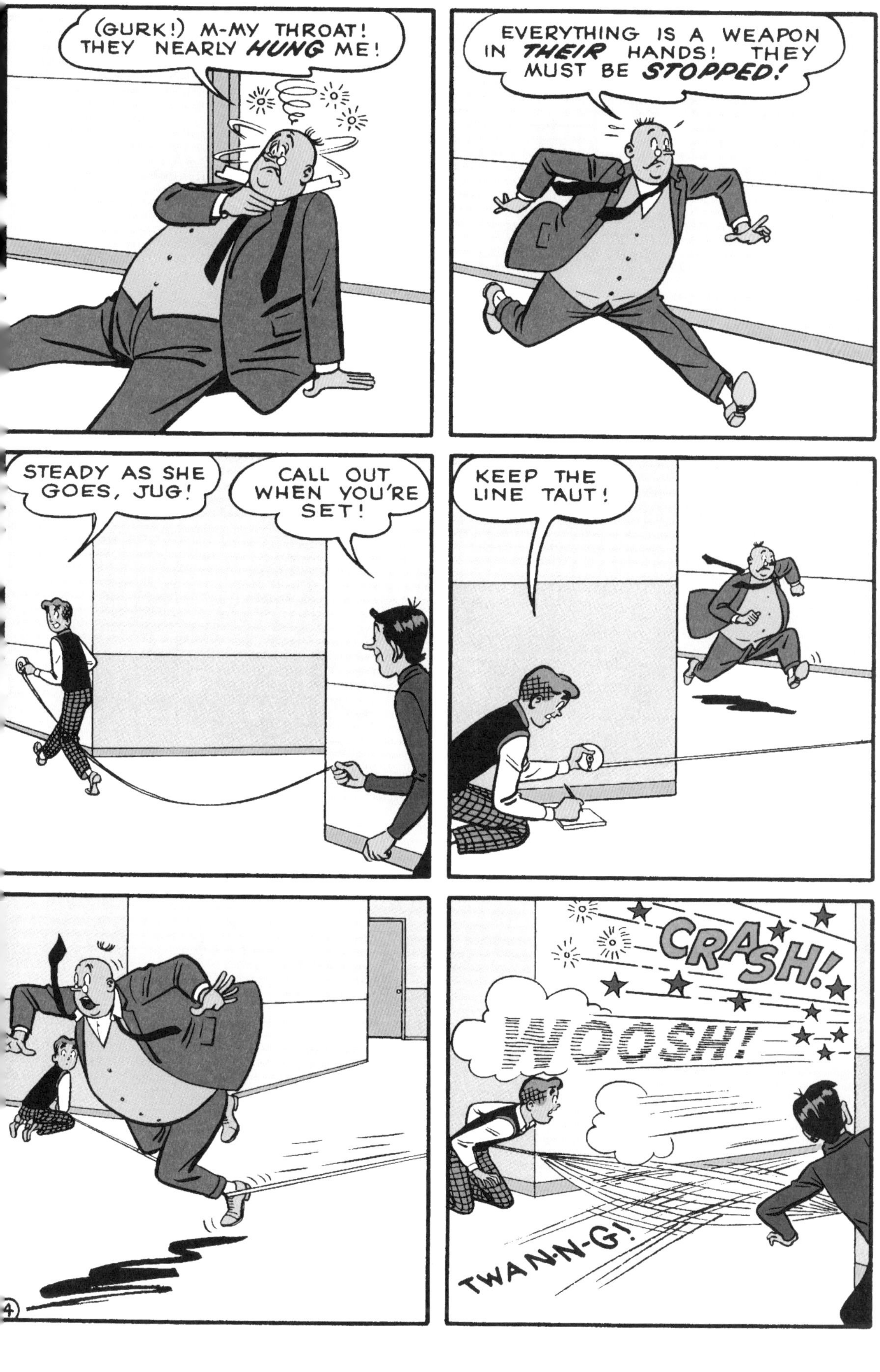
(GURK!) M-MY THROAT! THEY NEARLY HUNG ME!
EVERYTHING IS A WEAPON IN THEIR HANDS! THEY MUST BE STOPPED!
STEADY AS SHE GOES, JUG!
CALL OUT WHEN YOU'RE SET!
KEEP THE LINE TAUT!
CRASH!
WOOSH!
TWAN-N-G!
4

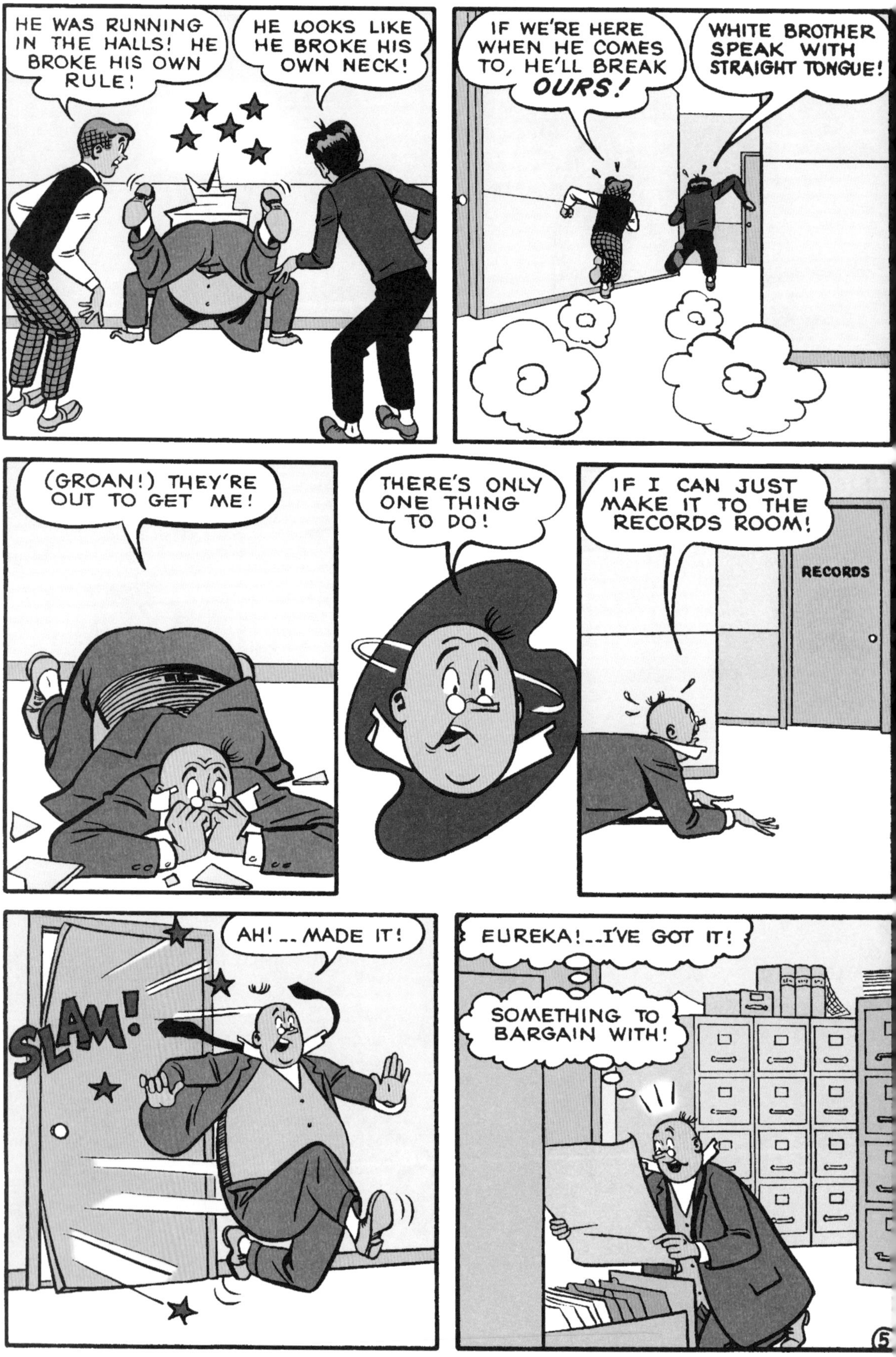
HE WAS RUNNING IN THE HALLS! HE BROKE HIS OWN RULE!
HE LOOKS LIKE HE BROKE HIS OWN NECK!
IF WE'RE HERE WHEN HE COMES TO, HE'LL BREAK OURS!
WHITE BROTHER SPEAK WITH STRAIGHT TONGUE!
(GROAN!) THEY'RE OUT TO GET ME!
THERE'S ONLY ONE THING TO DO!
IF I CAN JUST MAKE IT TO THE RECORDS ROOM!
RECORDS
AH! -- MADE IT!
SLAM!
EUREKA! -- I'VE GOT IT!
SOMETHING TO BARGAIN WITH!
5

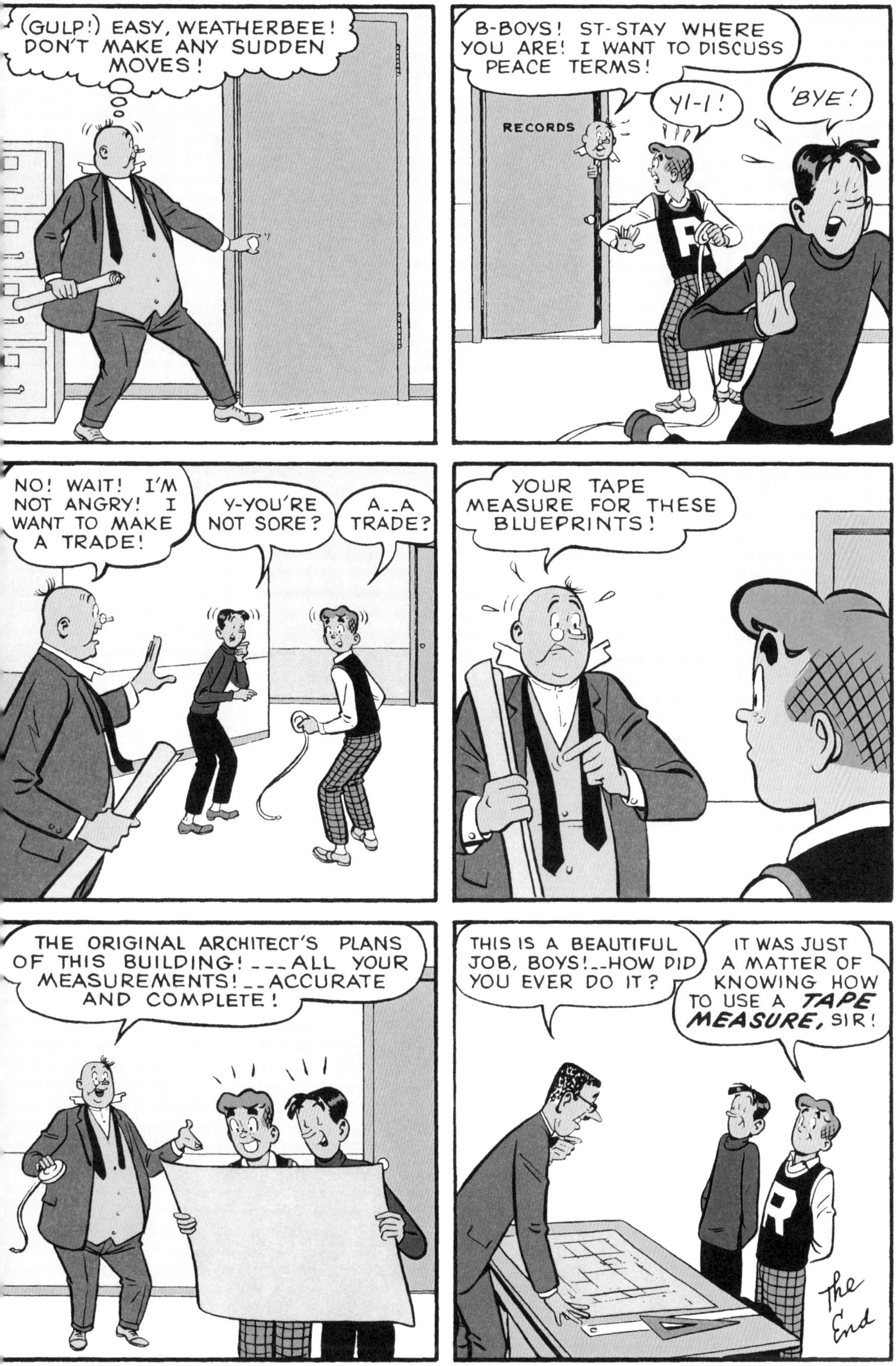
(GULP!) EASY, WEATHERBEE! DON'T MAKE ANY SUDDEN MOVES!
B-BOYS! ST-STAY WHERE YOU ARE! I WANT TO DISCUSS PEACE TERMS!
RECORDS
YI-I!
'BYE!
NO! WAIT! I'M NOT ANGRY! I WANT TO MAKE A TRADE!
Y-YOU'RE NOT SORE?
A..A TRADE?
YOUR TAPE MEASURE FOR THESE BLUEPRINTS!
THE ORIGINAL ARCHITECT'S PLANS OF THIS BUILDING! ...ALL YOUR MEASUREMENTS! ..ACCURATE AND COMPLETE!
THIS IS A BEAUTIFUL JOB, BOYS!..HOW DID YOU EVER DO IT?
IT WAS JUST A MATTER OF KNOWING HOW TO USE A TAPE MEASURE, SIR!
The End

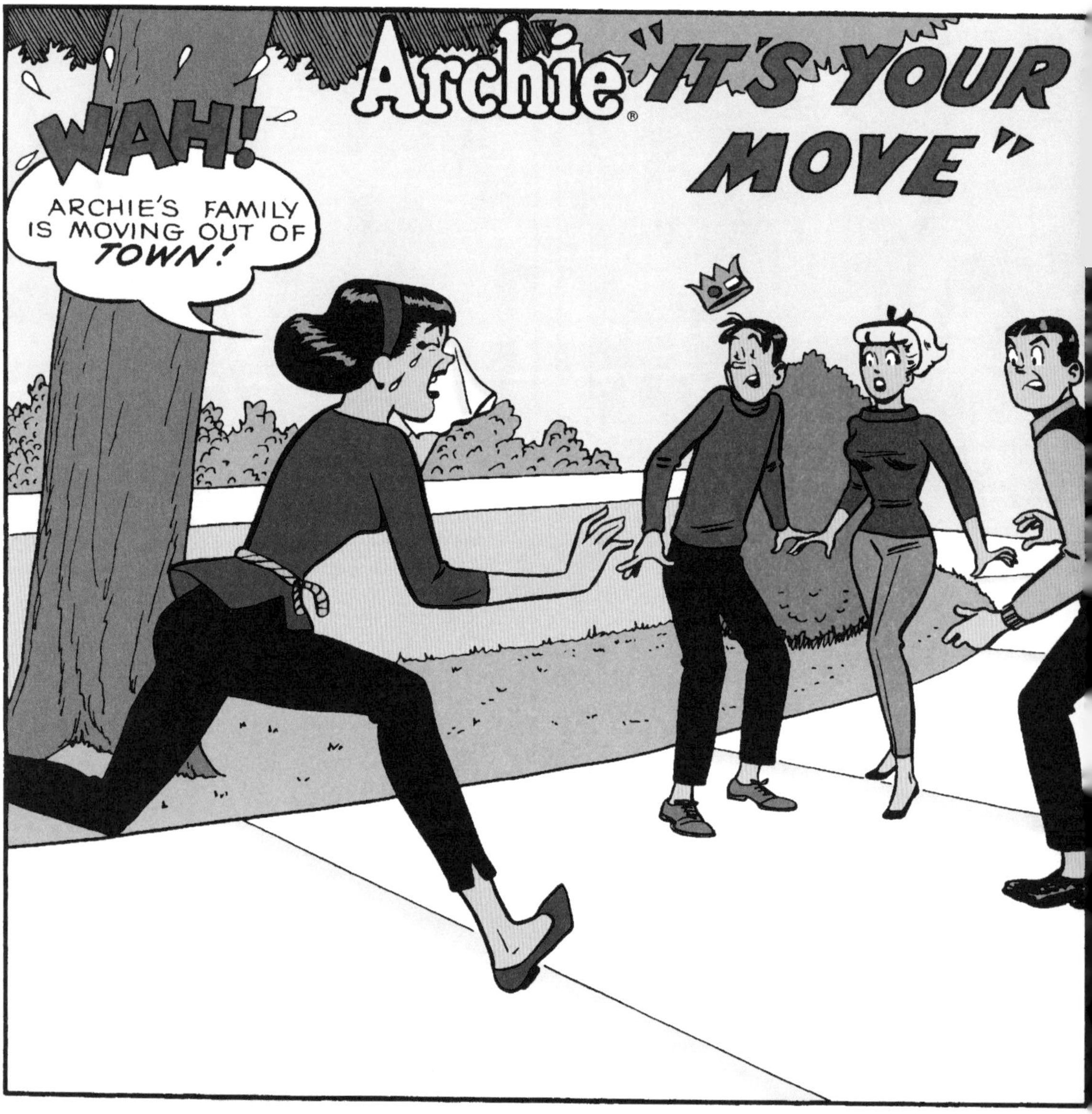
Archie®
"IT'S YOUR MOVE"
WAH!
ARCHIE'S FAMILY IS MOVING OUT OF TOWN!

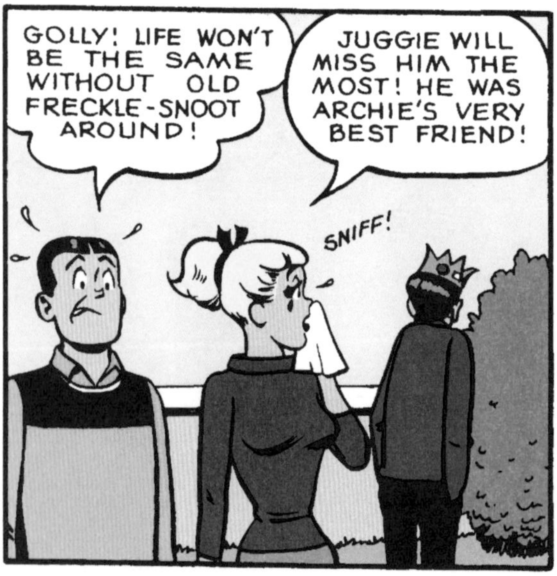
GOLLY! LIFE WON'T BE THE SAME WITHOUT OLD FRECKLE-SNOOT AROUND!
JUGGIE WILL MISS HIM THE MOST! HE WAS ARCHIE'S VERY BEST FRIEND!
SNIFF!

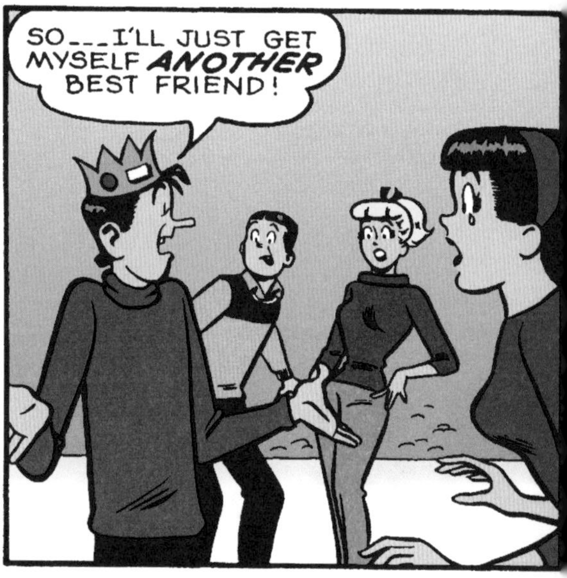
SO---I'LL JUST GET MYSELF ANOTHER BEST FRIEND!

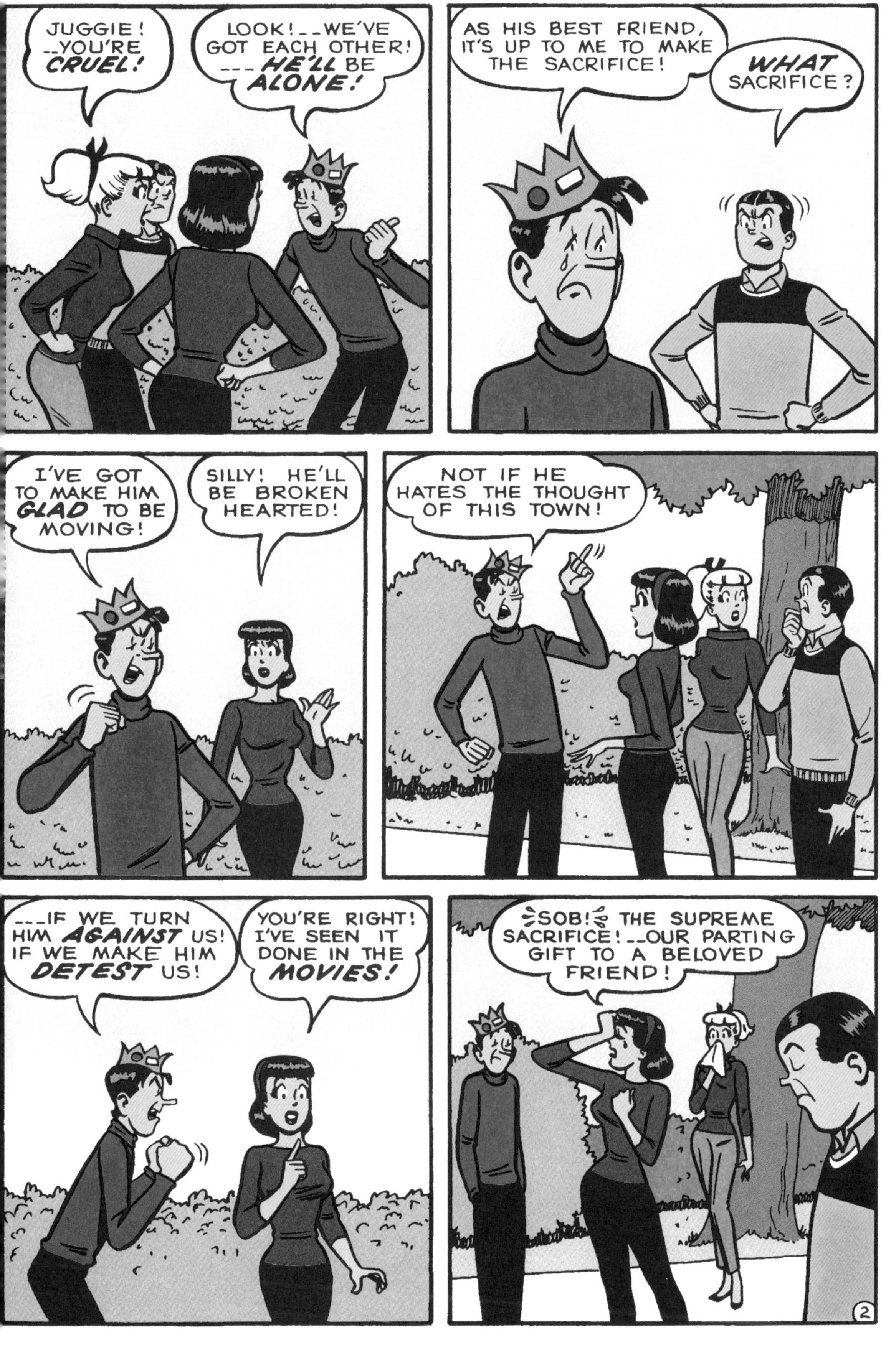
JUGGIE! --YOU'RE CRUEL!
LOOK!--WE'VE GOT EACH OTHER! ---HE'LL BE ALONE!
AS HIS BEST FRIEND, IT'S UP TO ME TO MAKE THE SACRIFICE!
WHAT SACRIFICE?
I'VE GOT TO MAKE HIM GLAD TO BE MOVING!
SILLY! HE'LL BE BROKEN HEARTED!
NOT IF HE HATES THE THOUGHT OF THIS TOWN!
---IF WE TURN HIM AGAINST US! IF WE MAKE HIM DETEST US!
YOU'RE RIGHT! I'VE SEEN IT DONE IN THE MOVIES!
SOB! THE SUPREME SACRIFICE!--OUR PARTING GIFT TO A BELOVED FRIEND!
2

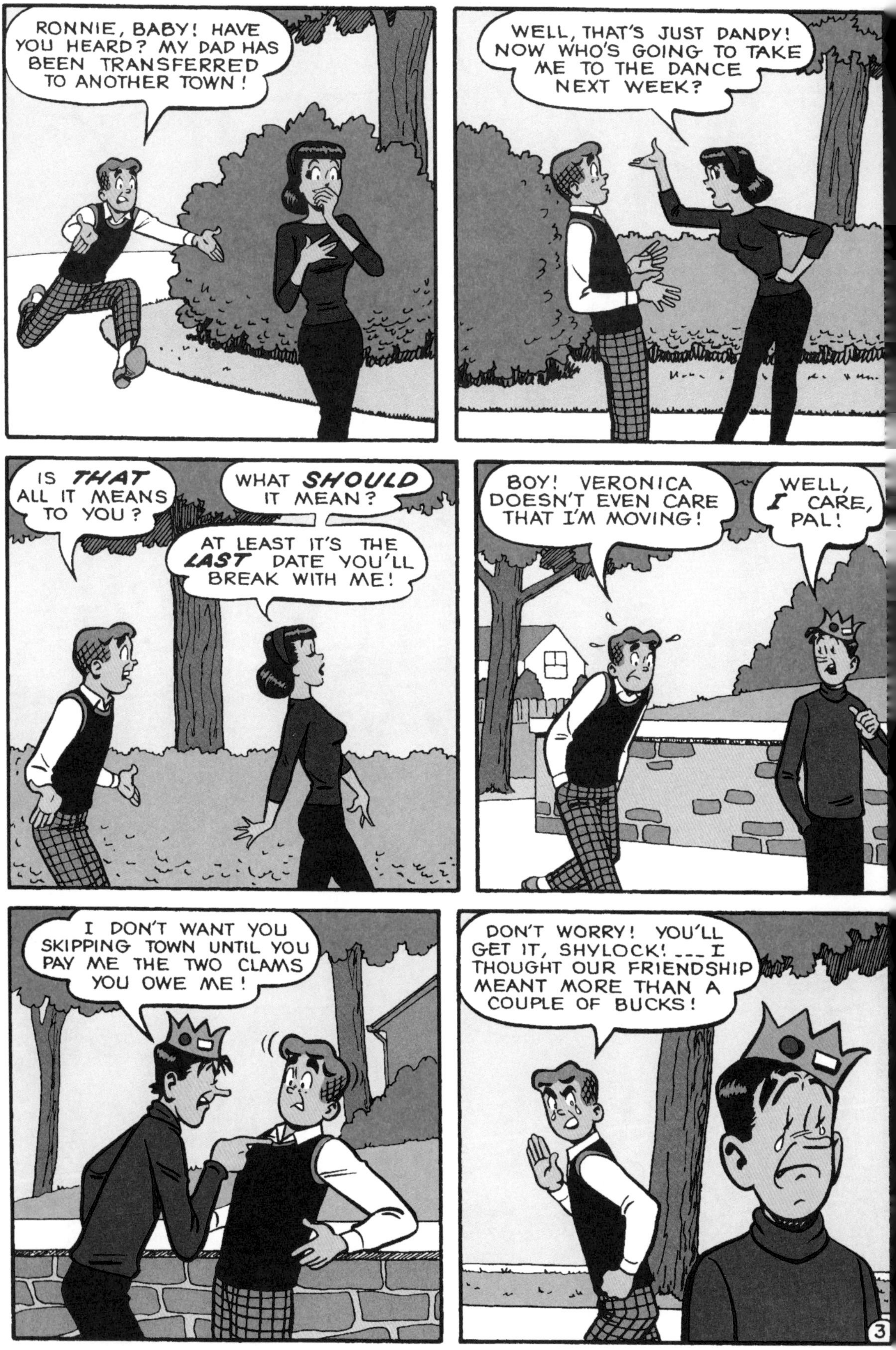
RONNIE, BABY! HAVE YOU HEARD? MY DAD HAS BEEN TRANSFERRED TO ANOTHER TOWN!
WELL, THAT'S JUST DANDY! NOW WHO'S GOING TO TAKE ME TO THE DANCE NEXT WEEK?
IS THAT ALL IT MEANS TO YOU?
WHAT SHOULD IT MEAN?
AT LEAST IT'S THE LAST DATE YOU'LL BREAK WITH ME!
BOY! VERONICA DOESN'T EVEN CARE THAT I'M MOVING!
WELL, I CARE, PAL!
I DON'T WANT YOU SKIPPING TOWN UNTIL YOU PAY ME THE TWO CLAMS YOU OWE ME!
DON'T WORRY! YOU'LL GET IT, SHYLOCK! --- I THOUGHT OUR FRIENDSHIP MEANT MORE THAN A COUPLE OF BUCKS!
3

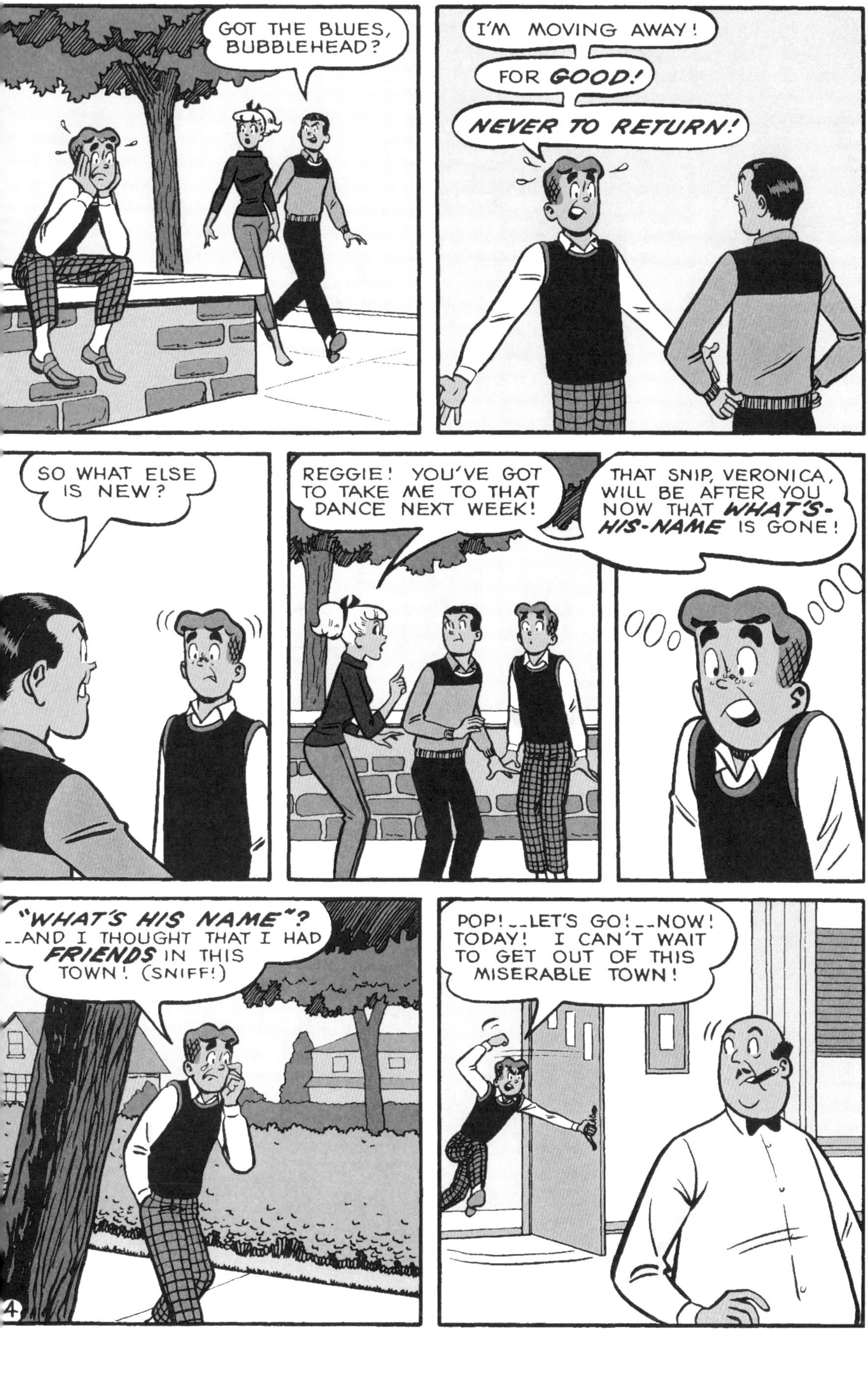
GOT THE BLUES, BUBBLEHEAD?
I'M MOVING AWAY!
FOR GOOD!
NEVER TO RETURN!
SO WHAT ELSE IS NEW?
REGGIE! YOU'VE GOT TO TAKE ME TO THAT DANCE NEXT WEEK!
THAT SNIP, VERONICA, WILL BE AFTER YOU NOW THAT WHAT'S-HIS-NAME IS GONE!
"WHAT'S HIS NAME"? ..AND I THOUGHT THAT I HAD FRIENDS IN THIS TOWN! (SNIFF!)
POP!..LET'S GO!..NOW! TODAY! I CAN'T WAIT TO GET OUT OF THIS MISERABLE TOWN!
4

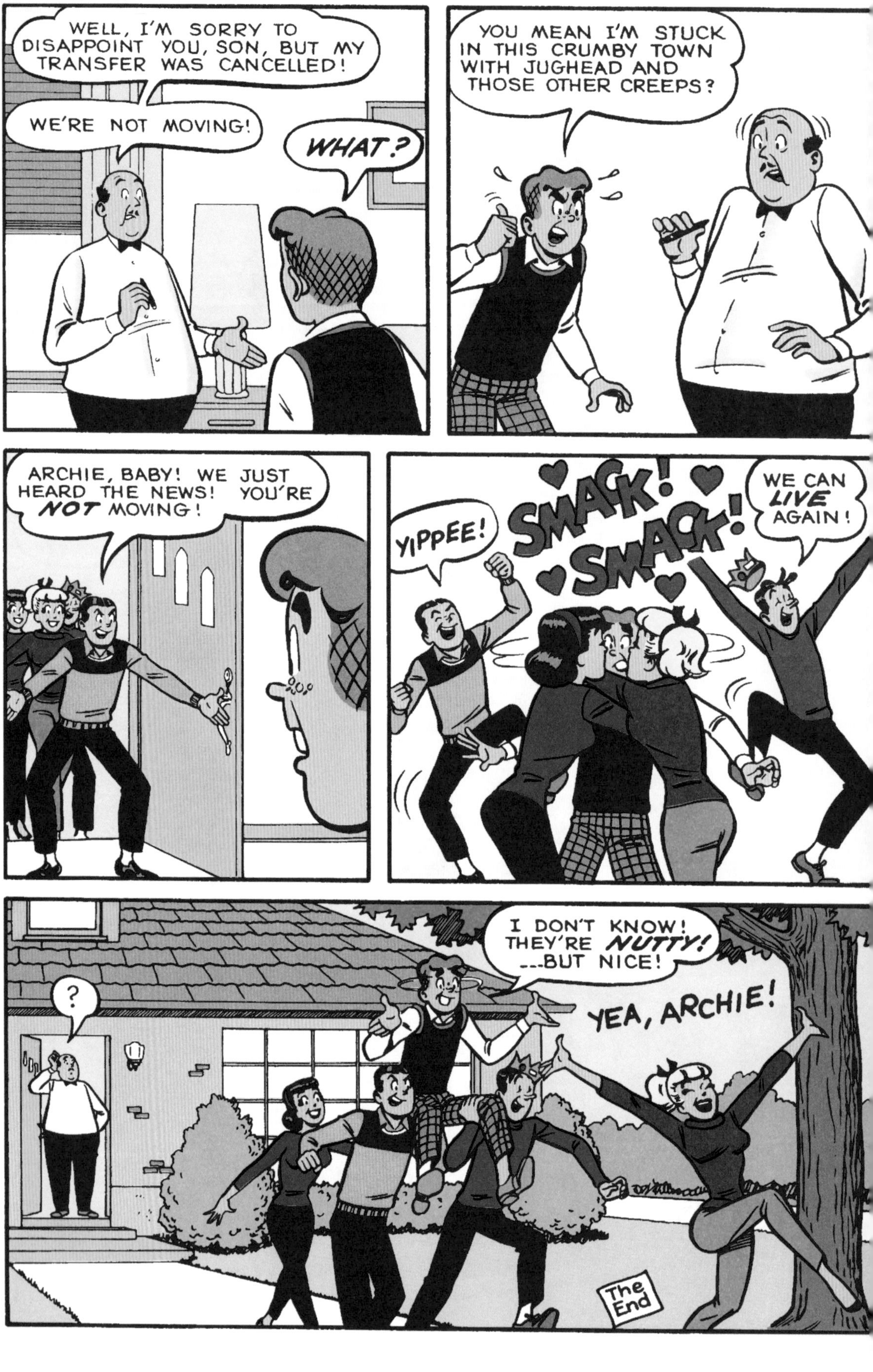
WELL, I'M SORRY TO DISAPPOINT YOU, SON, BUT MY TRANSFER WAS CANCELLED!
WE'RE NOT MOVING!
WHAT?
YOU MEAN I'M STUCK IN THIS CRUMBY TOWN WITH JUGHEAD AND THOSE OTHER CREEPS?
ARCHIE, BABY! WE JUST HEARD THE NEWS! YOU'RE NOT MOVING!
YIPPEE!
SMACK! SMACK!
WE CAN LIVE AGAIN!
?
I DON'T KNOW! THEY'RE NUTTY! ---BUT NICE!
YEA, ARCHIE!
The End

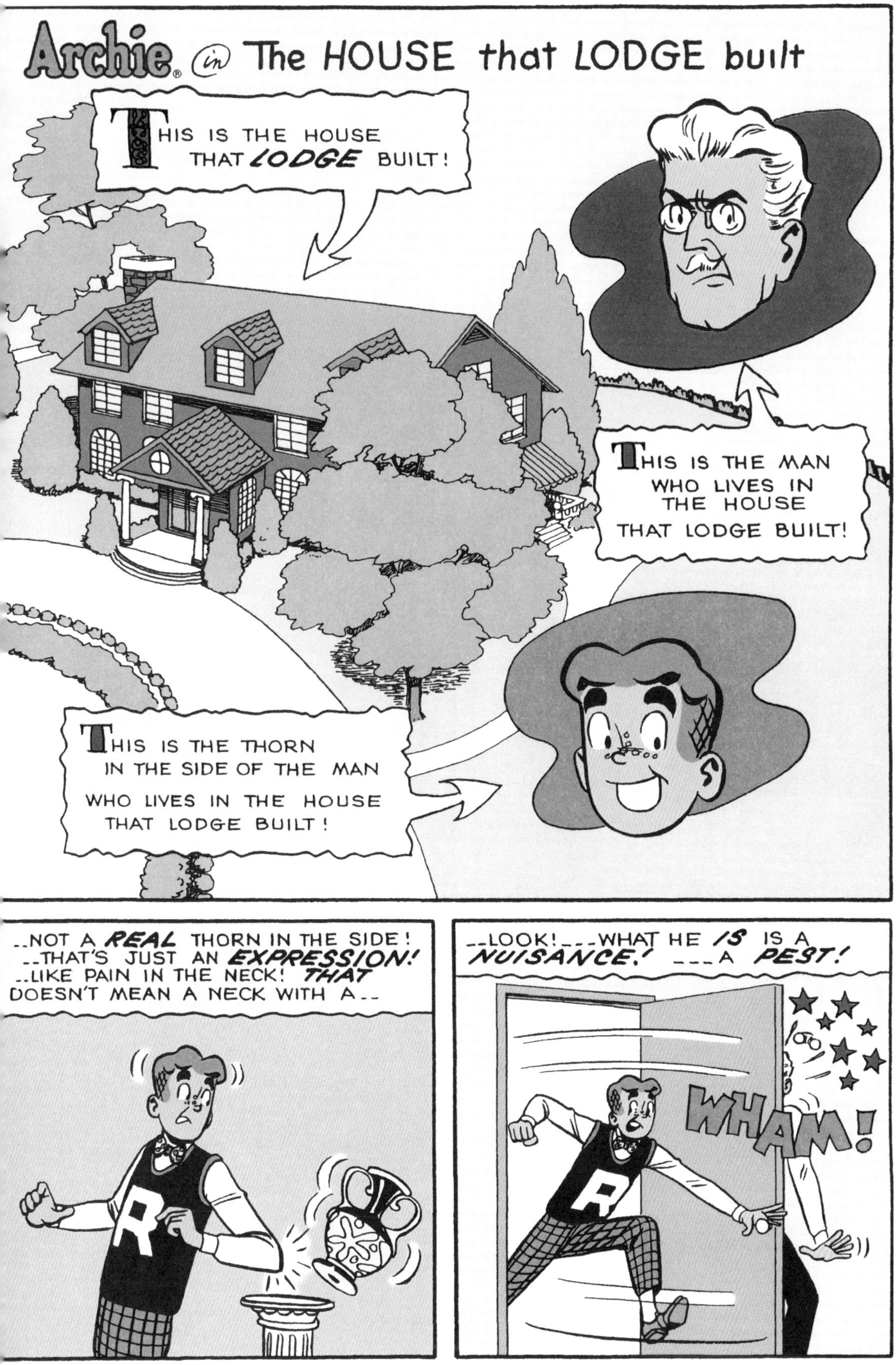
Archie in The HOUSE that LODGE built
THIS IS THE HOUSE THAT LODGE BUILT!
THIS IS THE MAN WHO LIVES IN THE HOUSE THAT LODGE BUILT!
THIS IS THE THORN IN THE SIDE OF THE MAN WHO LIVES IN THE HOUSE THAT LODGE BUILT!
..NOT A REAL THORN IN THE SIDE! ..THAT'S JUST AN EXPRESSION! ..LIKE PAIN IN THE NECK! THAT DOESN'T MEAN A NECK WITH A..
..LOOK!...WHAT HE IS IS A NUISANCE! ...A PEST!
WHAM!

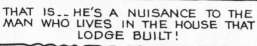

THAT IS-- HE'S A NUISANCE TO THE MAN WHO LIVES IN THE HOUSE THAT LODGE BUILT!

BUT NOT TO THE *DAUGHTER* OF THE MAN WHO LIVES IN THE HOUSE THAT LODGE BUILT!

THE MAN WHO LIVES IN THE---ETC. YOU KNOW!---*LODGE!* --WOULD BE *LOST* WITHOUT THIS PEST!

IN FACT, HE *ENJOYS* THIS THORN-IN-SIDE, PAIN-IN-NECK, NUISANCE!

HI, MISTER LODGE!

IT'S LIKE HAVING AN ITCH YOU CAN *SCRATCH!*   HE ACTUALLY LOOKS FOR-WARD TO ARCHIE'S VISITS, BECAUSE IT FEELS SO GOOD TO *EJECT* HIM!

2

AND ANOTHER OF ARCHIE'S VISITS TO THE HOUSE THAT LODGE BUILT COMES TO ITS INEVITABLE CONCLUSION!

AND *STAY* OUT!

SLAM!

HAPPY?___ CONTENT?___JUST LOOK AT THAT GRIN!

BUT FATE* HAS A WAY OF SPOILING EVERY-ONE'S FUN!

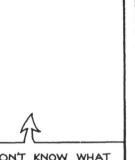

*WE DON'T KNOW WHAT FATE LOOKS LIKE, SO DRAW YOUR OWN PICTURE IN HERE!

JUST WAIT! SOMEDAY HE'LL APPRECIATE ME!

I'M AFRAID NOT, ARCHIEKINS!

WE MAY AS WELL GIVE UP SEEING EACH OTHER!

NO!__NOT *THAT!*

YOU WATCH! YOUNG LOVE ALWAYS WINS OUT IN THESE KIND OF STORIES!

YOU'RE A DREAMER, DARLING! DADDY WILL NEVER APPROVE OF YOU!

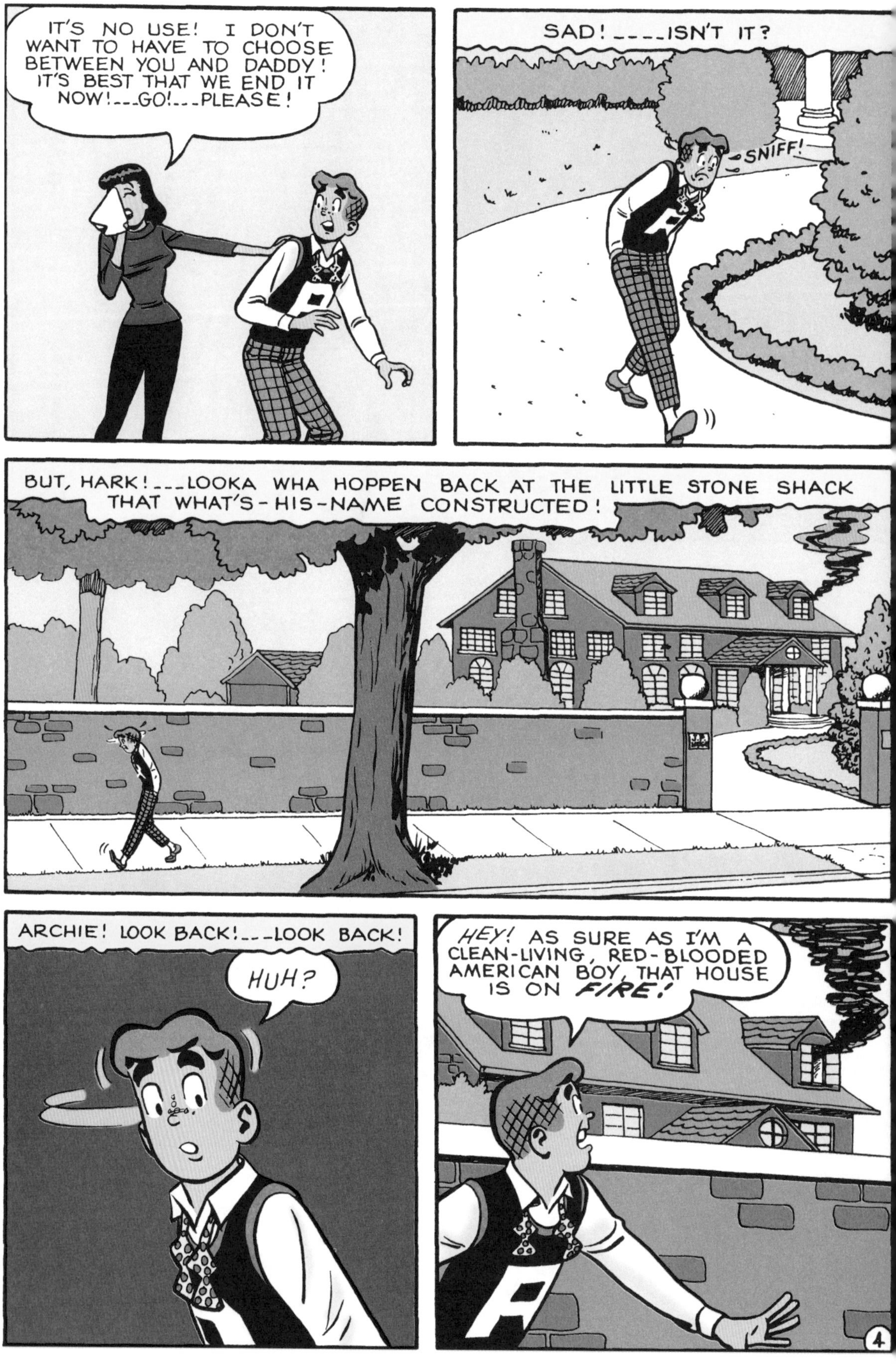
IT'S NO USE! I DON'T WANT TO HAVE TO CHOOSE BETWEEN YOU AND DADDY! IT'S BEST THAT WE END IT NOW!---GO!---PLEASE!
SAD! ----ISN'T IT?
SNIFF!
BUT, HARK!---LOOKA WHA HOPPEN BACK AT THE LITTLE STONE SHACK THAT WHAT'S-HIS-NAME CONSTRUCTED!
ARCHIE! LOOK BACK!---LOOK BACK!
HUH?
HEY! AS SURE AS I'M A CLEAN-LIVING, RED-BLOODED AMERICAN BOY, THAT HOUSE IS ON FIRE!
4

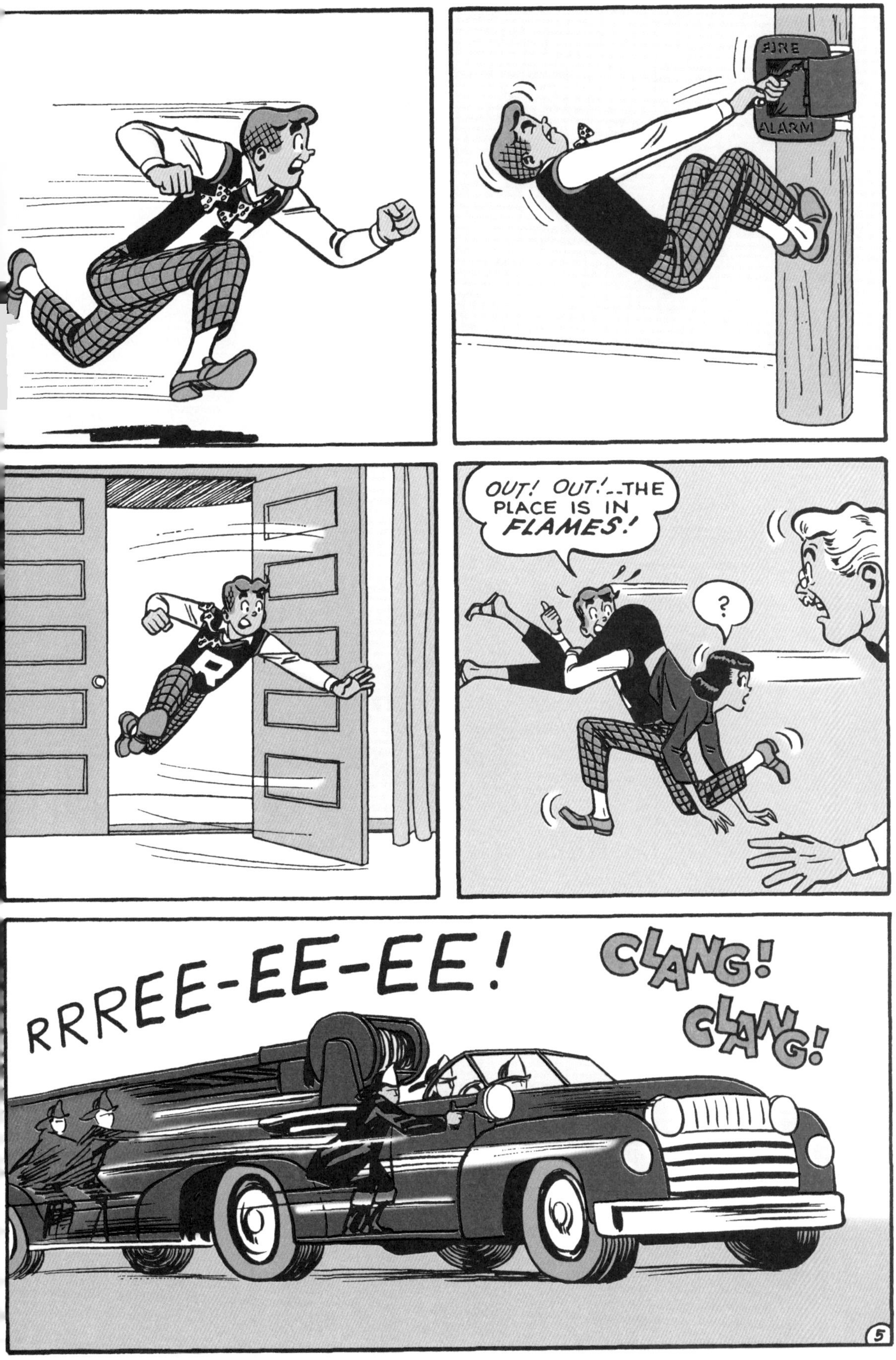
FIRE
ALARM
OUT! OUT!..THE PLACE IS IN FLAMES!
?
RRREE-EE-EE!
CLANG!
CLANG!
5

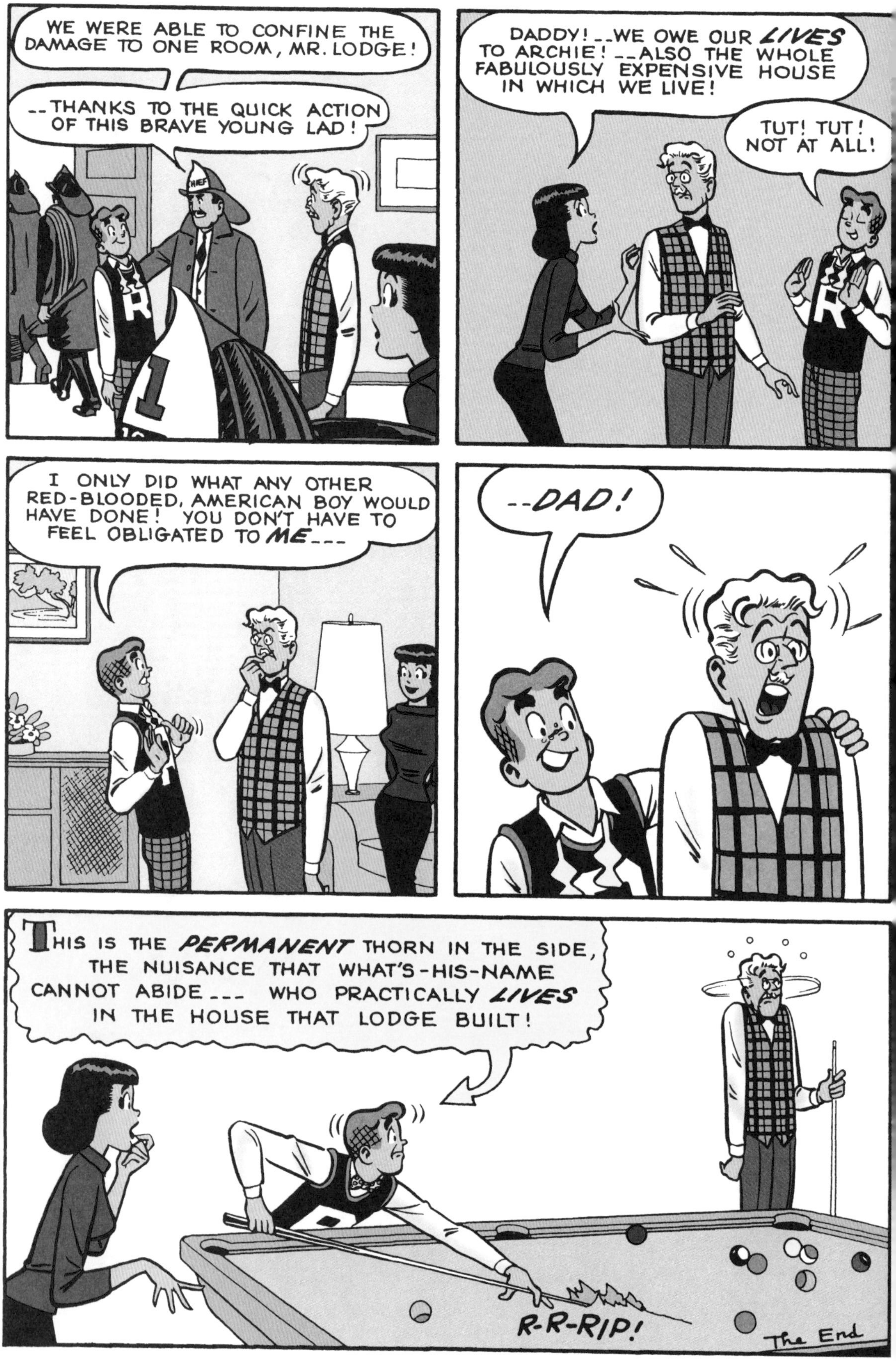
WE WERE ABLE TO CONFINE THE DAMAGE TO ONE ROOM, MR. LODGE!
--THANKS TO THE QUICK ACTION OF THIS BRAVE YOUNG LAD!
CHIEF
DADDY! --WE OWE OUR LIVES TO ARCHIE! --ALSO THE WHOLE FABULOUSLY EXPENSIVE HOUSE IN WHICH WE LIVE!
TUT! TUT! NOT AT ALL!
I ONLY DID WHAT ANY OTHER RED-BLOODED, AMERICAN BOY WOULD HAVE DONE! YOU DON'T HAVE TO FEEL OBLIGATED TO ME---
--DAD!
THIS IS THE PERMANENT THORN IN THE SIDE, THE NUISANCE THAT WHAT'S-HIS-NAME CANNOT ABIDE--- WHO PRACTICALLY LIVES IN THE HOUSE THAT LODGE BUILT!
R-R-RIP!
The End

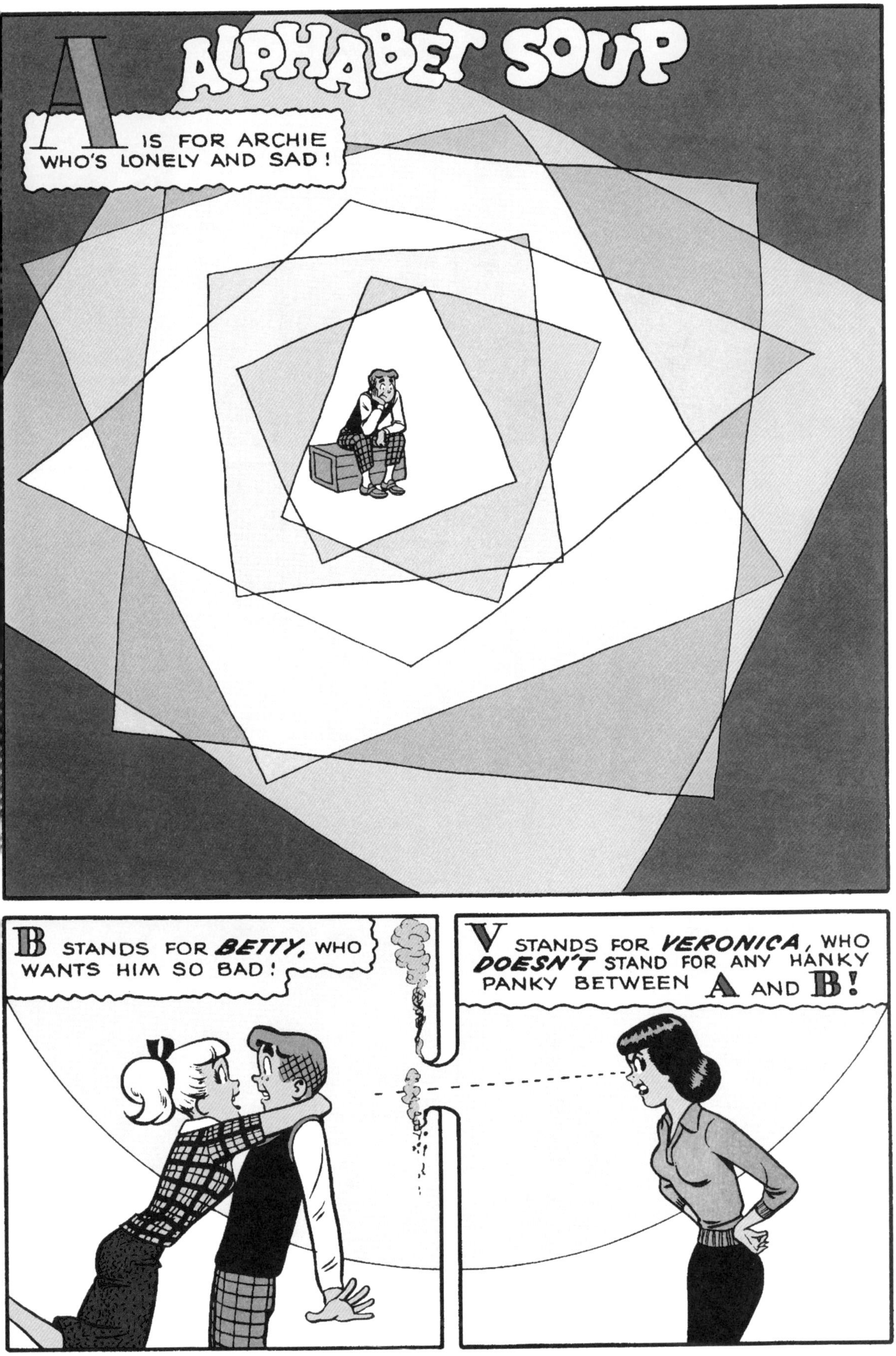
ALPHABET SOUP
A IS FOR ARCHIE WHO'S LONELY AND SAD!
B STANDS FOR BETTY, WHO WANTS HIM SO BAD!
V STANDS FOR VERONICA, WHO DOESN'T STAND FOR ANY HANKY PANKY BETWEEN A AND B!

---THIS IS THE LITTLE FINGER OF VERONICA ---

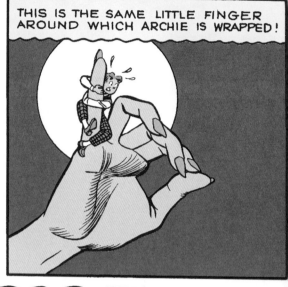

THIS IS THE SAME LITTLE FINGER AROUND WHICH ARCHIE IS WRAPPED!

THIS IS THE *THUMB* OF VERONICA...

THIS IS THE SAME THUMB UNDER WHICH IS ----GUESS WHO?

THAT IS, --- WHEN HE'S NOT WRAPPED AROUND THE *LITTLE* FINGER!

(GROAN!) SEE ABOVE!

J STANDS FOR *JUGHEAD*-- ARCHIE'S PAL...JUGHEAD WILL STAND FOR *ANYTHING!*

---AS LONG AS IT IS SMOTHERED WITH KETCHUP!

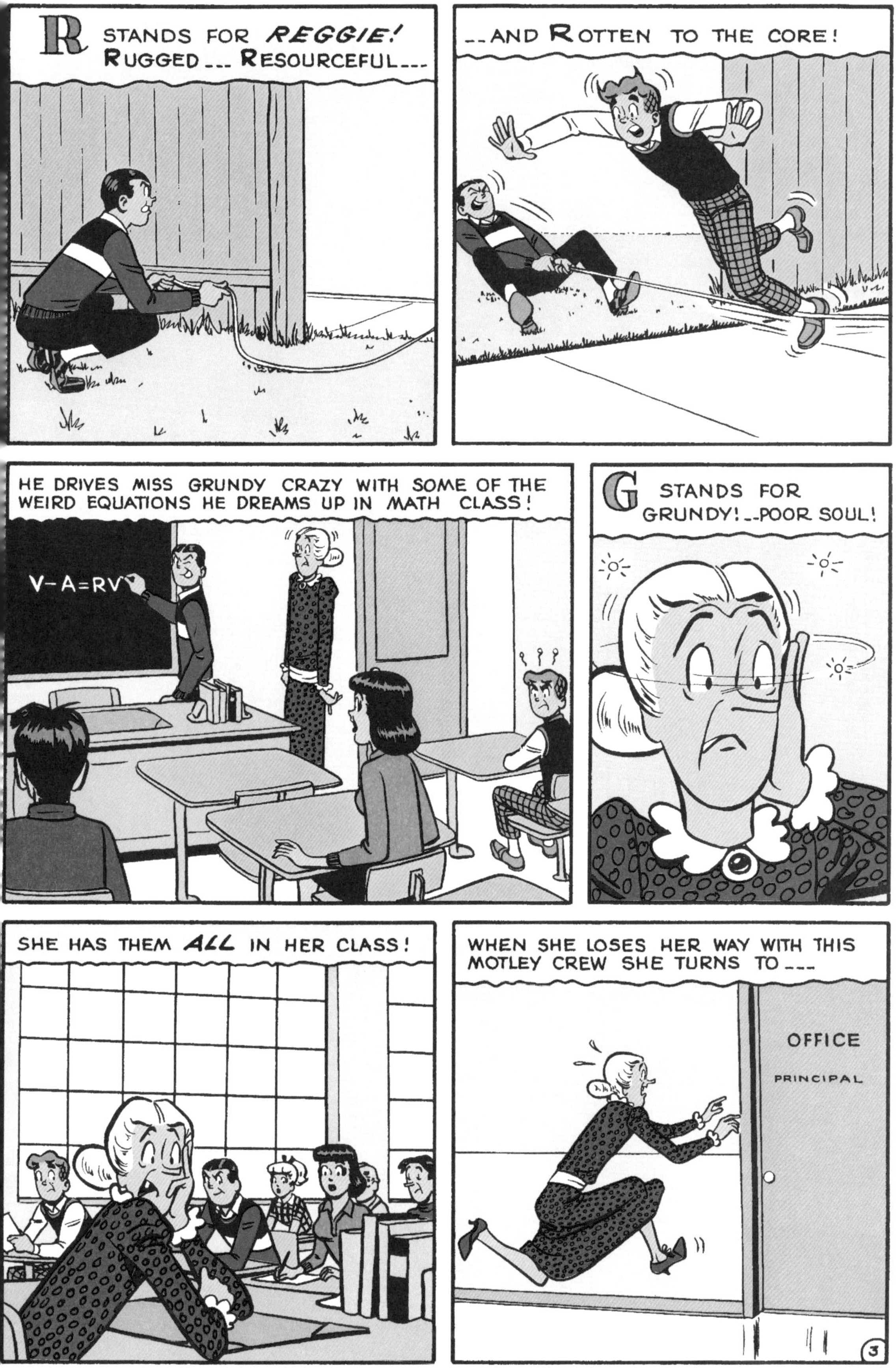
R STANDS FOR REGGIE! RUGGED --- RESOURCEFUL---
--AND ROTTEN TO THE CORE!
HE DRIVES MISS GRUNDY CRAZY WITH SOME OF THE WEIRD EQUATIONS HE DREAMS UP IN MATH CLASS!
V-A=RV
G STANDS FOR GRUNDY! --POOR SOUL!
SHE HAS THEM ALL IN HER CLASS!
WHEN SHE LOSES HER WAY WITH THIS MOTLEY CREW SHE TURNS TO ---
OFFICE
PRINCIPAL

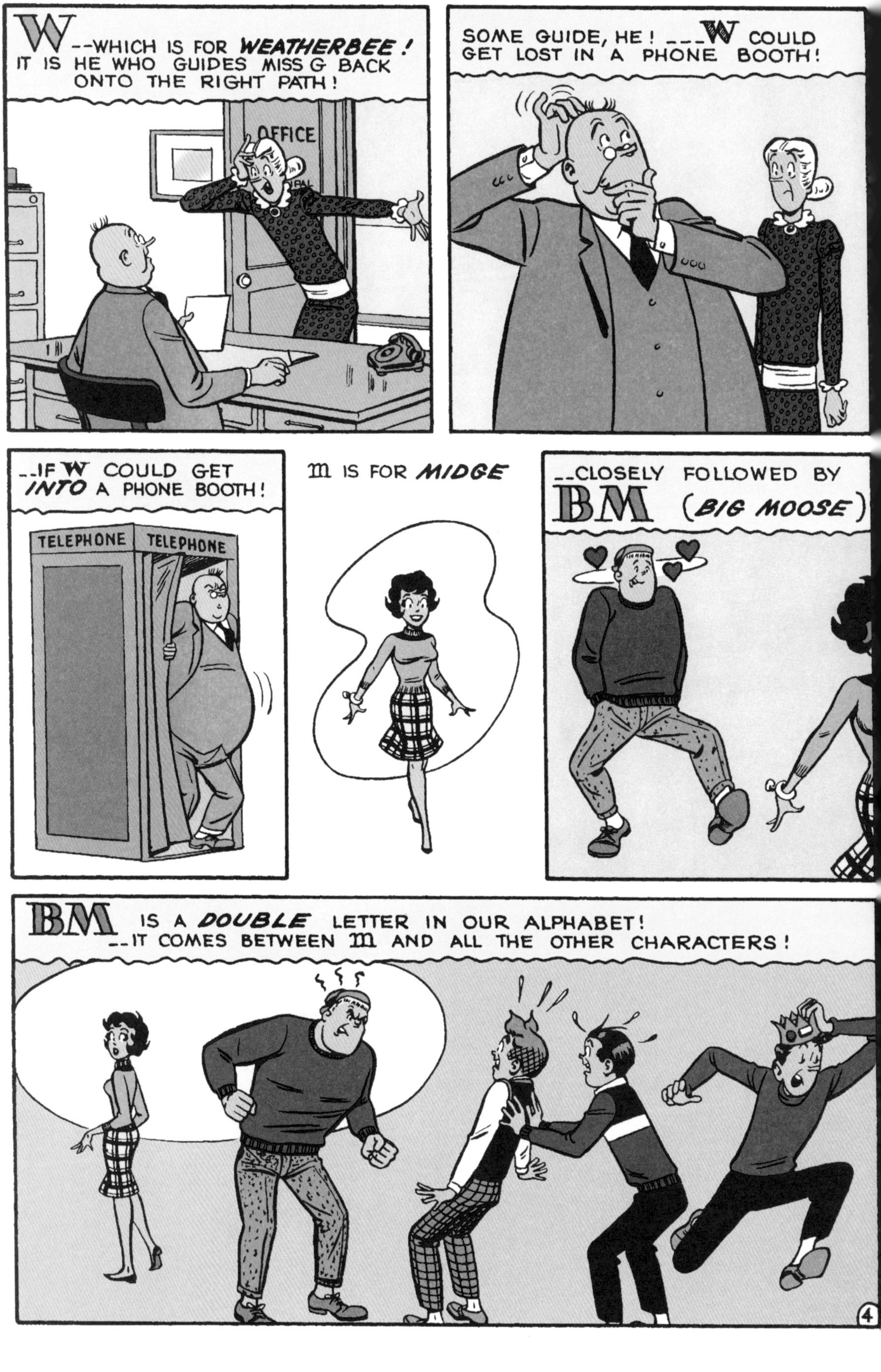
W--WHICH IS FOR WEATHERBEE! IT IS HE WHO GUIDES MISS G BACK ONTO THE RIGHT PATH!
OFFICE
SOME GUIDE, HE! ---W COULD GET LOST IN A PHONE BOOTH!
--IF W COULD GET INTO A PHONE BOOTH!
TELEPHONE
TELEPHONE
m IS FOR MIDGE
--CLOSELY FOLLOWED BY BM (BIG MOOSE)
BM IS A DOUBLE LETTER IN OUR ALPHABET! --IT COMES BETWEEN m AND ALL THE OTHER CHARACTERS!
4

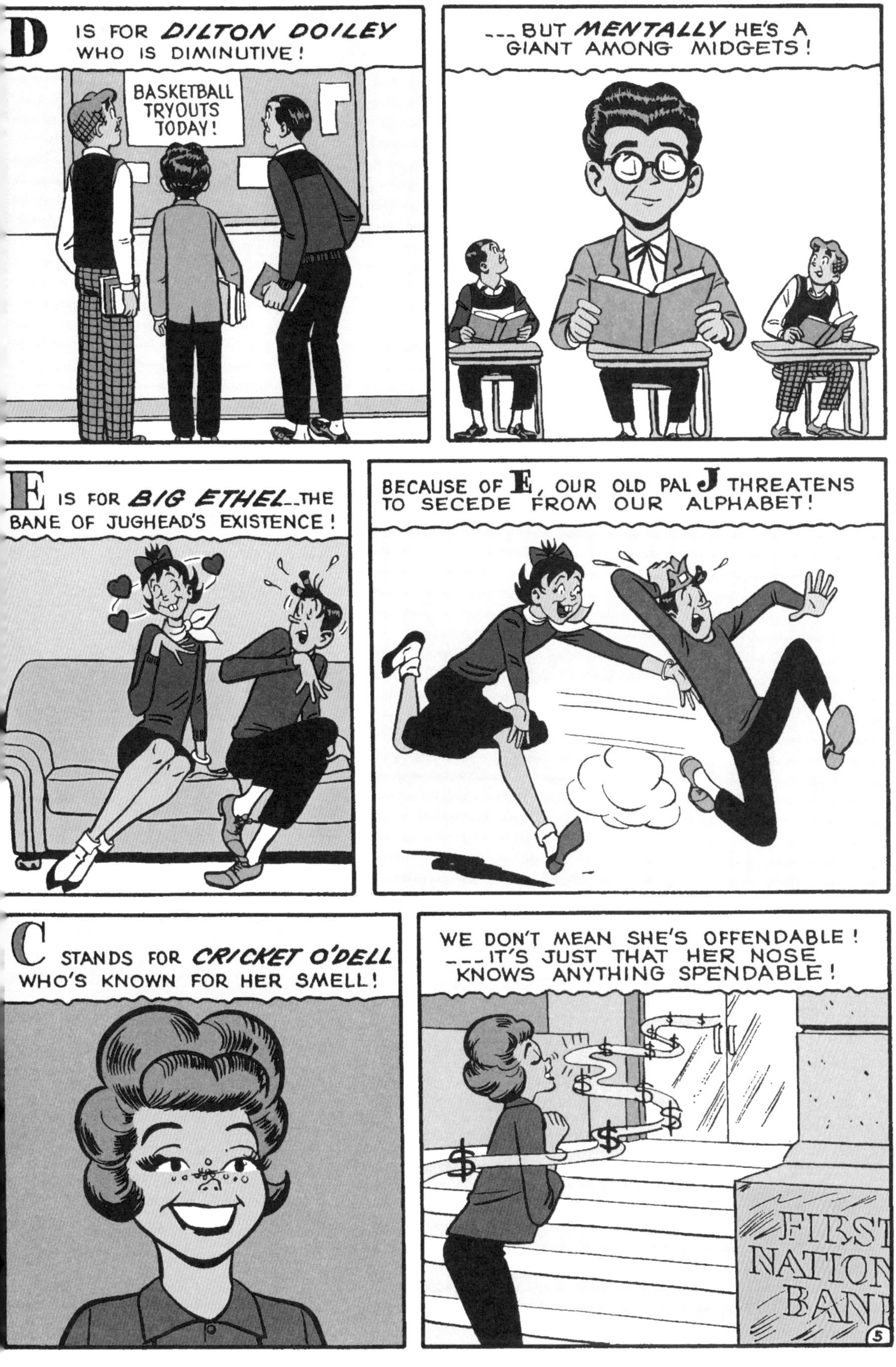
D IS FOR DILTON DOILEY WHO IS DIMINUTIVE!
BASKETBALL TRYOUTS TODAY!
---BUT MENTALLY HE'S A GIANT AMONG MIDGETS!
E IS FOR BIG ETHEL--THE BANE OF JUGHEAD'S EXISTENCE!
BECAUSE OF E, OUR OLD PAL J THREATENS TO SECEDE FROM OUR ALPHABET!
C STANDS FOR CRICKET O'DELL WHO'S KNOWN FOR HER SMELL!
WE DON'T MEAN SHE'S OFFENDABLE! ---IT'S JUST THAT HER NOSE KNOWS ANYTHING SPENDABLE!
FIRST NATION BAN
5

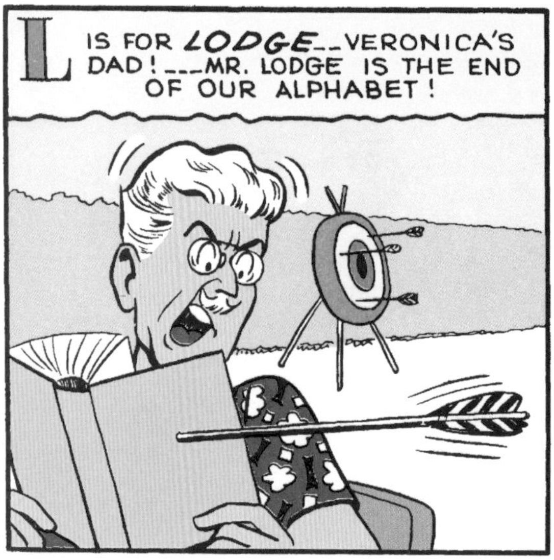
L IS FOR LODGE--VERONICA'S DAD! ---MR. LODGE IS THE END OF OUR ALPHABET!

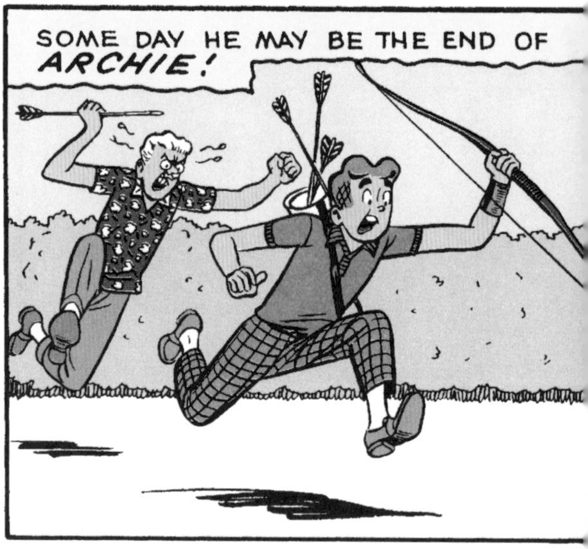
SOME DAY HE MAY BE THE END OF ARCHIE!

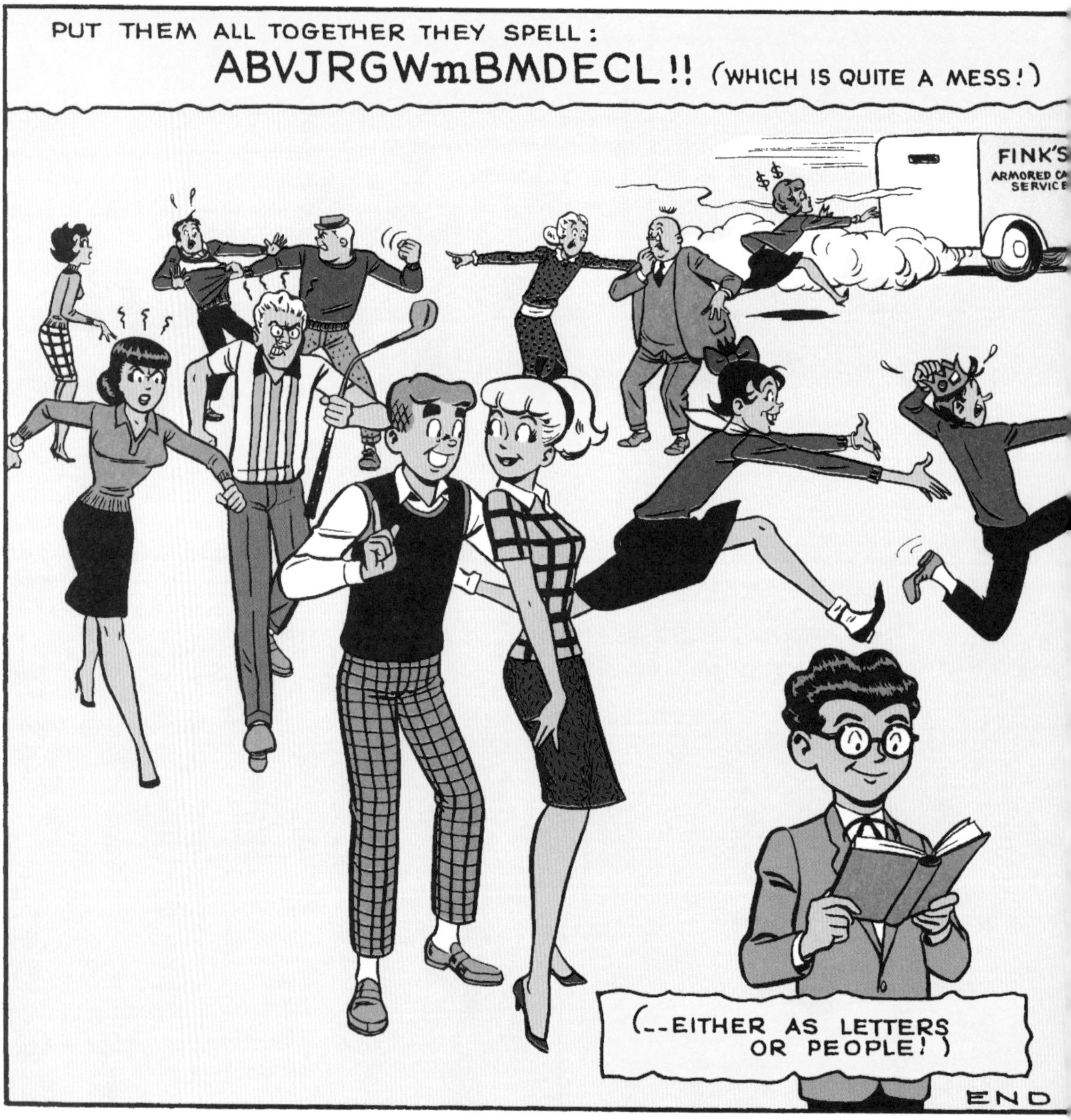
PUT THEM ALL TOGETHER THEY SPELL:
ABVJRGWmBMDECL!! (WHICH IS QUITE A MESS!)
FINK'S
(--EITHER AS LETTERS OR PEOPLE!)
END

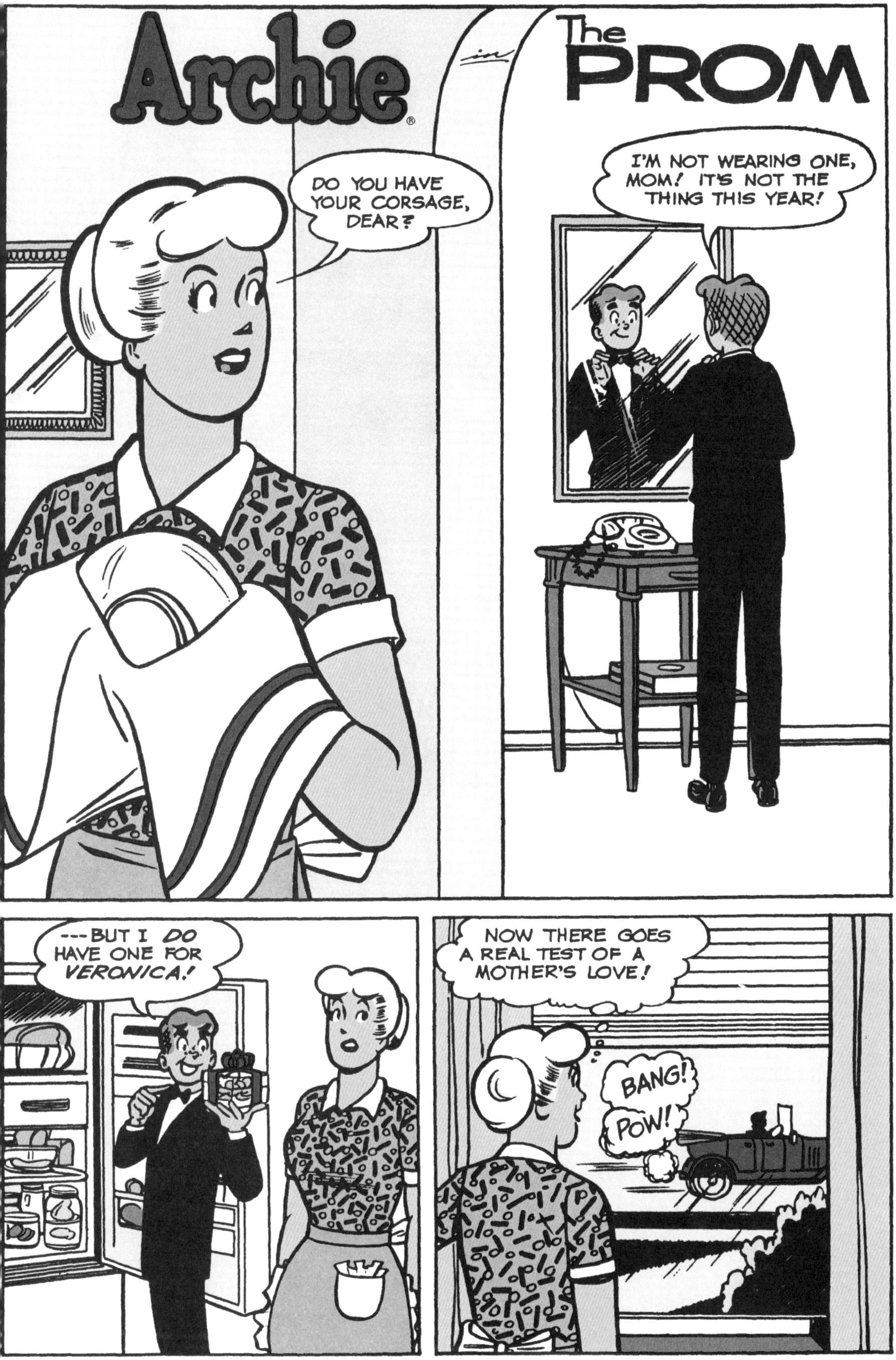
Archie
in
The PROM
DO YOU HAVE YOUR CORSAGE, DEAR?
I'M NOT WEARING ONE, MOM! IT'S NOT THE THING THIS YEAR!
---BUT I DO HAVE ONE FOR VERONICA!
NOW THERE GOES A REAL TEST OF A MOTHER'S LOVE!
BANG!
POW!

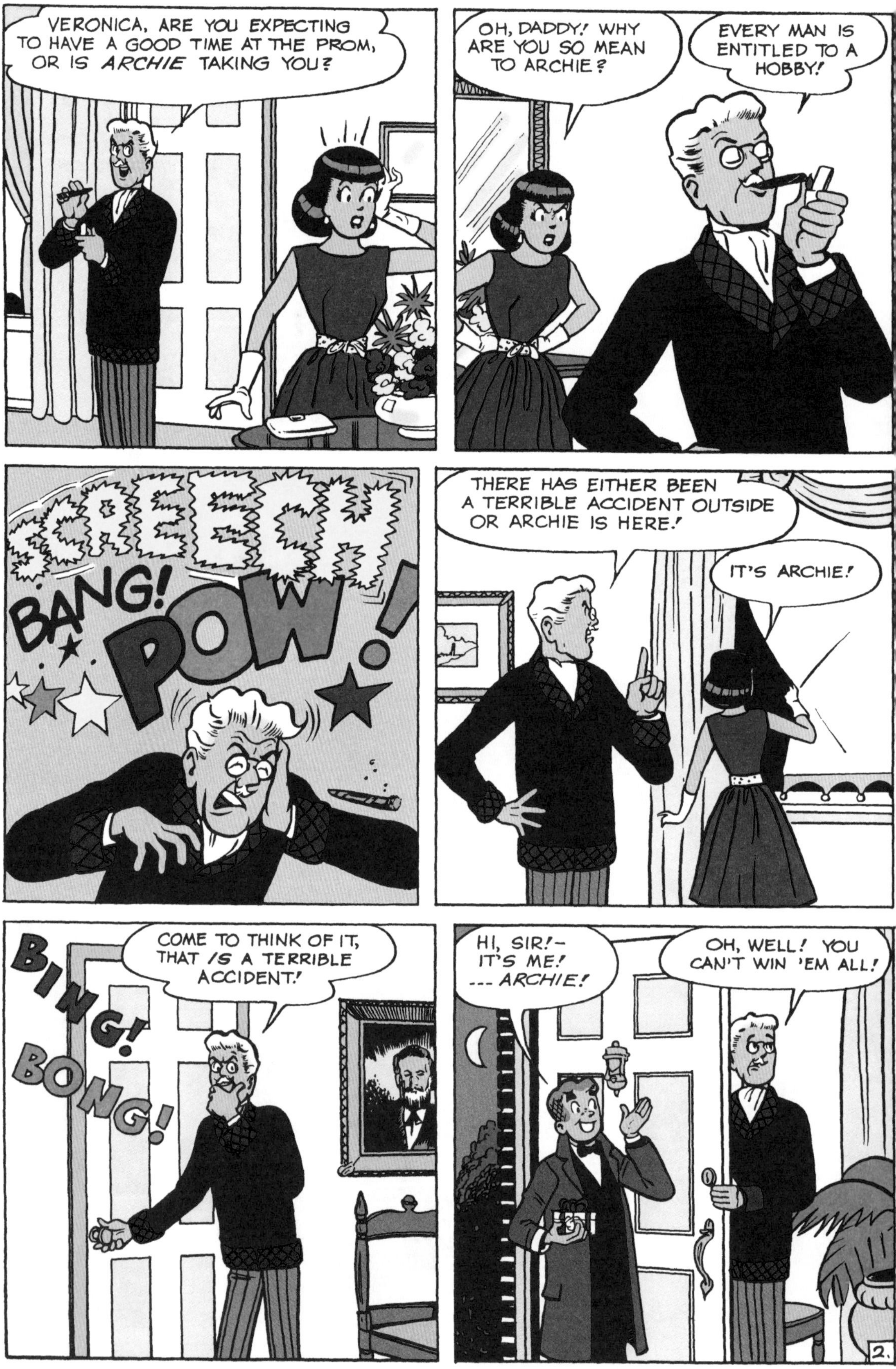
VERONICA, ARE YOU EXPECTING TO HAVE A GOOD TIME AT THE PROM, OR IS *ARCHIE* TAKING YOU?
OH, DADDY! WHY ARE YOU SO MEAN TO ARCHIE?
EVERY MAN IS ENTITLED TO A HOBBY!
SCREECH!
BANG!
POW!
THERE HAS EITHER BEEN A TERRIBLE ACCIDENT OUTSIDE OR ARCHIE IS HERE!
IT'S ARCHIE!
BING! BONG!
COME TO THINK OF IT, THAT *IS* A TERRIBLE ACCIDENT!
HI, SIR!– IT'S ME! --- *ARCHIE!*
OH, WELL! YOU CAN'T WIN 'EM ALL!
2.

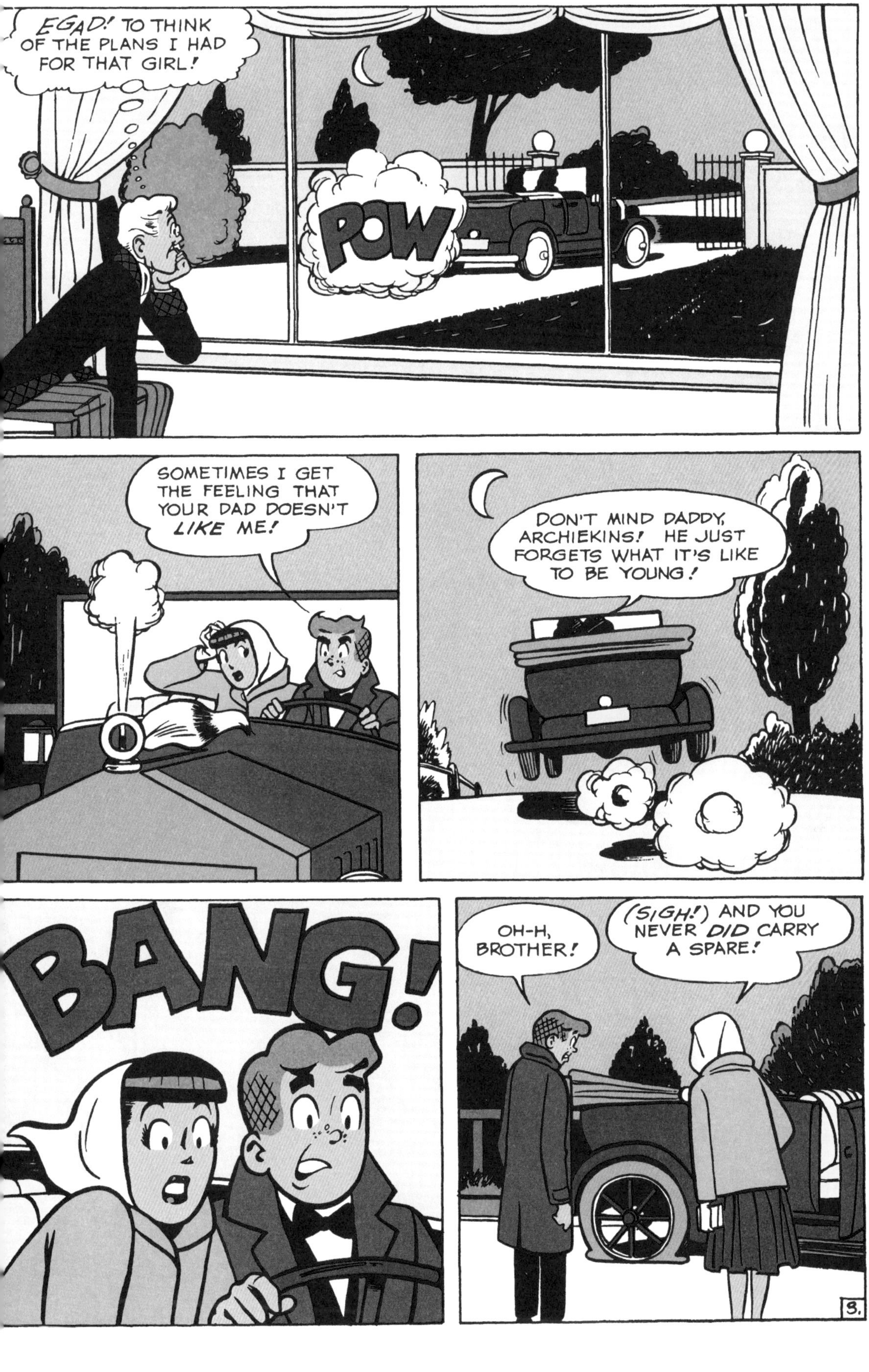
EGAD! TO THINK OF THE PLANS I HAD FOR THAT GIRL!
POW
SOMETIMES I GET THE FEELING THAT YOUR DAD DOESN'T LIKE ME!
DON'T MIND DADDY, ARCHIEKINS! HE JUST FORGETS WHAT IT'S LIKE TO BE YOUNG!
BANG!
OH-H, BROTHER!
(SIGH!) AND YOU NEVER DID CARRY A SPARE!
3.

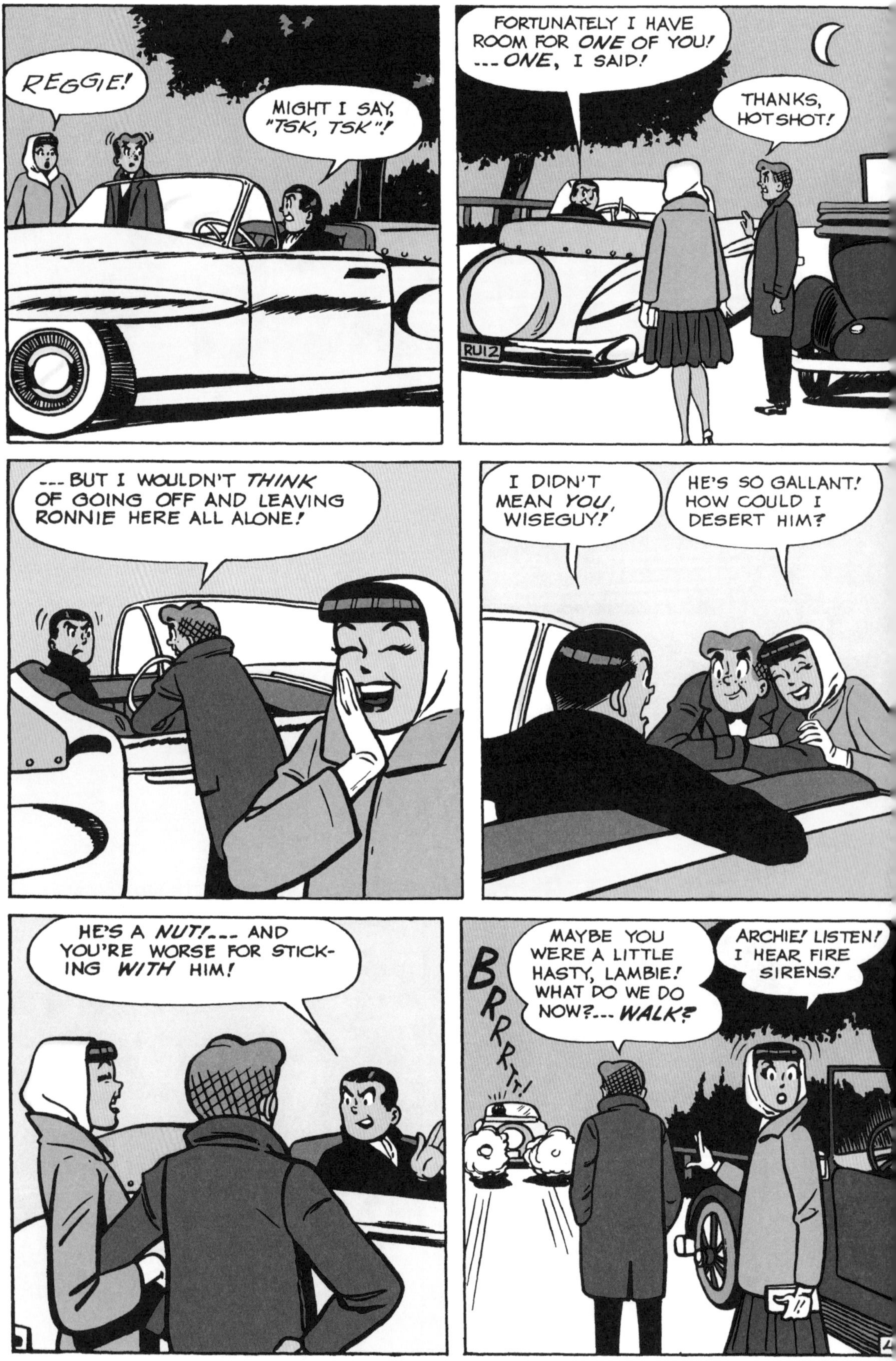
REGGIE!
MIGHT I SAY, "TSK, TSK"!
FORTUNATELY I HAVE ROOM FOR ONE OF YOU! ... ONE, I SAID!
THANKS, HOTSHOT!
RU12
... BUT I WOULDN'T THINK OF GOING OFF AND LEAVING RONNIE HERE ALL ALONE!
I DIDN'T MEAN YOU, WISEGUY!
HE'S SO GALLANT! HOW COULD I DESERT HIM?
HE'S A NUT! ... AND YOU'RE WORSE FOR STICKING WITH HIM!
BRRRRTT!
MAYBE YOU WERE A LITTLE HASTY, LAMBIE! WHAT DO WE DO NOW? ... WALK?
ARCHIE! LISTEN! I HEAR FIRE SIRENS!

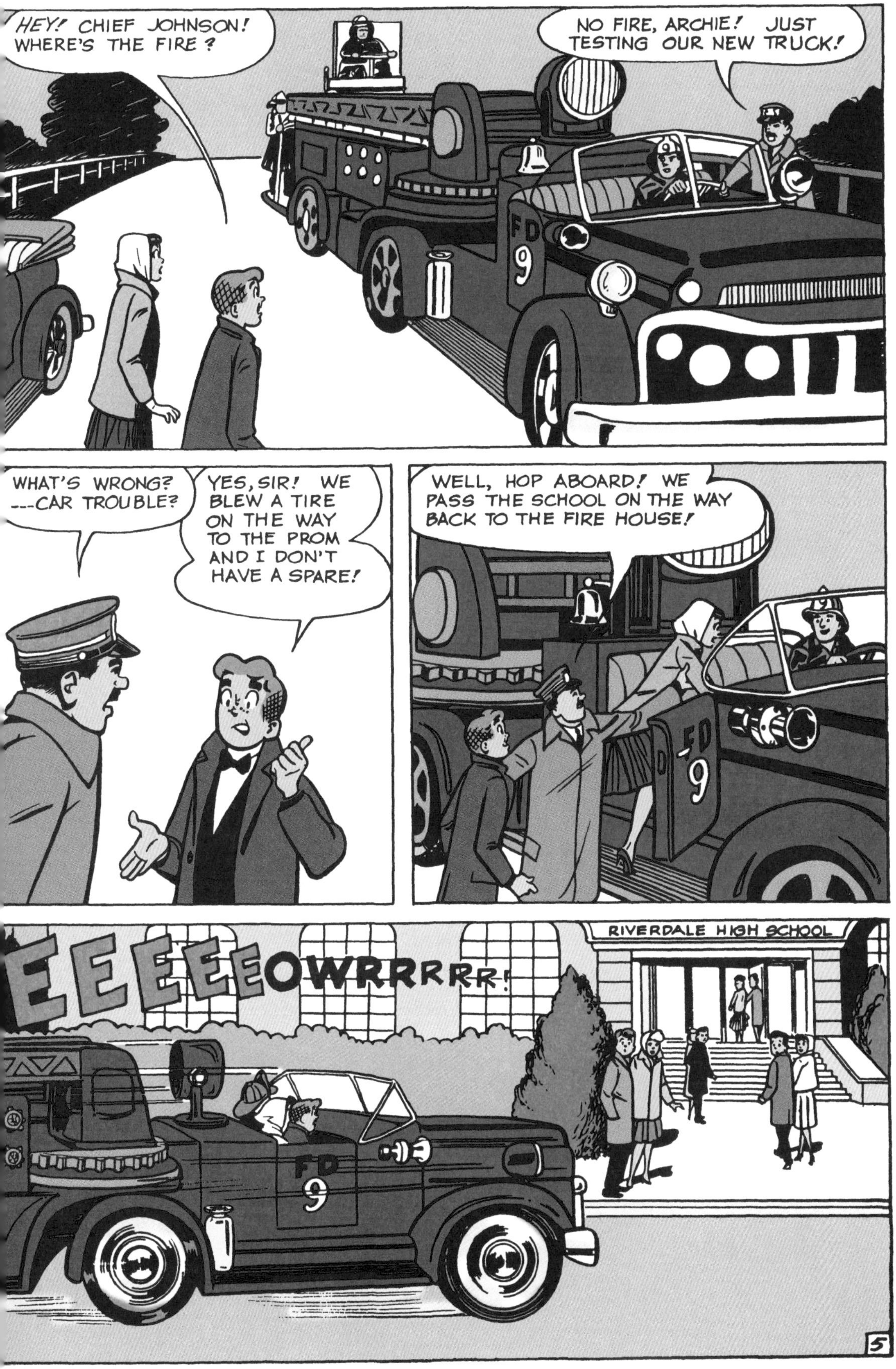
HEY! CHIEF JOHNSON! WHERE'S THE FIRE?
NO FIRE, ARCHIE! JUST TESTING OUR NEW TRUCK!
WHAT'S WRONG? ---CAR TROUBLE?
YES, SIR! WE BLEW A TIRE ON THE WAY TO THE PROM AND I DON'T HAVE A SPARE!
WELL, HOP ABOARD! WE PASS THE SCHOOL ON THE WAY BACK TO THE FIRE HOUSE!
EEEEEOWRRRRR!
RIVERDALE HIGH SCHOOL
5

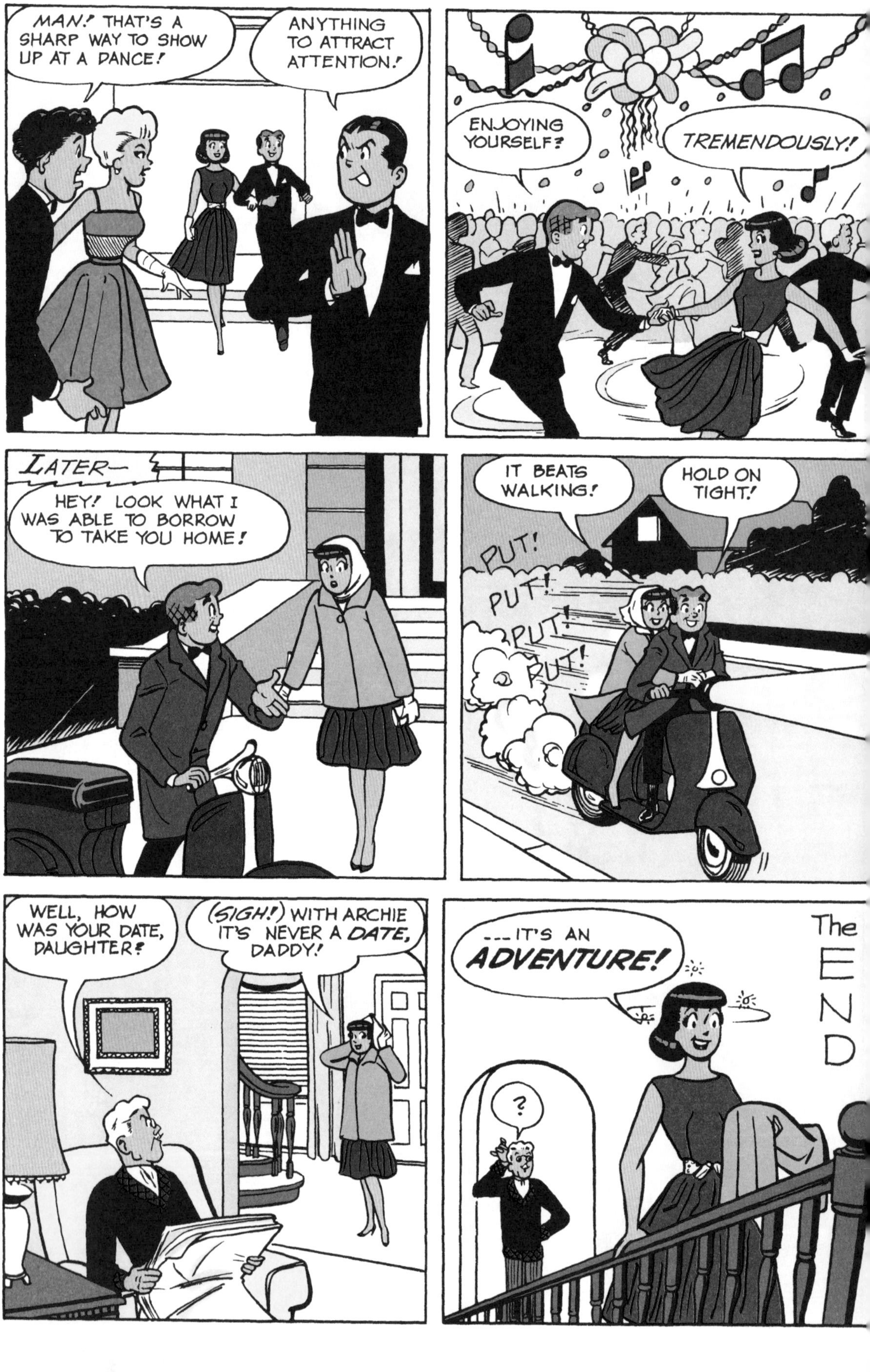
MAN! THAT'S A SHARP WAY TO SHOW UP AT A DANCE!
ANYTHING TO ATTRACT ATTENTION!
ENJOYING YOURSELF?
TREMENDOUSLY!
LATER—
HEY! LOOK WHAT I WAS ABLE TO BORROW TO TAKE YOU HOME!
IT BEATS WALKING!
HOLD ON TIGHT!
PUT! PUT! PUT! PUT!
WELL, HOW WAS YOUR DATE, DAUGHTER?
(SIGH!) WITH ARCHIE IT'S NEVER A DATE, DADDY!
---IT'S AN ADVENTURE!
?
The END

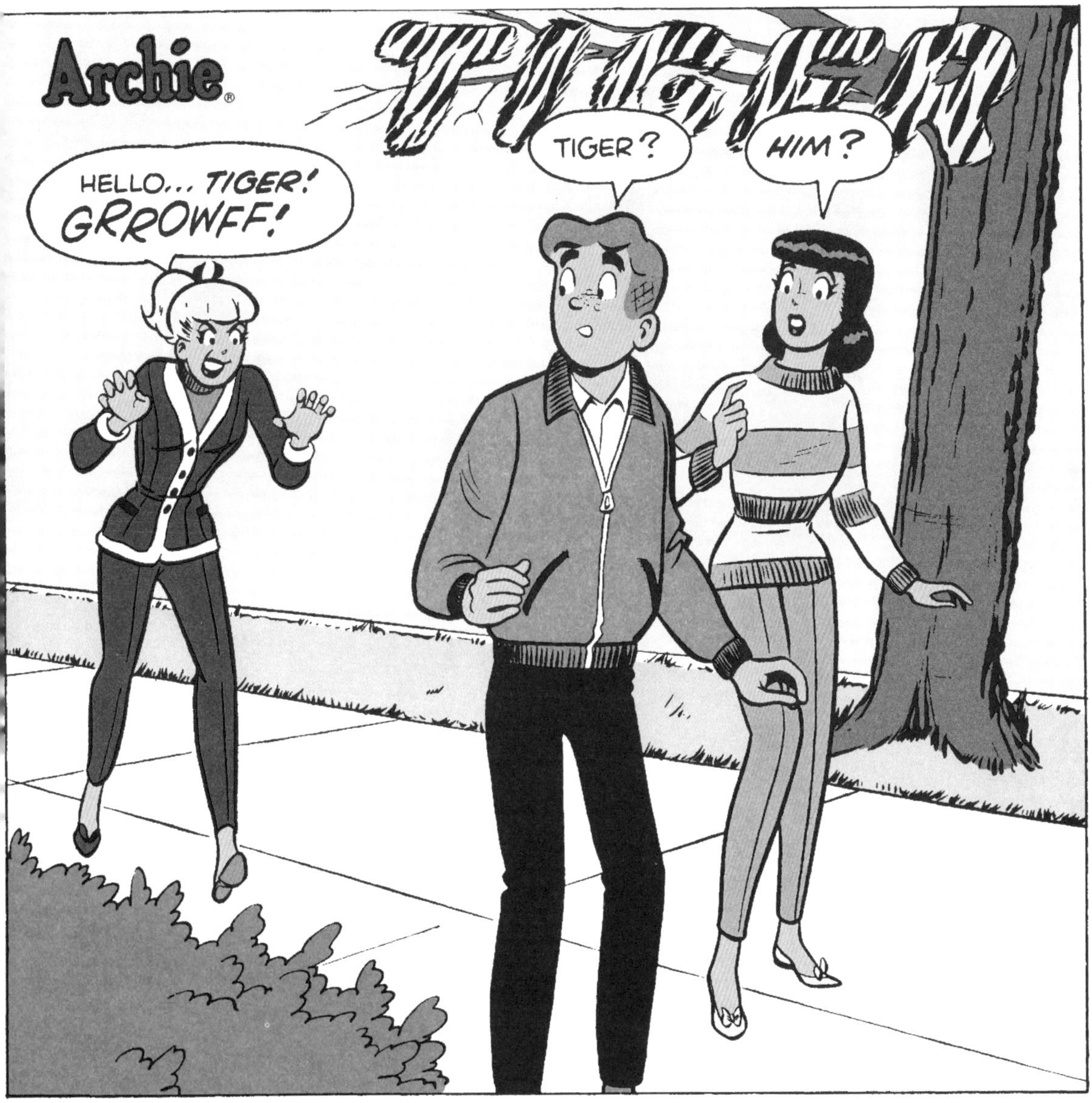
Archie
TIGER
HELLO... TIGER! GRROWFF!
TIGER?
HIM?

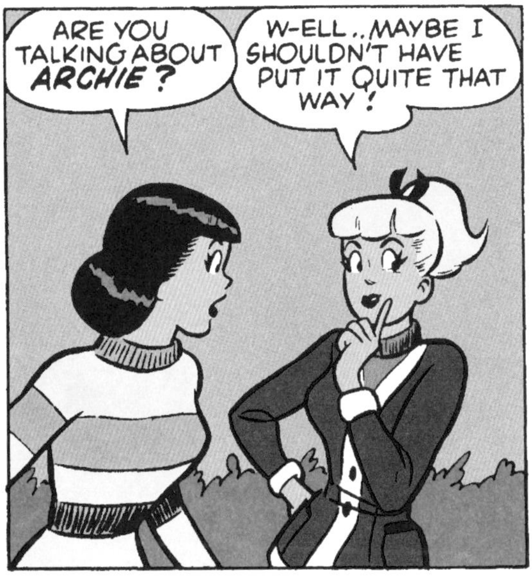
ARE YOU TALKING ABOUT ARCHIE?
W-ELL.. MAYBE I SHOULDN'T HAVE PUT IT QUITE THAT WAY!

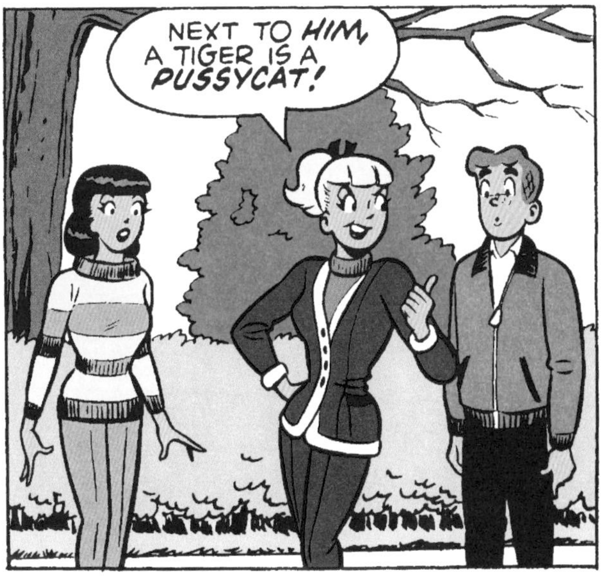
NEXT TO HIM, A TIGER IS A PUSSYCAT!

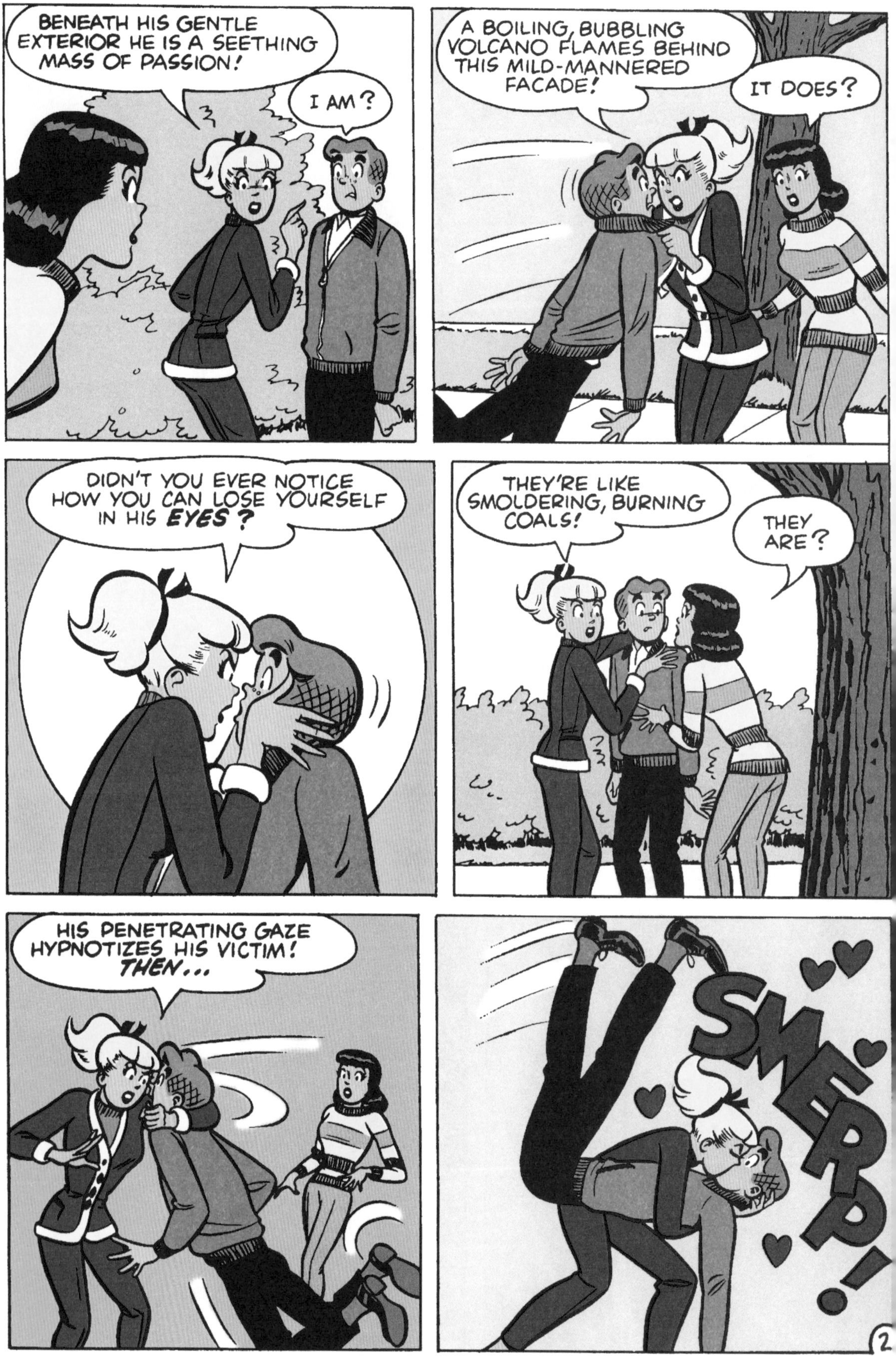
BENEATH HIS GENTLE EXTERIOR HE IS A SEETHING MASS OF PASSION!
I AM?
A BOILING, BUBBLING VOLCANO FLAMES BEHIND THIS MILD-MANNERED FACADE!
IT DOES?
DIDN'T YOU EVER NOTICE HOW YOU CAN LOSE YOURSELF IN HIS EYES?
THEY'RE LIKE SMOLDERING, BURNING COALS!
THEY ARE?
HIS PENETRATING GAZE HYPNOTIZES HIS VICTIM! THEN...
SMERP!

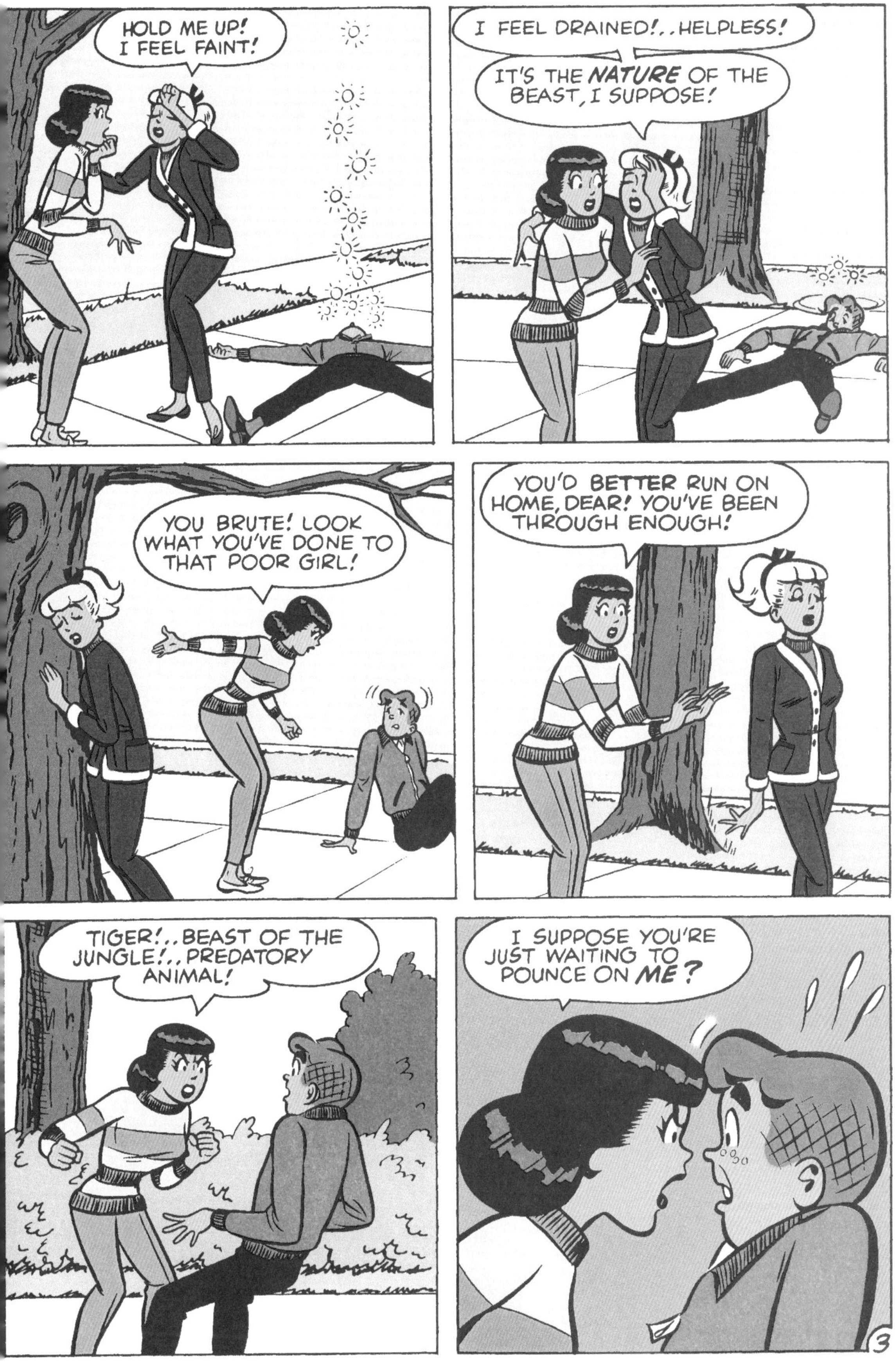
HOLD ME UP! I FEEL FAINT!
I FEEL DRAINED!..HELPLESS!
IT'S THE NATURE OF THE BEAST, I SUPPOSE!
YOU BRUTE! LOOK WHAT YOU'VE DONE TO THAT POOR GIRL!
YOU'D BETTER RUN ON HOME, DEAR! YOU'VE BEEN THROUGH ENOUGH!
TIGER!..BEAST OF THE JUNGLE!..PREDATORY ANIMAL!
I SUPPOSE YOU'RE JUST WAITING TO POUNCE ON ME?
3

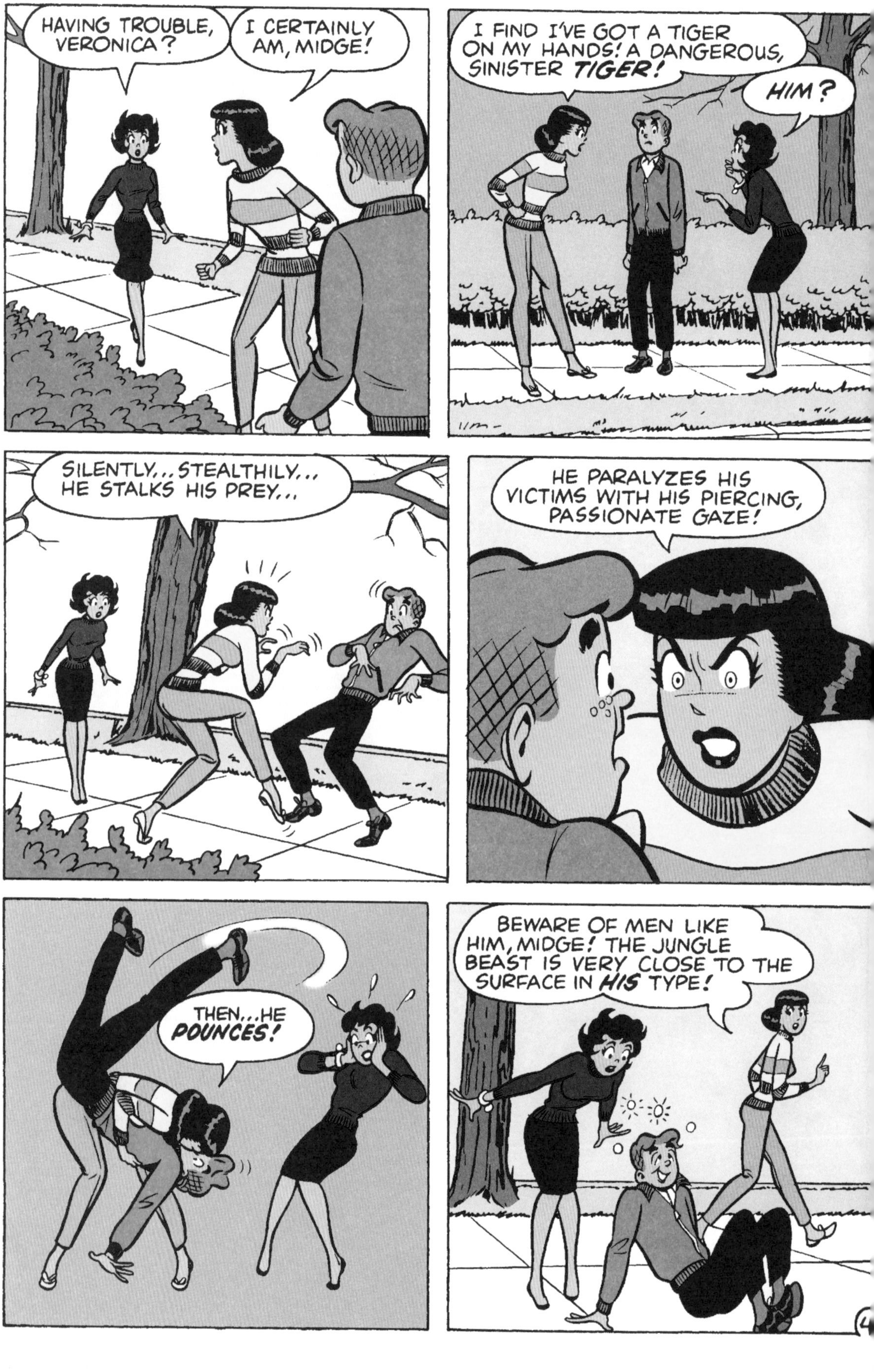
HAVING TROUBLE, VERONICA?
I CERTAINLY AM, MIDGE!
I FIND I'VE GOT A TIGER ON MY HANDS! A DANGEROUS, SINISTER TIGER!
HIM?
SILENTLY... STEALTHILY... HE STALKS HIS PREY...
HE PARALYZES HIS VICTIMS WITH HIS PIERCING, PASSIONATE GAZE!
THEN... HE POUNCES!
BEWARE OF MEN LIKE HIM, MIDGE! THE JUNGLE BEAST IS VERY CLOSE TO THE SURFACE IN HIS TYPE!
4

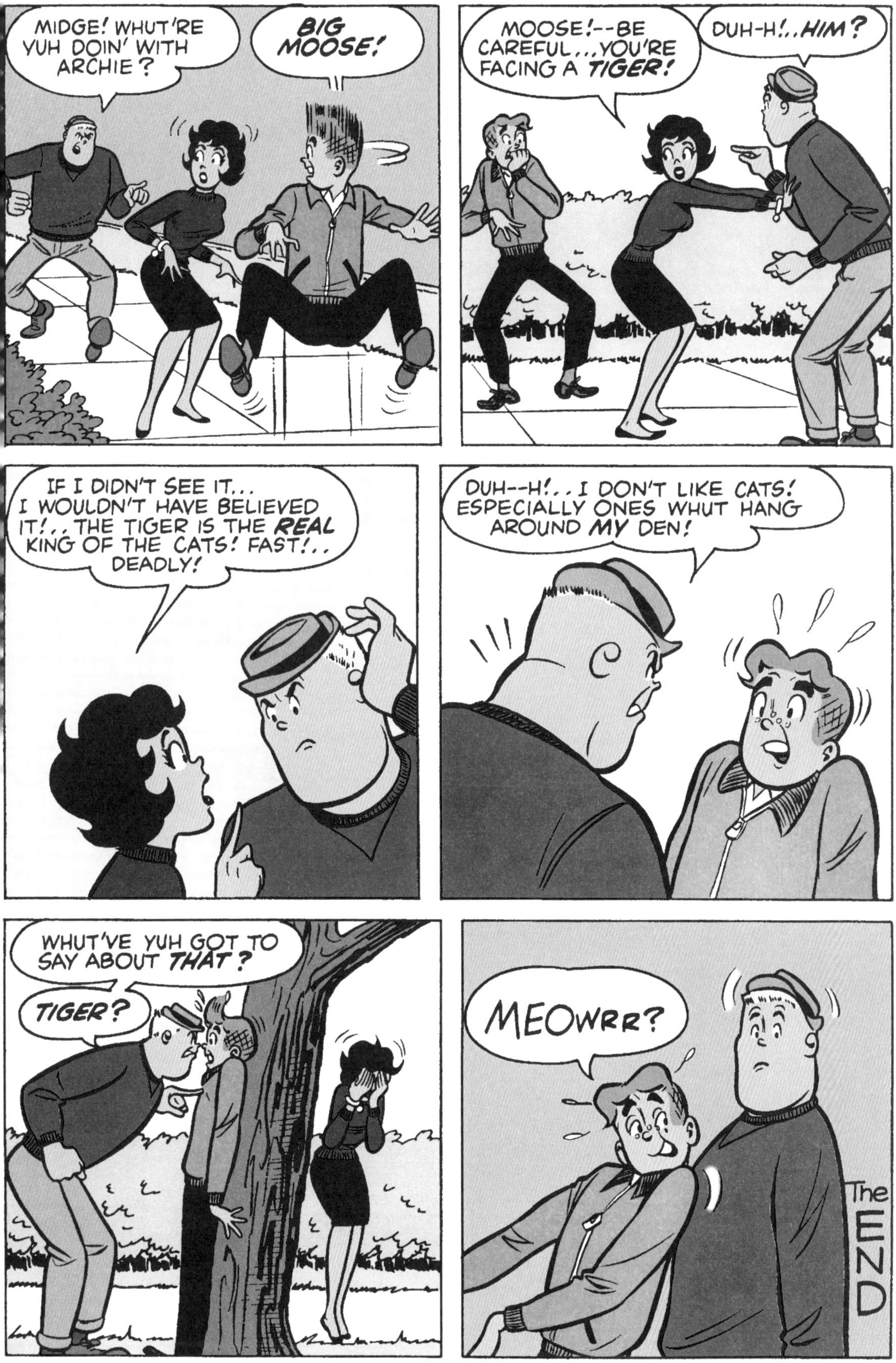
MIDGE! WHUT'RE YUH DOIN' WITH ARCHIE?
BIG MOOSE!
MOOSE!--BE CAREFUL...YOU'RE FACING A TIGER!
DUH-H!..HIM?
IF I DIDN'T SEE IT... I WOULDN'T HAVE BELIEVED IT!.. THE TIGER IS THE REAL KING OF THE CATS! FAST!.. DEADLY!
DUH--H!..I DON'T LIKE CATS! ESPECIALLY ONES WHUT HANG AROUND MY DEN!
WHUT'VE YUH GOT TO SAY ABOUT THAT?
TIGER?
MEOWRR?
The END

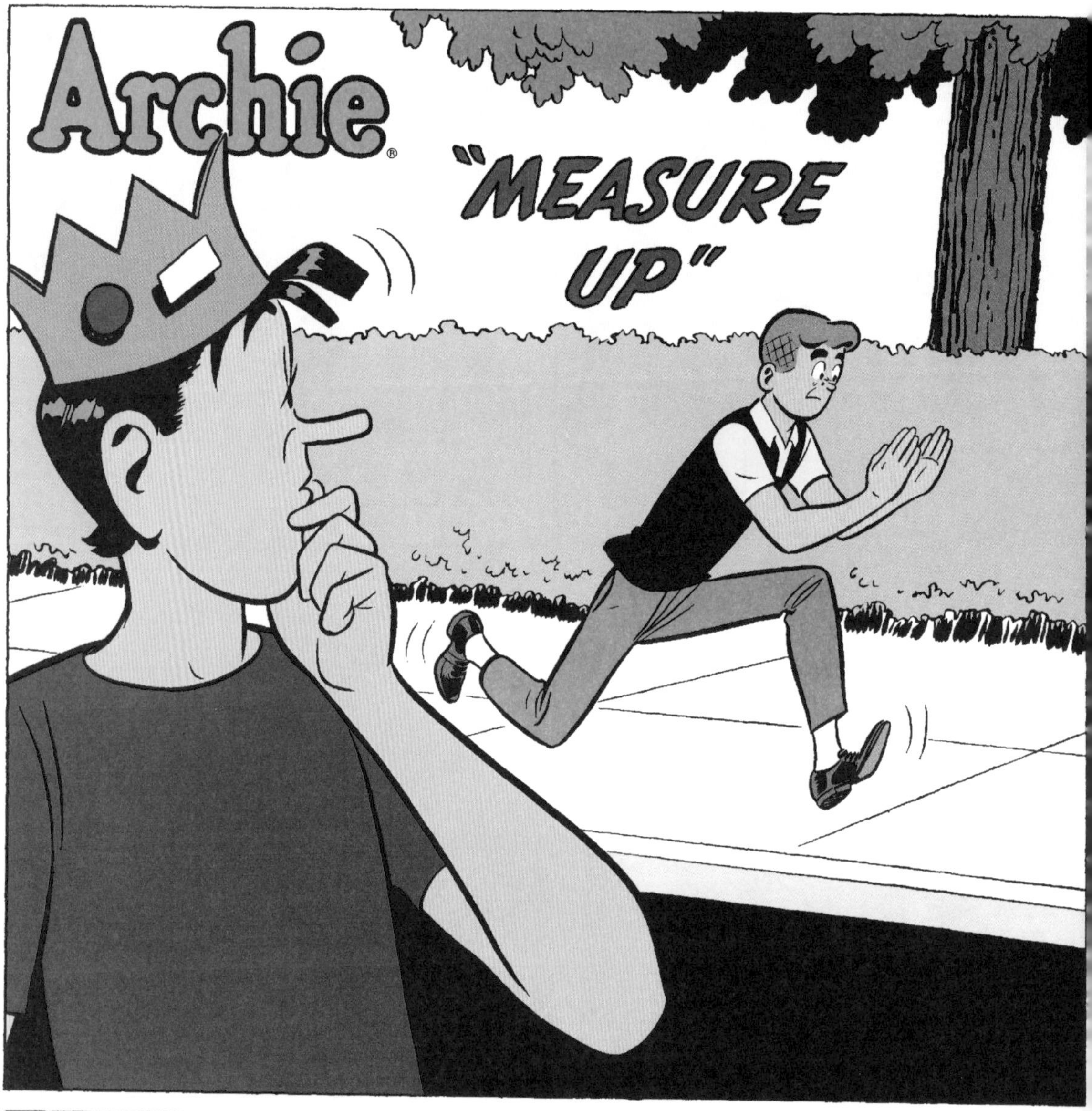
Archie
"MEASURE UP"

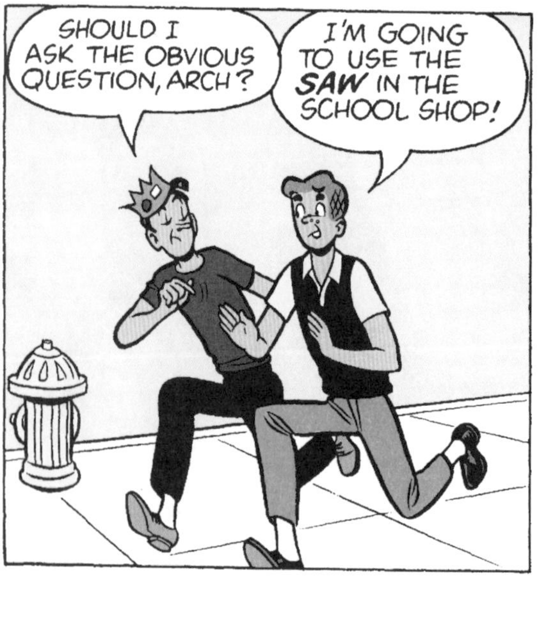
SHOULD I ASK THE OBVIOUS QUESTION, ARCH?
I'M GOING TO USE THE SAW IN THE SCHOOL SHOP!

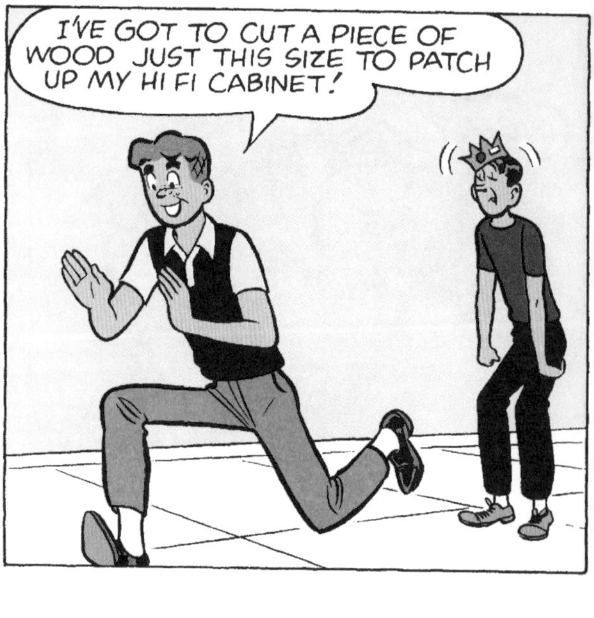
I'VE GOT TO CUT A PIECE OF WOOD JUST THIS SIZE TO PATCH UP MY HI FI CABINET!

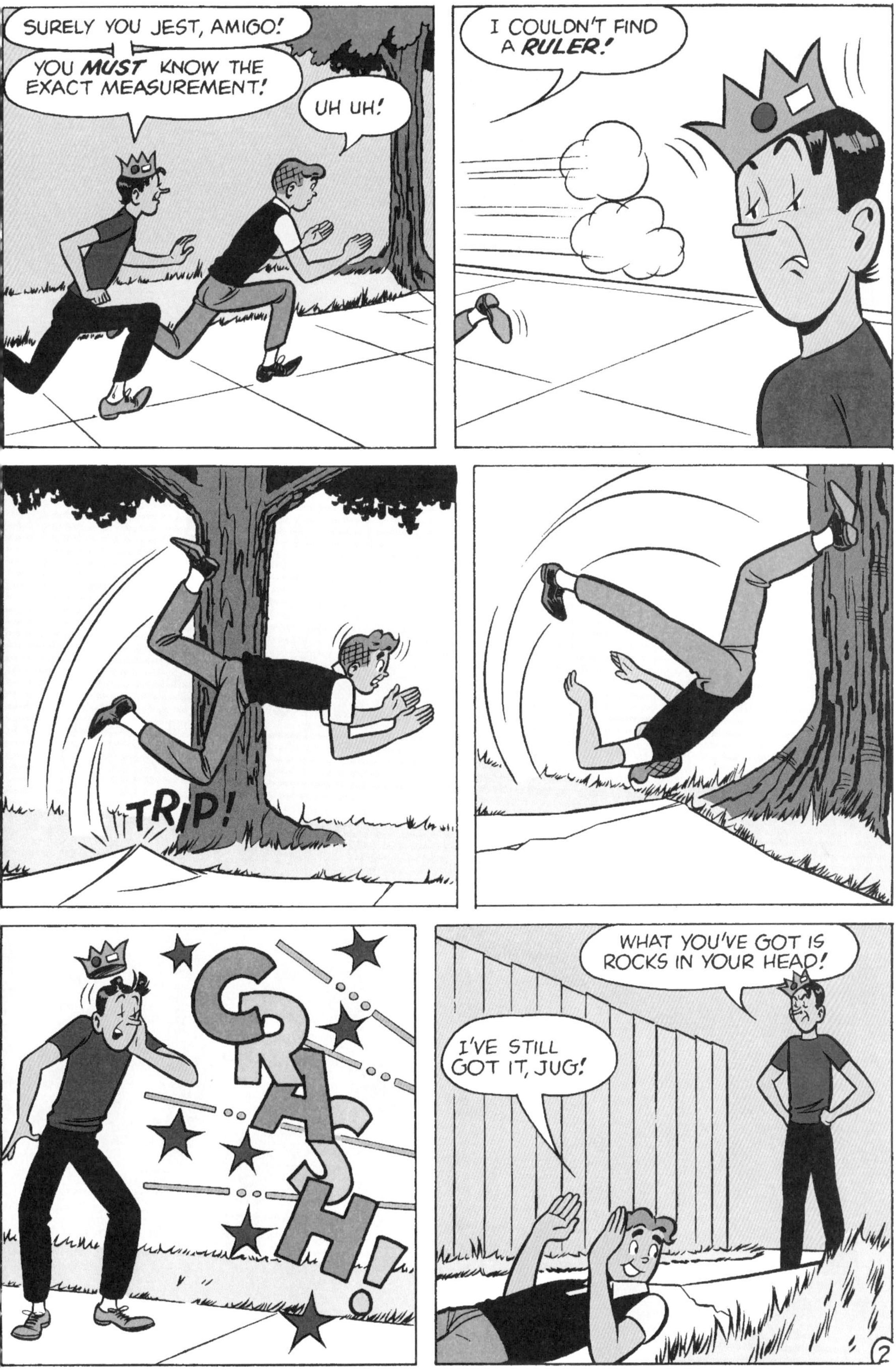
SURELY YOU JEST, AMIGO!
YOU MUST KNOW THE EXACT MEASUREMENT!
UH UH!
I COULDN'T FIND A RULER!
TRIP!
CRASH!
WHAT YOU'VE GOT IS ROCKS IN YOUR HEAD!
I'VE STILL GOT IT, JUG!
2

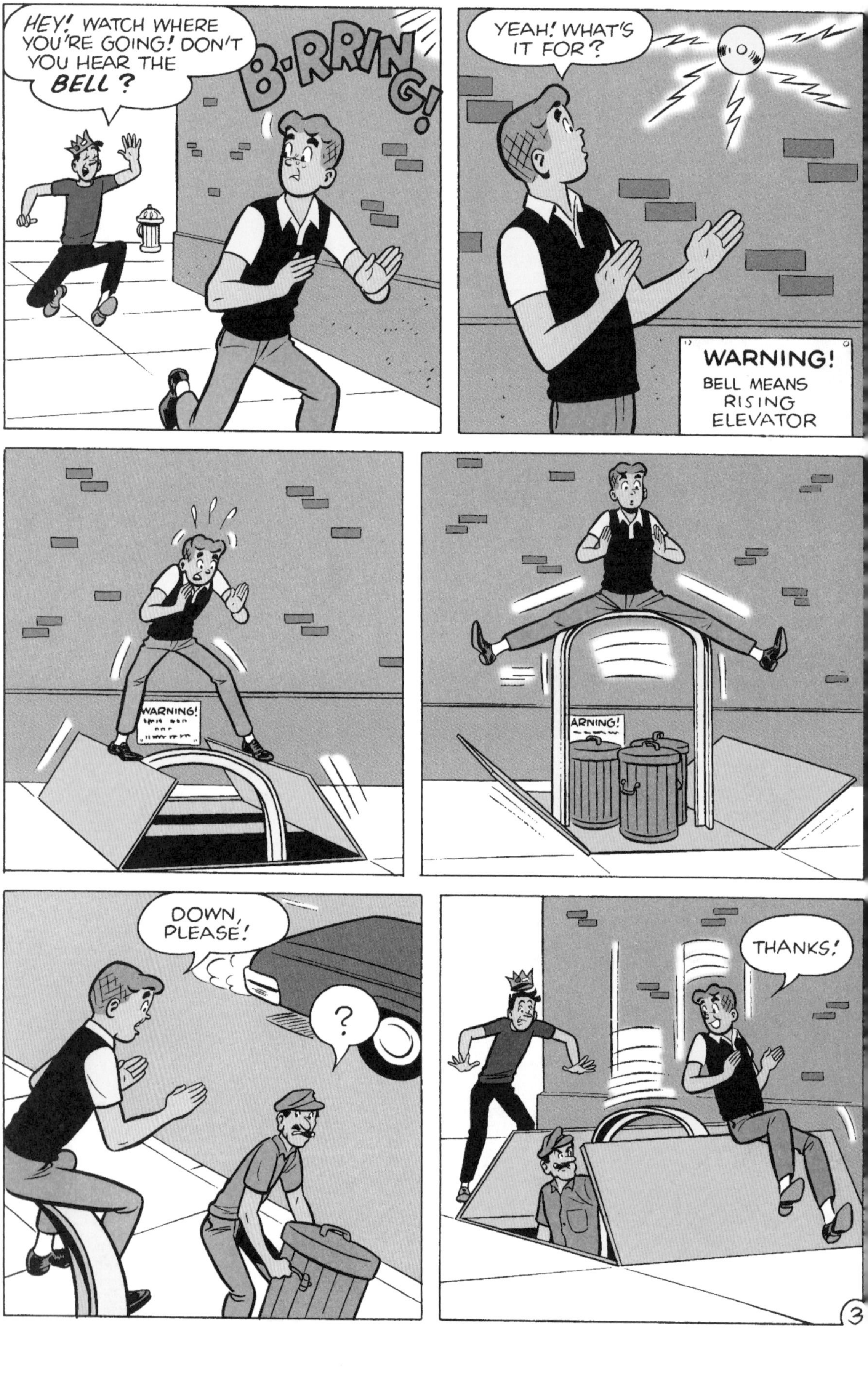

HEY! WATCH WHERE YOU'RE GOING! DON'T YOU HEAR THE BELL?
B-RRING!
YEAH! WHAT'S IT FOR?
WARNING! BELL MEANS RISING ELEVATOR
WARNING!
DOWN, PLEASE!
?
THANKS!
3

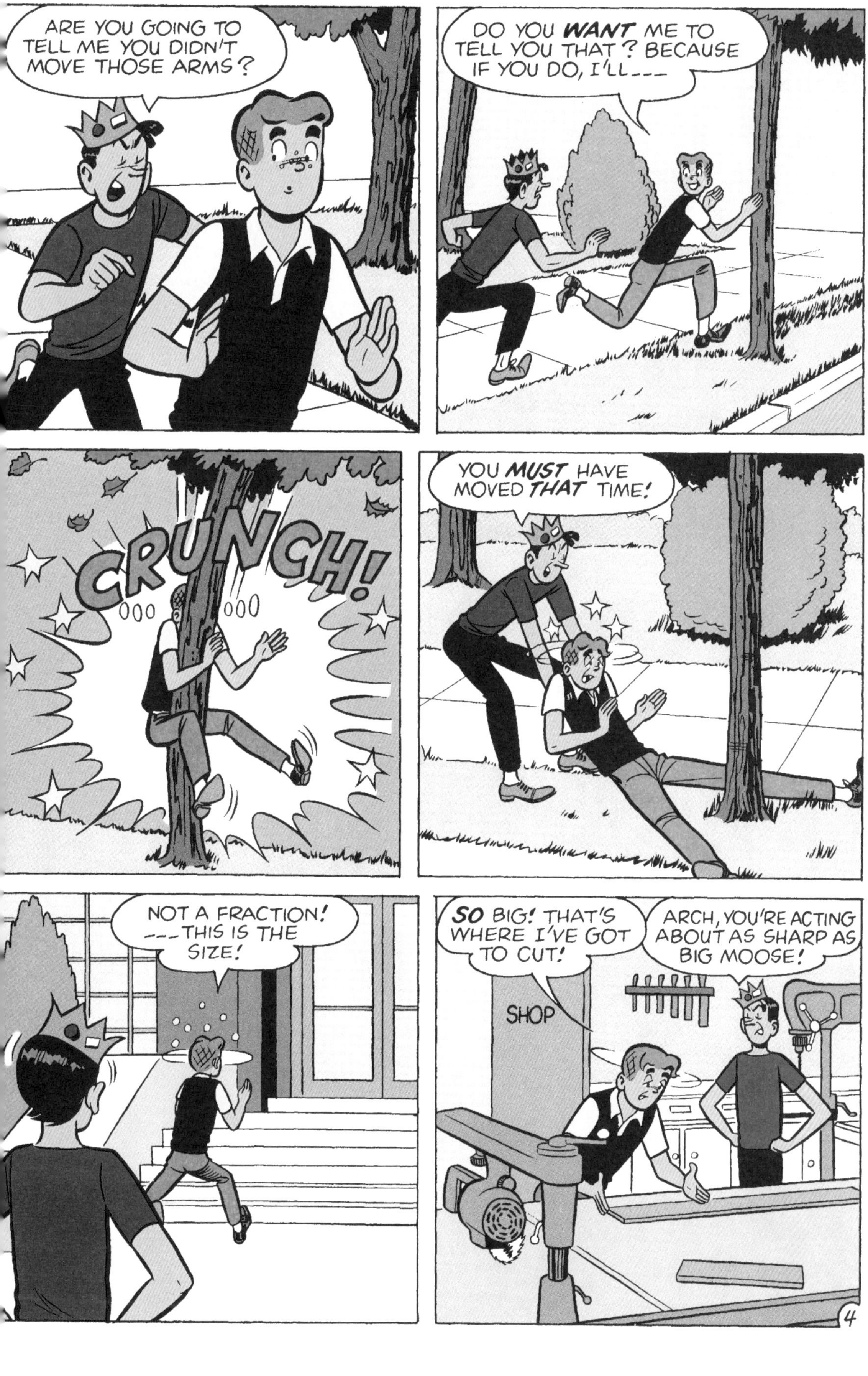
ARE YOU GOING TO TELL ME YOU DIDN'T MOVE THOSE ARMS?
DO YOU WANT ME TO TELL YOU THAT? BECAUSE IF YOU DO, I'LL---
CRUNCH!
OOO
OOO
YOU MUST HAVE MOVED THAT TIME!
NOT A FRACTION! ---THIS IS THE SIZE!
SO BIG! THAT'S WHERE I'VE GOT TO CUT!
ARCH, YOU'RE ACTING ABOUT AS SHARP AS BIG MOOSE!
SHOP
4

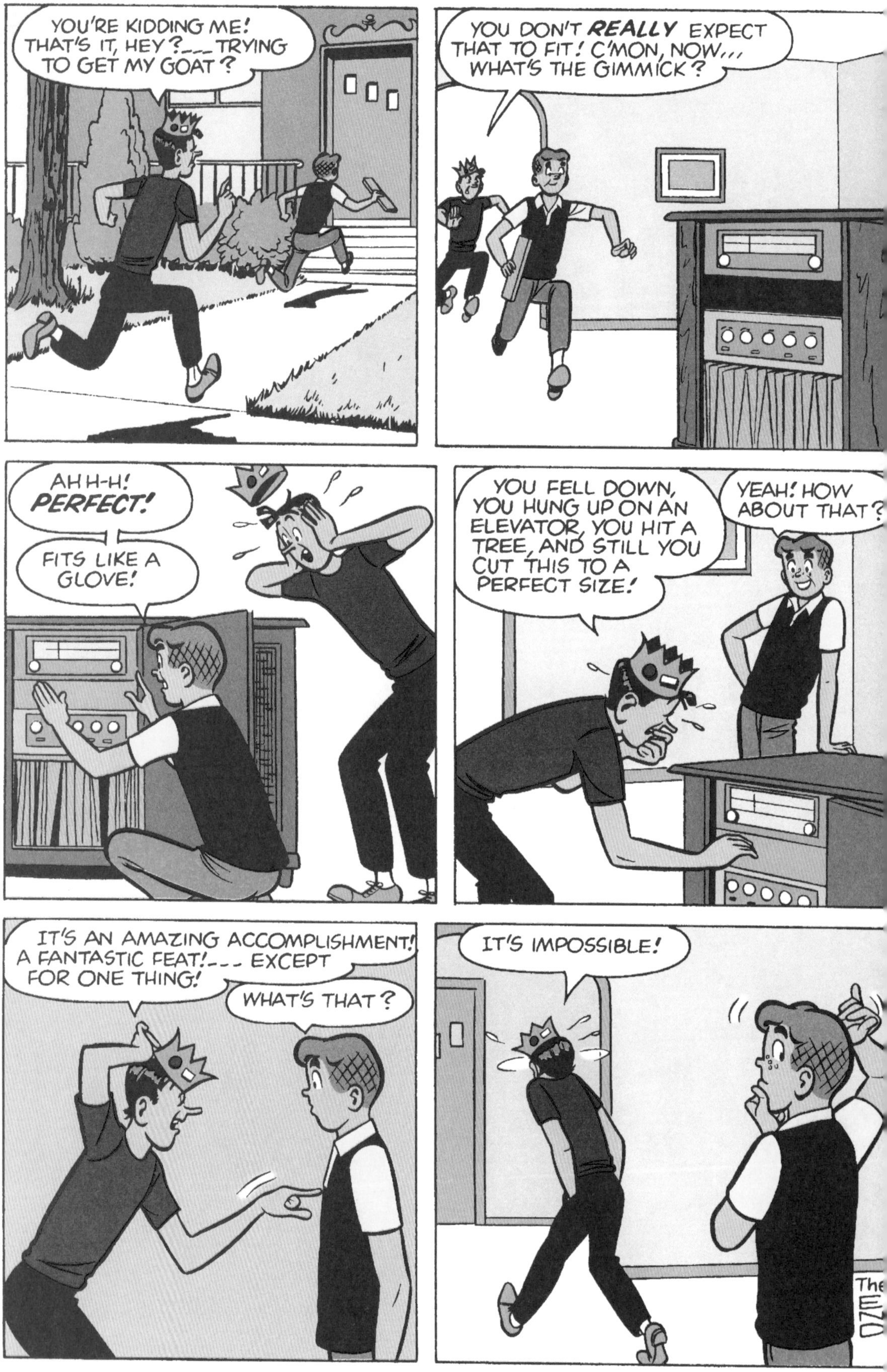
YOU'RE KIDDING ME! THAT'S IT, HEY?--- TRYING TO GET MY GOAT?
YOU DON'T REALLY EXPECT THAT TO FIT! C'MON, NOW... WHAT'S THE GIMMICK?
AHH-H! PERFECT!
FITS LIKE A GLOVE!
YOU FELL DOWN, YOU HUNG UP ON AN ELEVATOR, YOU HIT A TREE, AND STILL YOU CUT THIS TO A PERFECT SIZE!
YEAH! HOW ABOUT THAT?
IT'S AN AMAZING ACCOMPLISHMENT! A FANTASTIC FEAT!--- EXCEPT FOR ONE THING!
WHAT'S THAT?
IT'S IMPOSSIBLE!
The END

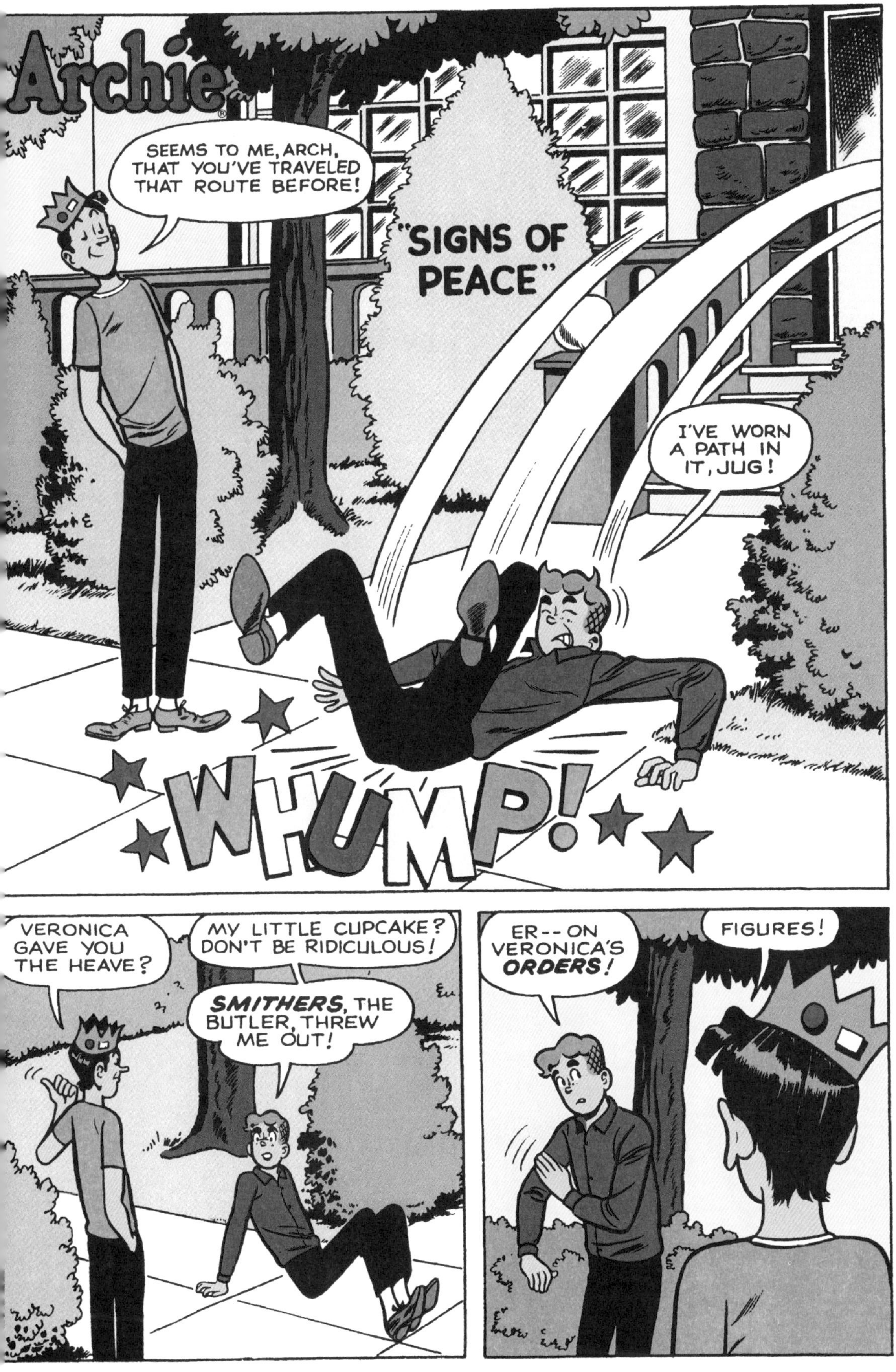
Archie
"SIGNS OF PEACE"
SEEMS TO ME, ARCH, THAT YOU'VE TRAVELED THAT ROUTE BEFORE!
I'VE WORN A PATH IN IT, JUG!
WHUMP!
VERONICA GAVE YOU THE HEAVE?
MY LITTLE CUPCAKE? DON'T BE RIDICULOUS!
SMITHERS, THE BUTLER, THREW ME OUT!
ER-- ON VERONICA'S ORDERS!
FIGURES!

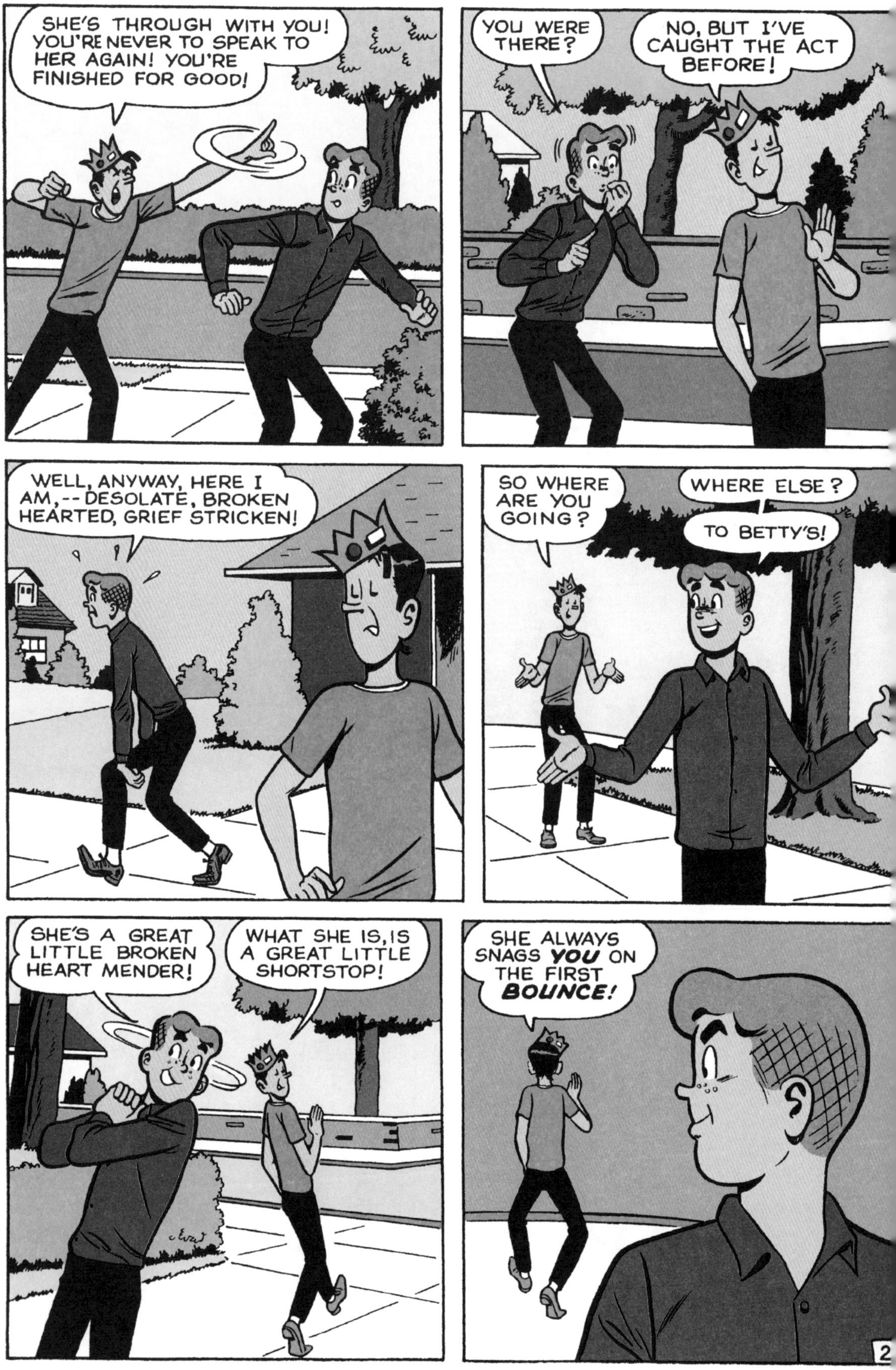
SHE'S THROUGH WITH YOU! YOU'RE NEVER TO SPEAK TO HER AGAIN! YOU'RE FINISHED FOR GOOD!
YOU WERE THERE?
NO, BUT I'VE CAUGHT THE ACT BEFORE!
WELL, ANYWAY, HERE I AM,-- DESOLATE, BROKEN HEARTED, GRIEF STRICKEN!
SO WHERE ARE YOU GOING?
WHERE ELSE?
TO BETTY'S!
SHE'S A GREAT LITTLE BROKEN HEART MENDER!
WHAT SHE IS, IS A GREAT LITTLE SHORTSTOP!
SHE ALWAYS SNAGS **YOU** ON THE FIRST ***BOUNCE!***

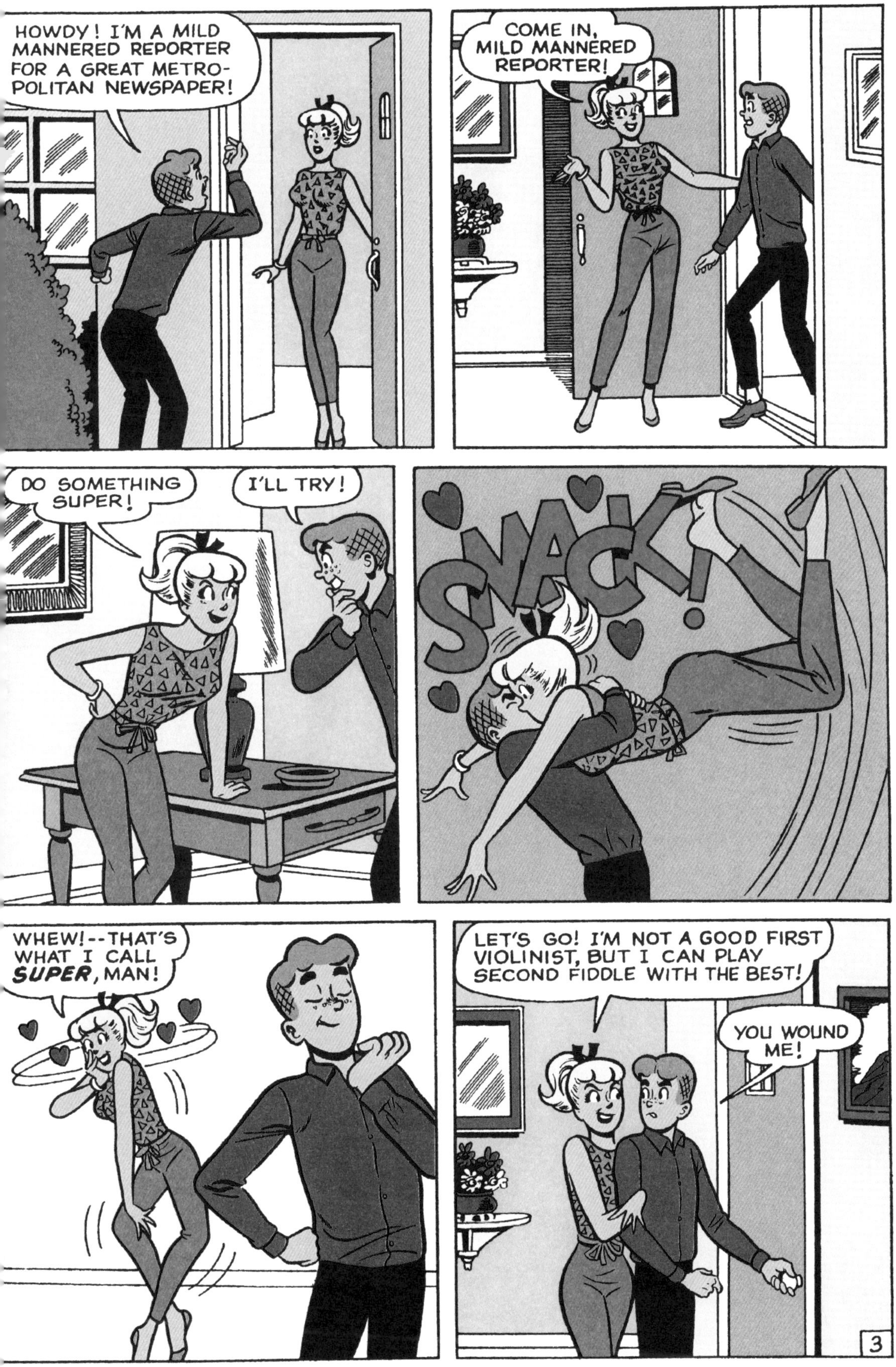
HOWDY! I'M A MILD MANNERED REPORTER FOR A GREAT METRO-POLITAN NEWSPAPER!
COME IN, MILD MANNERED REPORTER!
DO SOMETHING SUPER!
I'LL TRY!
SMACK!
WHEW!--THAT'S WHAT I CALL SUPER, MAN!
LET'S GO! I'M NOT A GOOD FIRST VIOLINIST, BUT I CAN PLAY SECOND FIDDLE WITH THE BEST!
YOU WOUND ME!
3

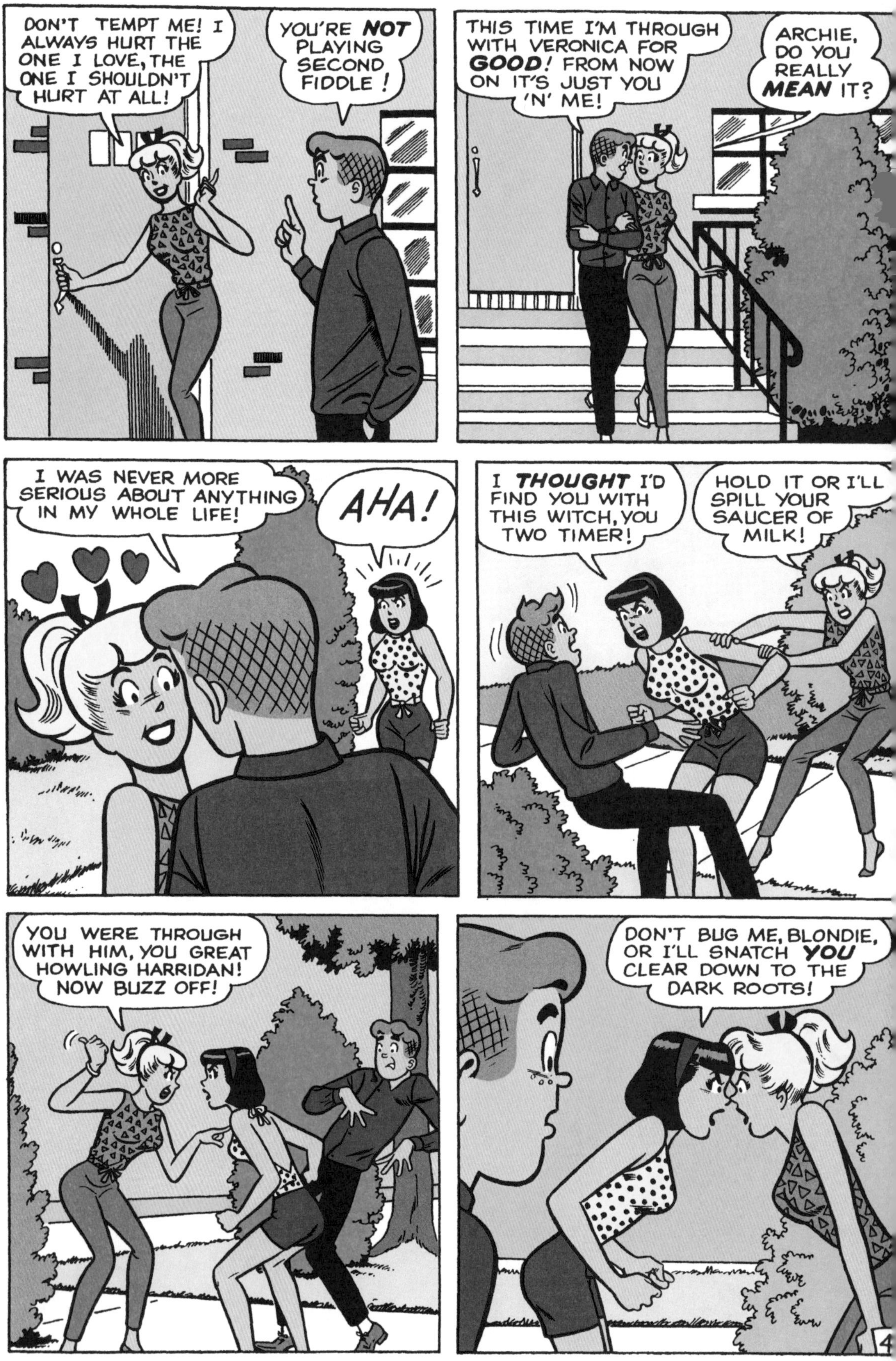
DON'T TEMPT ME! I ALWAYS HURT THE ONE I LOVE, THE ONE I SHOULDN'T HURT AT ALL!
YOU'RE NOT PLAYING SECOND FIDDLE!
THIS TIME I'M THROUGH WITH VERONICA FOR GOOD! FROM NOW ON IT'S JUST YOU 'N' ME!
ARCHIE, DO YOU REALLY MEAN IT?
I WAS NEVER MORE SERIOUS ABOUT ANYTHING IN MY WHOLE LIFE!
AHA!
I THOUGHT I'D FIND YOU WITH THIS WITCH, YOU TWO TIMER!
HOLD IT OR I'LL SPILL YOUR SAUCER OF MILK!
YOU WERE THROUGH WITH HIM, YOU GREAT HOWLING HARRIDAN! NOW BUZZ OFF!
DON'T BUG ME, BLONDIE, OR I'LL SNATCH YOU CLEAR DOWN TO THE DARK ROOTS!
4

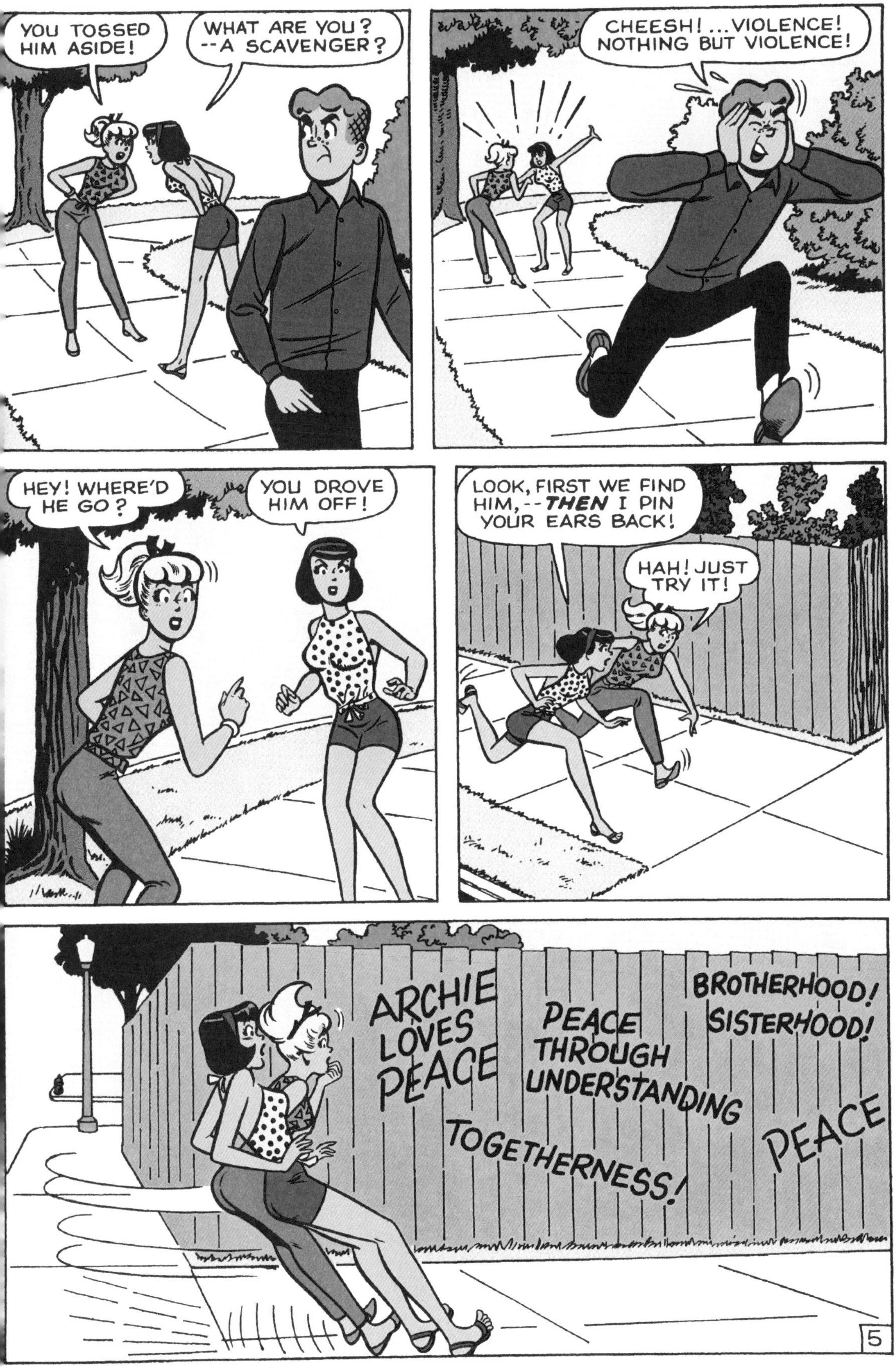
YOU TOSSED HIM ASIDE!
WHAT ARE YOU? --A SCAVENGER?
CHEESH! ...VIOLENCE! NOTHING BUT VIOLENCE!
HEY! WHERE'D HE GO?
YOU DROVE HIM OFF!
LOOK, FIRST WE FIND HIM, --THEN I PIN YOUR EARS BACK!
HAH! JUST TRY IT!
ARCHIE LOVES PEACE
PEACE THROUGH UNDERSTANDING
BROTHERHOOD! SISTERHOOD!
TOGETHERNESS!
PEACE
5

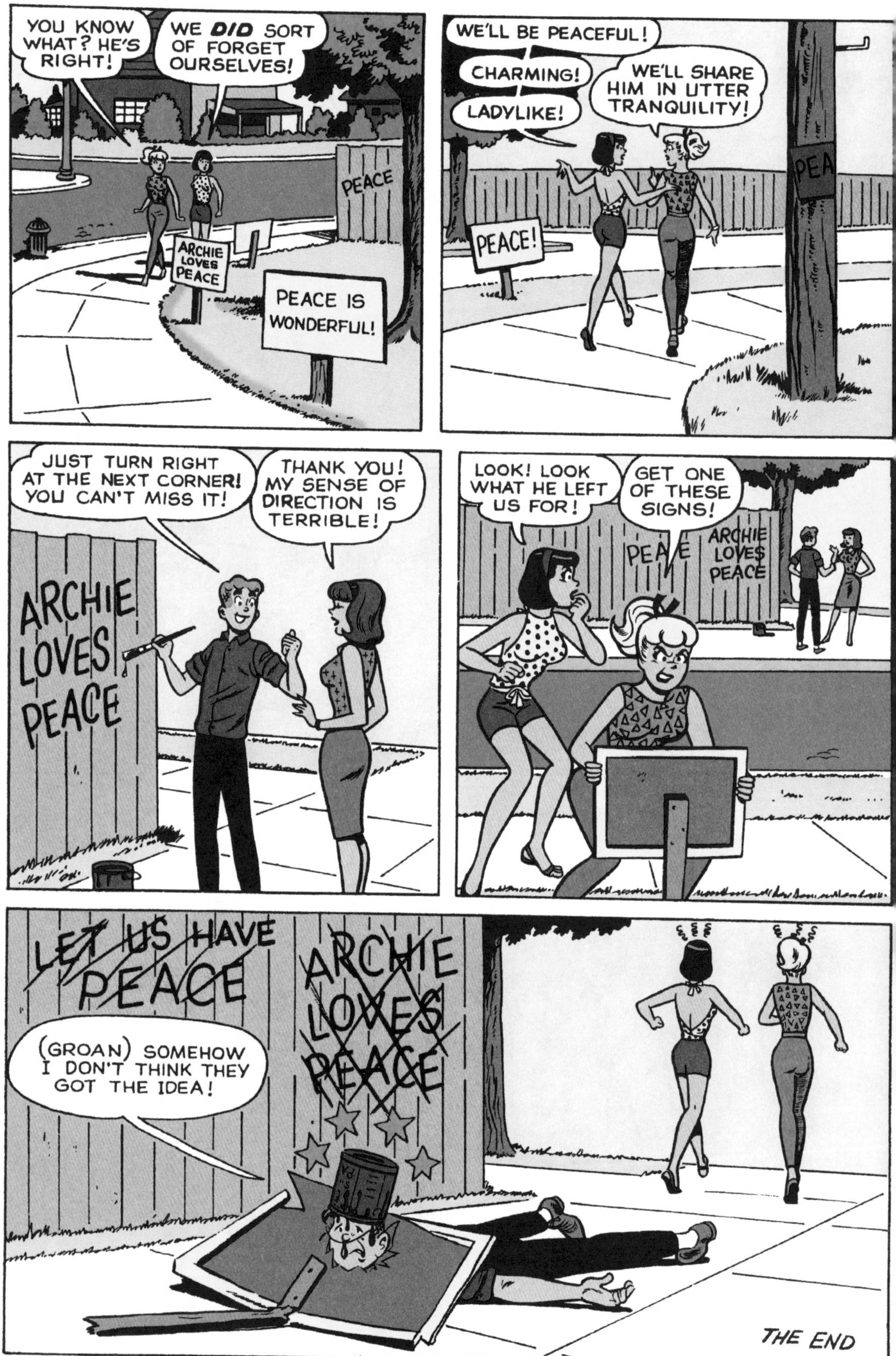
YOU KNOW WHAT? HE'S RIGHT!
WE DID SORT OF FORGET OURSELVES!
PEACE
ARCHIE LOVES PEACE
PEACE IS WONDERFUL!
WE'LL BE PEACEFUL!
CHARMING!
LADYLIKE!
WE'LL SHARE HIM IN UTTER TRANQUILITY!
PEACE!
PEA
JUST TURN RIGHT AT THE NEXT CORNER! YOU CAN'T MISS IT!
THANK YOU! MY SENSE OF DIRECTION IS TERRIBLE!
ARCHIE LOVES PEACE
LOOK! LOOK WHAT HE LEFT US FOR!
GET ONE OF THESE SIGNS!
PEA E
ARCHIE LOVES PEACE
LET US HAVE PEACE
ARCHIE LOVES PEACE
(GROAN) SOMEHOW I DON'T THINK THEY GOT THE IDEA!
THE END

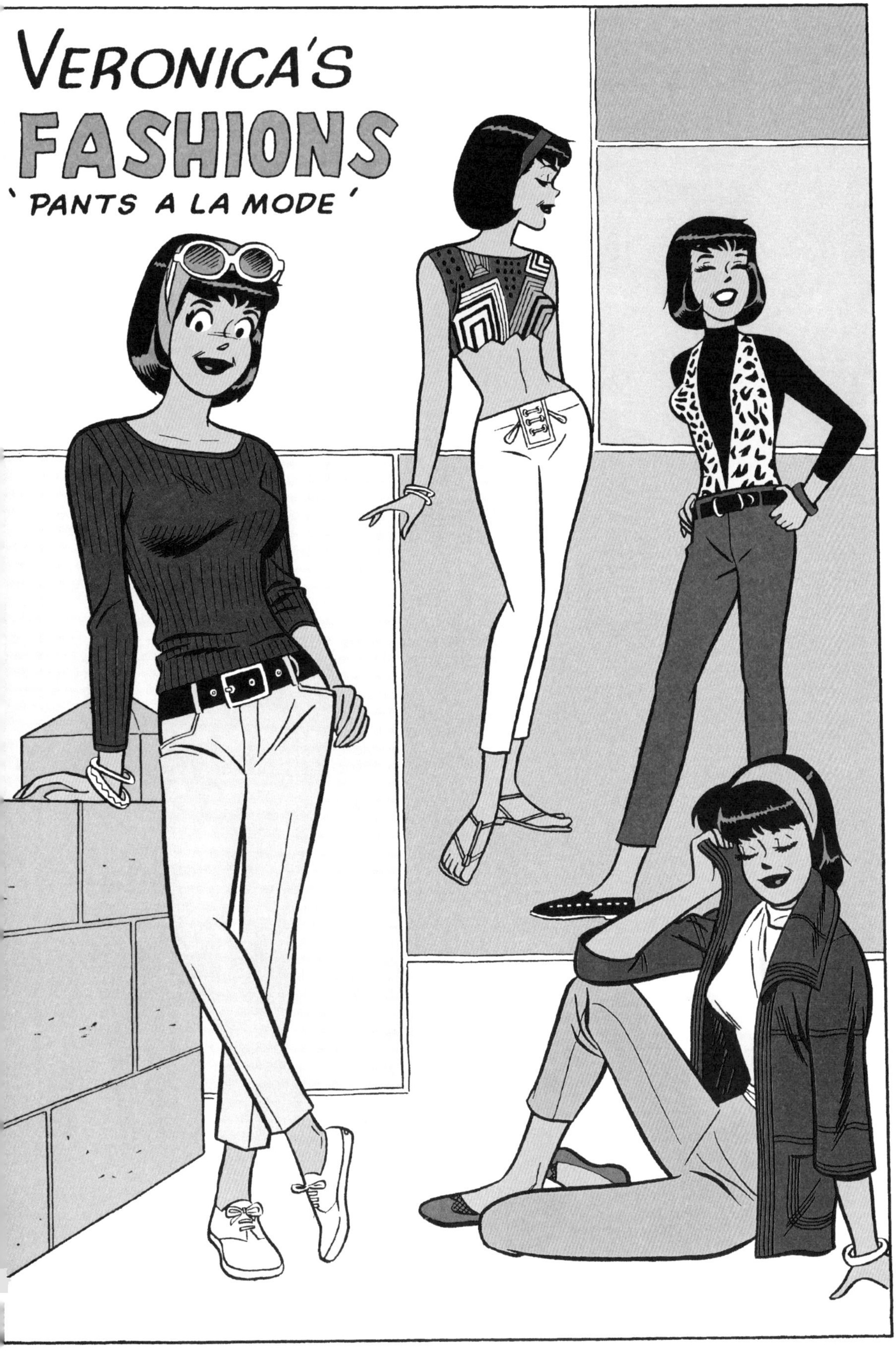
VERONICA'S
FASHIONS
'PANTS A LA MODE'

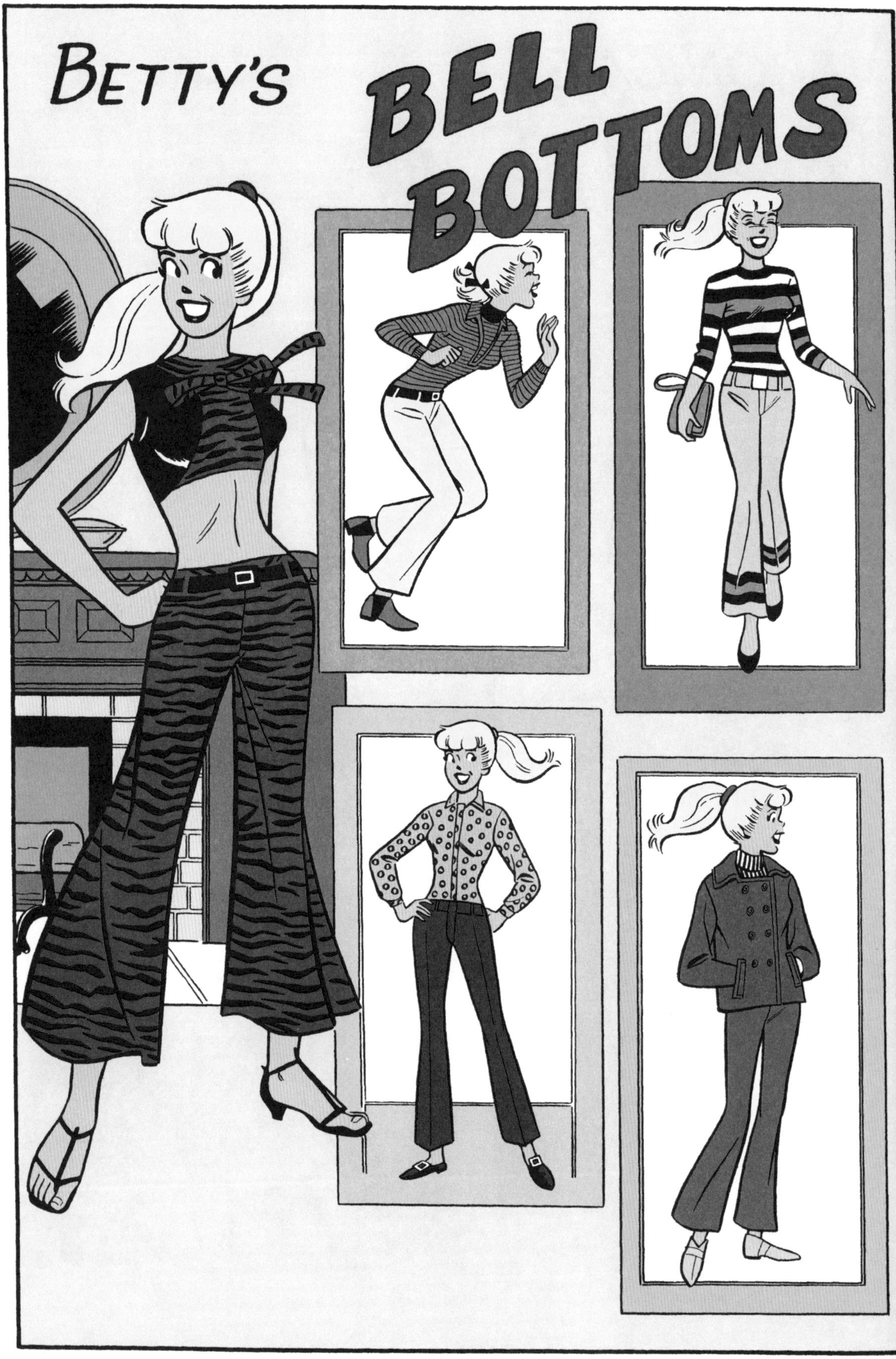
BETTY'S
BELL BOTTOMS

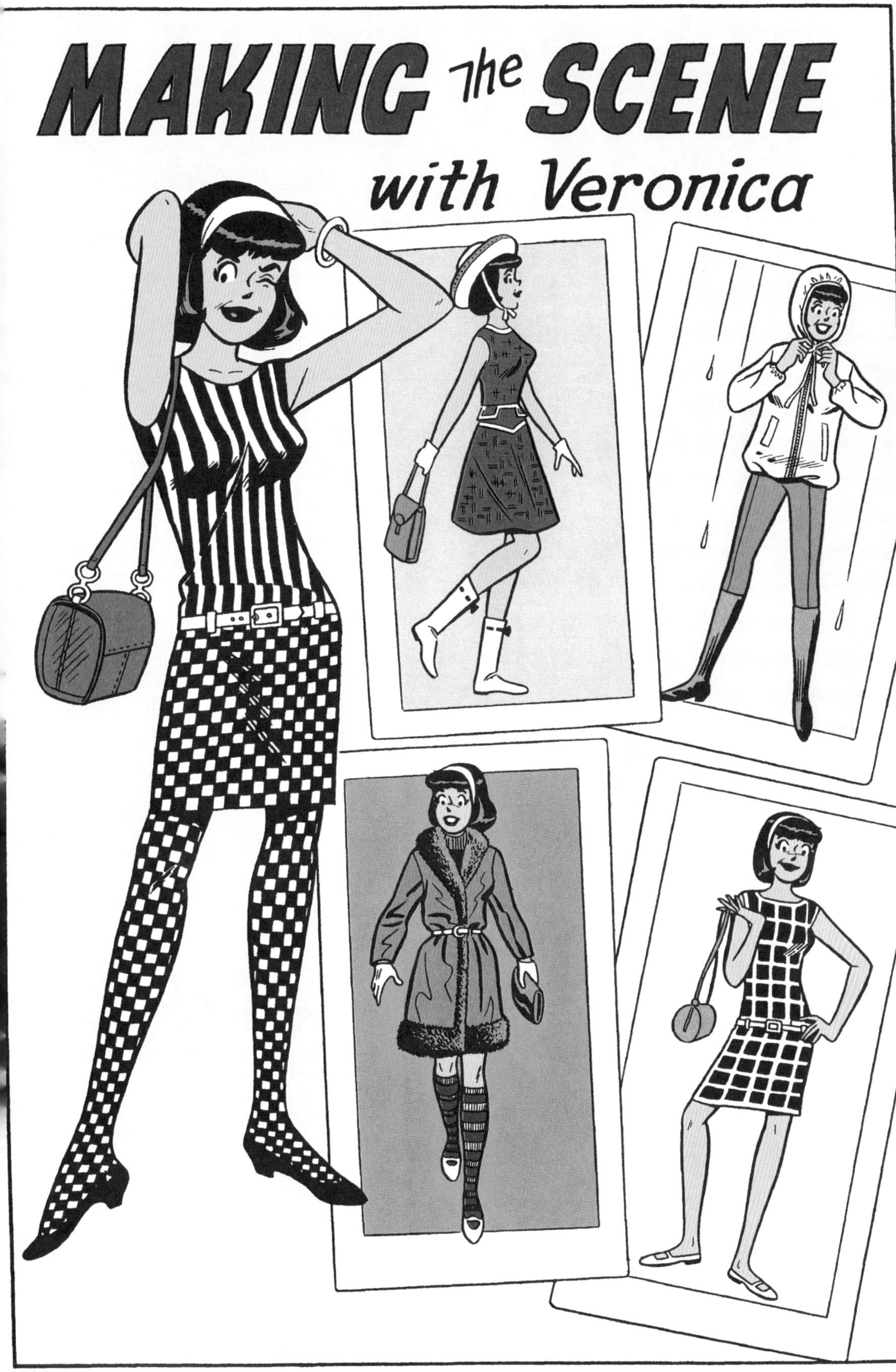
MAKING the SCENE
with Veronica

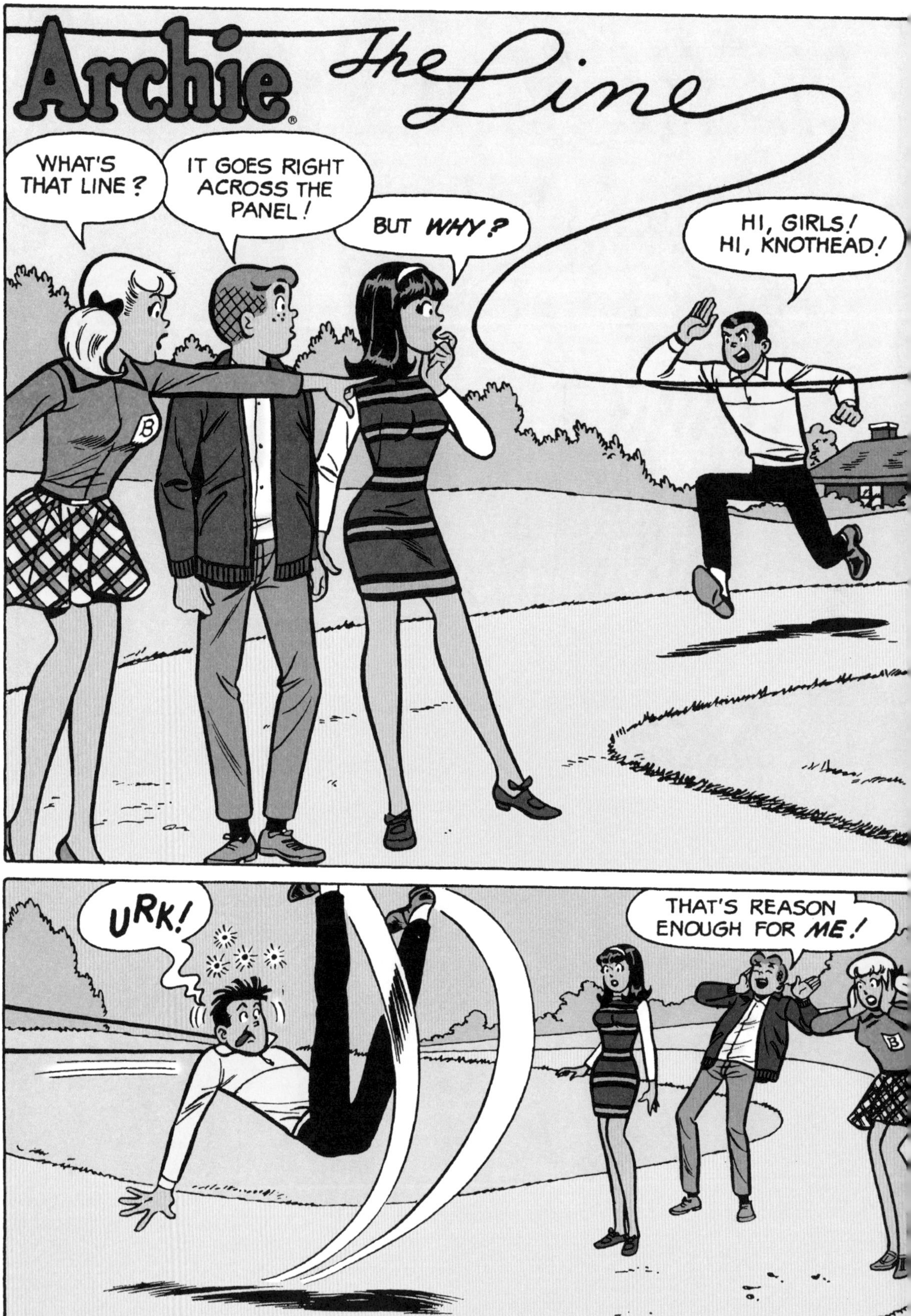
Archie®
The Line
WHAT'S THAT LINE?
IT GOES RIGHT ACROSS THE PANEL!
BUT WHY?
HI, GIRLS! HI, KNOTHEAD!
URK!
THAT'S REASON ENOUGH FOR ME!

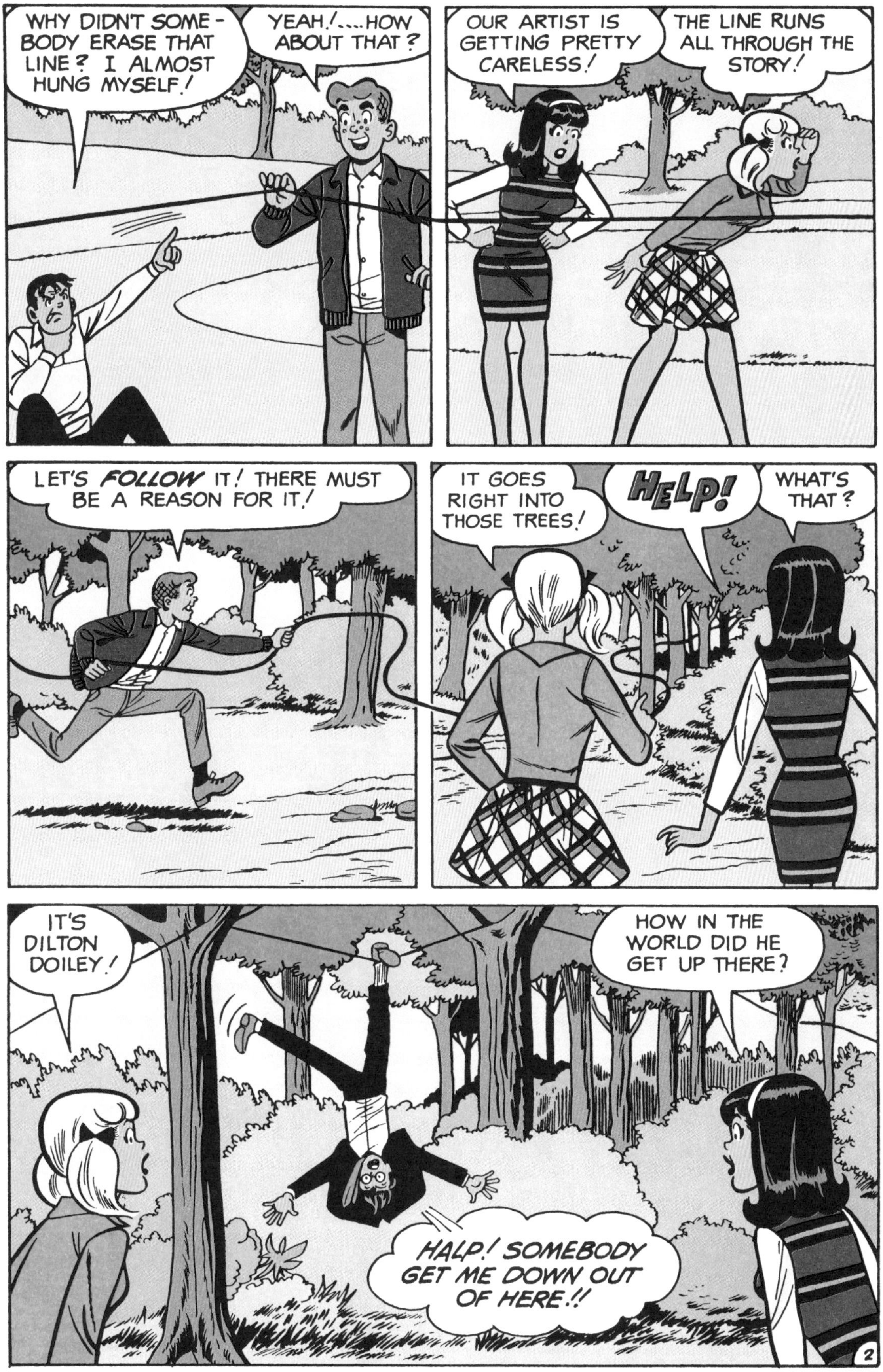
WHY DIDN'T SOMEBODY ERASE THAT LINE? I ALMOST HUNG MYSELF!
YEAH!....HOW ABOUT THAT?
OUR ARTIST IS GETTING PRETTY CARELESS!
THE LINE RUNS ALL THROUGH THE STORY!
LET'S FOLLOW IT! THERE MUST BE A REASON FOR IT!
IT GOES RIGHT INTO THOSE TREES!
HELP!
WHAT'S THAT?
IT'S DILTON DOILEY!
HOW IN THE WORLD DID HE GET UP THERE?
HALP! SOMEBODY GET ME DOWN OUT OF HERE!!
2

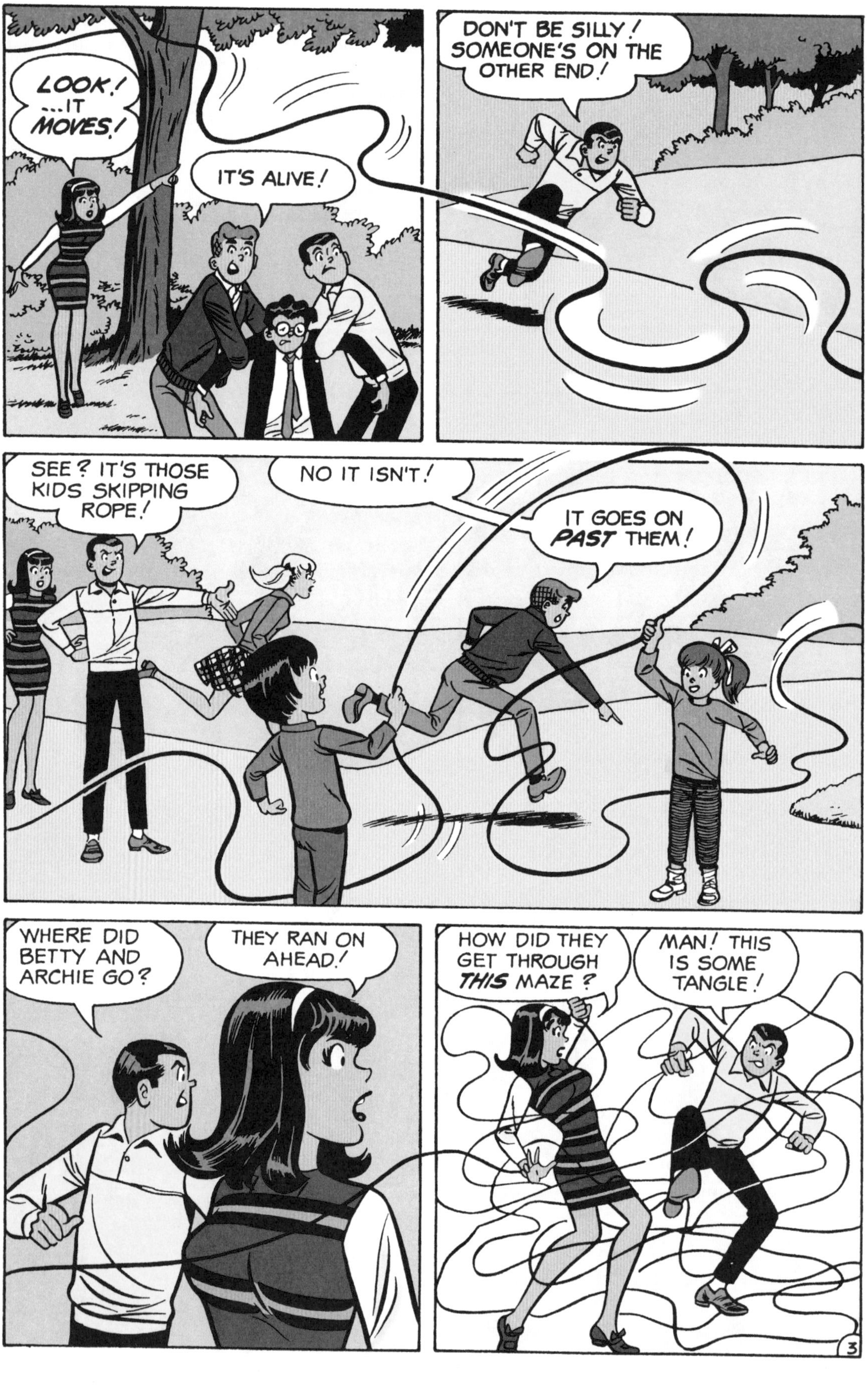
LOOK! ...IT MOVES!
IT'S ALIVE!
DON'T BE SILLY! SOMEONE'S ON THE OTHER END!
SEE? IT'S THOSE KIDS SKIPPING ROPE!
NO IT ISN'T!
IT GOES ON PAST THEM!
WHERE DID BETTY AND ARCHIE GO?
THEY RAN ON AHEAD!
HOW DID THEY GET THROUGH THIS MAZE?
MAN! THIS IS SOME TANGLE!
3

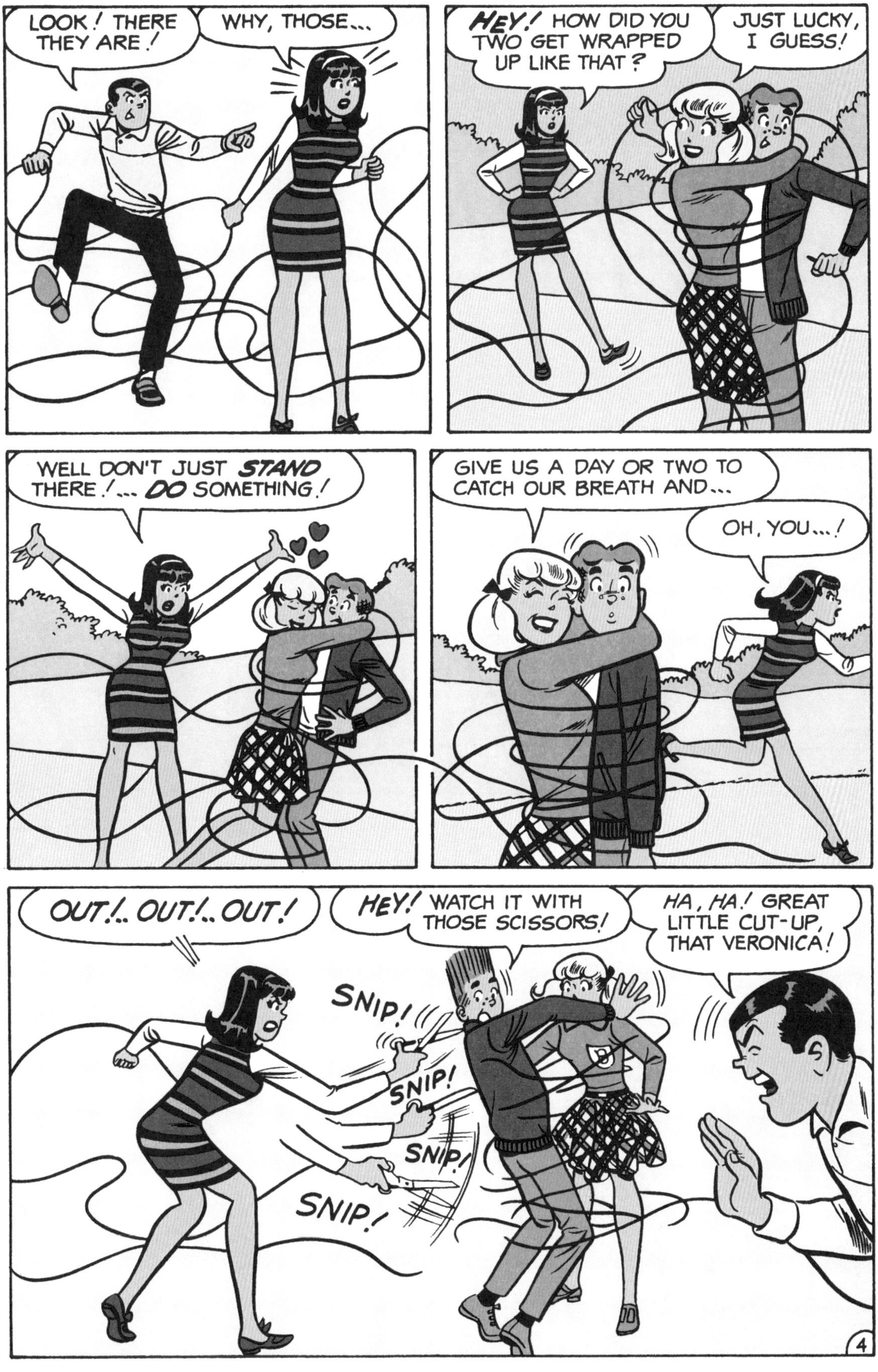
LOOK! THERE THEY ARE!
WHY, THOSE...
HEY! HOW DID YOU TWO GET WRAPPED UP LIKE THAT?
JUST LUCKY, I GUESS!
WELL DON'T JUST STAND THERE!... DO SOMETHING!
GIVE US A DAY OR TWO TO CATCH OUR BREATH AND...
OH, YOU...!
OUT!.. OUT!.. OUT!
HEY! WATCH IT WITH THOSE SCISSORS!
HA, HA! GREAT LITTLE CUT-UP, THAT VERONICA!
SNIP!
SNIP!
SNIP!
SNIP!
4

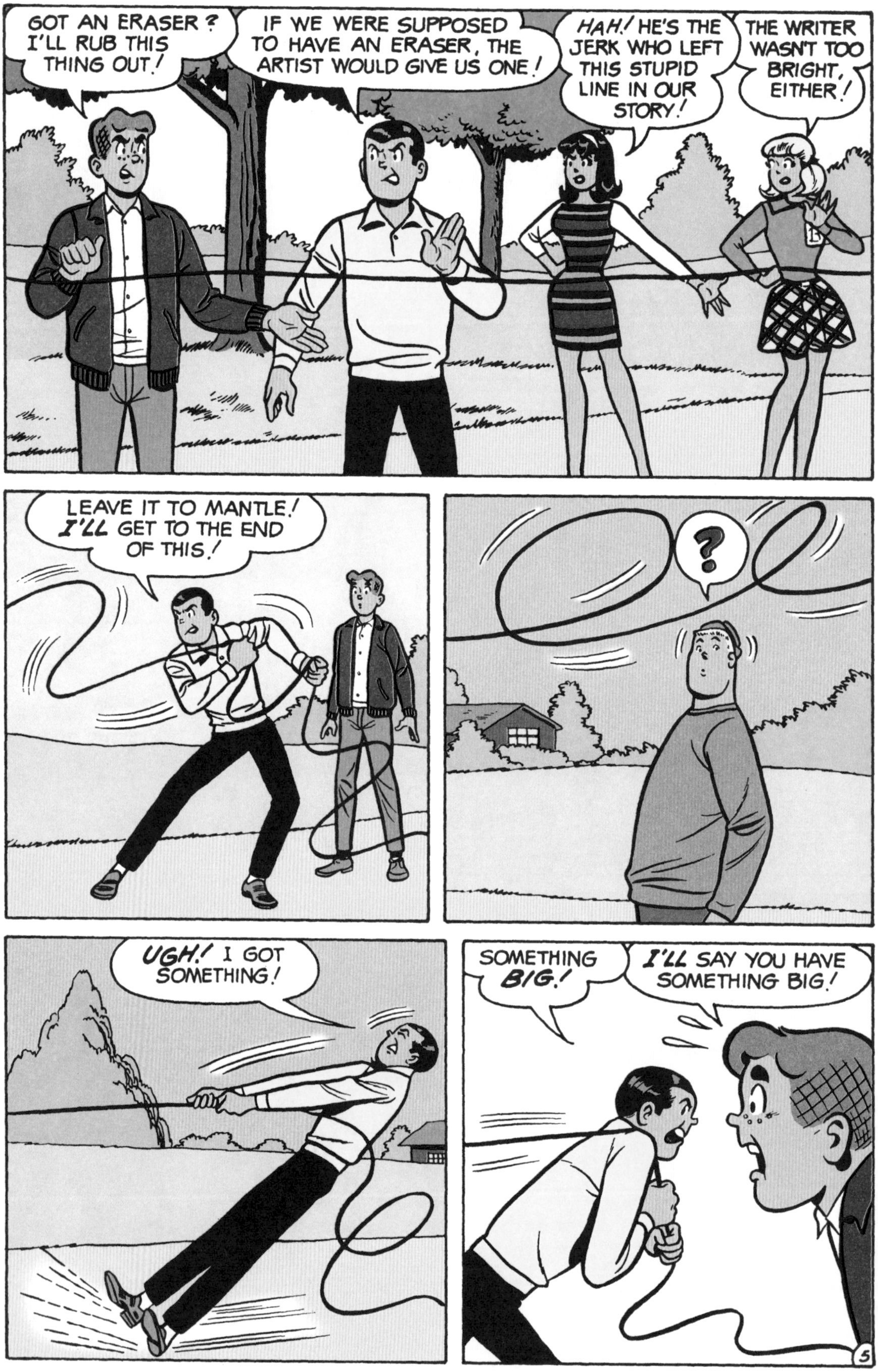
GOT AN ERASER? I'LL RUB THIS THING OUT!
IF WE WERE SUPPOSED TO HAVE AN ERASER, THE ARTIST WOULD GIVE US ONE!
HAH! HE'S THE JERK WHO LEFT THIS STUPID LINE IN OUR STORY!
THE WRITER WASN'T TOO BRIGHT, EITHER!
LEAVE IT TO MANTLE! I'LL GET TO THE END OF THIS!
?
UGH! I GOT SOMETHING!
SOMETHING BIG!
I'LL SAY YOU HAVE SOMETHING BIG!
5

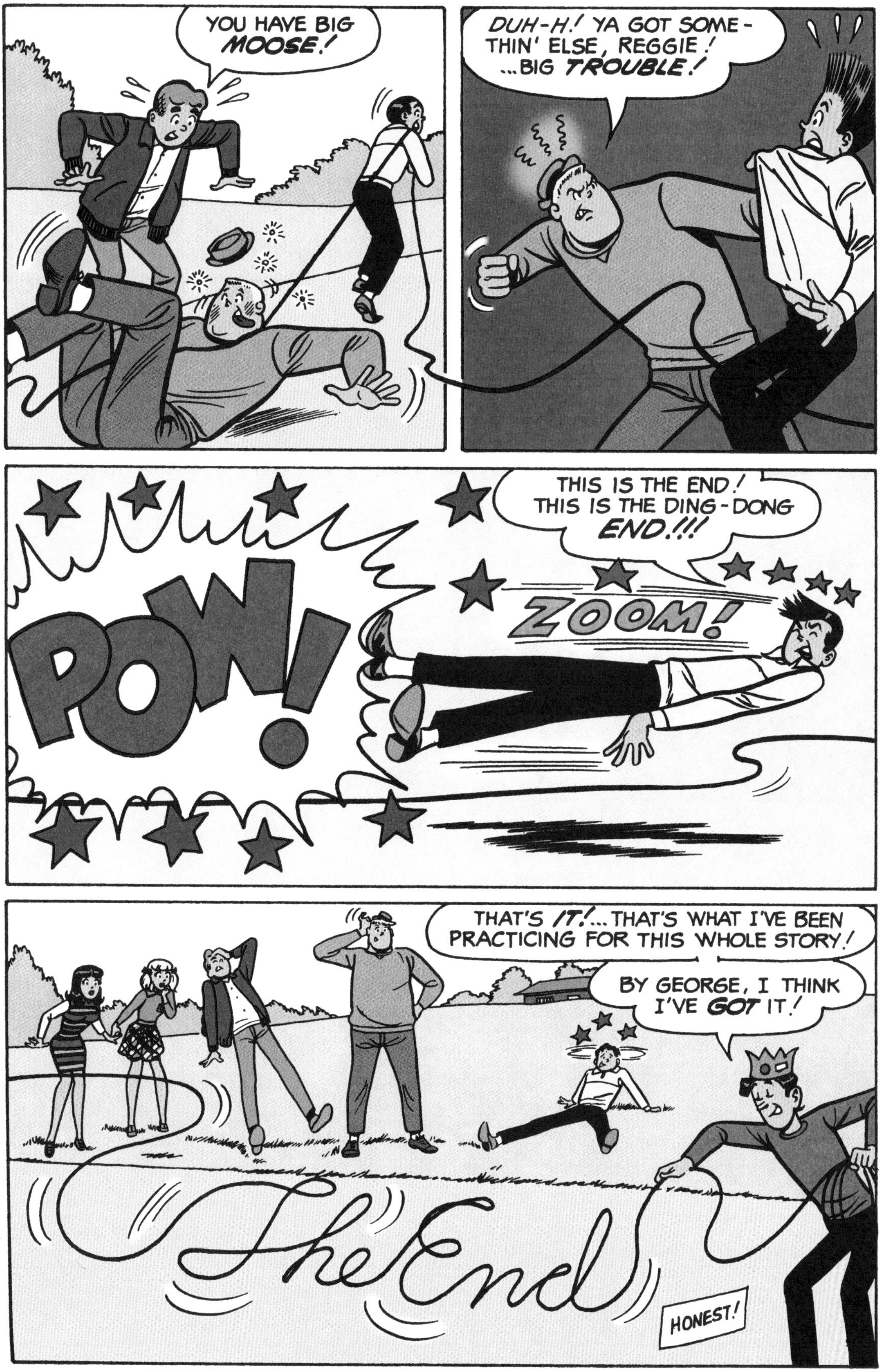
YOU HAVE BIG MOOSE!
DUH-H! YA GOT SOME-THIN' ELSE, REGGIE! ...BIG TROUBLE!
THIS IS THE END! THIS IS THE DING-DONG END!!!
POW!
ZOOM!
THAT'S IT!... THAT'S WHAT I'VE BEEN PRACTICING FOR THIS WHOLE STORY!
BY GEORGE, I THINK I'VE GOT IT!
The End
HONEST!

CHECK OUT THESE GREAT ARCHIE COMIC GRAPHIC NOVELS...